Advance Praise
Welcome Home, Caroline Kline

"An uplifting and sassy debut—with just enough Jersey attitude and plenty of heart—about family, love, finding yourself, and finding home base."

—Margarita Montimore, author of *Oona Out of Order* and *Acts of Violet*

"Original and unexpected, this second-chance romance is perfect for baseball lovers and lovers of deeply emotional, complicated relationships. I was cheering for Caroline Kline from the first page."

—Annabel Monaghan, author of *Nora Goes Off Script* and *Same Time Next Summer*

"Despite a total lack of athleticism, I'm hardwired to love a baseball story. But it's not just my affinity for fictional home runs that made me fall in love with *Welcome Home, Caroline Kline*. This book is wise and winning, a profound coming-of-age tale sharing the field with a thrilling and hilarious wallop of a sports saga. Courtney Preiss's debut didn't just make me root for the home team, it made me root for the very idea of home."

—Bobby Finger, author of *The Old Place*

"Preiss knocks it out of the park in her heartwarming, witty debut. When her life falls apart, feisty, jaded Caroline Kline returns to her New Jersey town and gets a second chance to discover the excitement of a good challenge, the joy of romance, and the wonder of home."

—Amy Poeppel, author of *The Sweet Spot*

"Courtney Preiss has written a laugh-out-loud original love letter to New Jersey and hit a home run with her debut novel. Wry and bighearted, *Welcome Home, Caroline Kline* is a sporty romp, a summer romance, and a thoughtful exploration of what it means to grow up. Playful with a game-face focus on what matters, Preiss had me at 'rec specs.'"

—Beck Dorey-Stein, author of *Rock the Boat*

"*Welcome Home, Caroline Kline* is a warm, bighearted novel about celebrating the people and places that are foundational in shaping our lives. Caroline might be dreading her return to New Jersey, but how lucky for readers that we get to accompany her back to her hometown. As she reconnects with a childhood love, rediscovers her love of baseball, and makes peace with her father, Caroline surprises herself by learning she can go home again—and that there is nowhere else she would rather be. An enormously fun and rewarding read."

—Kirthana Ramisetti, author of *Dava Shastri's Last Day*

"Watching Caroline's hesitant, brave, and acerbically funny transformation is exactly like watching a come-from-behind victory on the ballfield: beautiful and unexpected, riveting and memorable." —Katie Runde, author of *The Shore*

"Courtney Preiss's debut novel, *Welcome Home, Caroline Kline*, is lovely and engaging, funny and smart and sometimes sad. I rooted so hard for Caroline Kline, a young woman who makes a life for herself out in New York City, but somehow finds herself back in her childhood bedroom. This is a worst nightmare scenario to anyone who has grown up in New Jersey and also so very relatable. Her journey is a quiet triumph." —Marcy Dermansky, author of *Hurricane Girl*

"Brimming with warmth, humor, and wit, *Welcome Home, Caroline Kline* is an absolute home run of a novel. Courtney Preiss has written an unputdownable love letter to baseball, New Jersey, and the power of starting over, featuring an unforgettable heroine for whom you can't help but root." —Laura Hankin, author of *The Daydreams*

"With warmth, humor, and that special brand of New Jersey suburban splendor, *Welcome Home, Caroline Kline* is the perfect messy midtwenties coming-of-age story that should be required reading for anyone looking to find their place in the world. Preiss's prose absolutely shimmers as she sends Caroline on an endearing journey of discovery, from begrudgingly subbing for her ailing dad on his local men's softball league to reopening her recently broken heart to a romance of her youth. A novel that perfectly captures all those nostalgic yet life-affirming feelings that arise when returning to one's roots, Preiss's first publishing 'at bat' is a total home run. This is a debut not to be missed!"

—Becky Chalsen, author of *Kismet*

"*Welcome Home, Caroline Kline* is compulsively readable, riotously funny, and filled with sentences you'll want to read aloud to the person next to you. It's tender and hopeful, with a romance that will make you swoon. It's a laugh-out-loud love letter to baseball, New Jersey, and rock and roll. Most of all, it's life-affirming. You'll continue rooting for Caroline long after you finish the last page."

—Mandy Berman, author of *Perennials*

A Novel

Courtney Preiss

G. P. Putnam's Sons
New York

PUTNAM
— EST. 1838 —
G. P. Putnam's Sons
Publishers Since 1838
An imprint of Penguin Random House LLC
penguinrandomhouse.com

Library of Congress Cataloging-in-Publication Data

Names: Preiss, Courtney, author.
Title: Welcome home, Caroline Kline: a novel / Courtney Preiss.
Description: New York: G. P. Putnam's Sons, 2024.
Identifiers: LCCN 2023056472 (print) | LCCN 2023056473 (ebook) |
ISBN 9780593715413 (trade paperback) | ISBN 9780593715420 (ebook)
Subjects: LCGFT: Sports fiction. | Romance fiction. | Novels.
Classification: LCC PS3616.R443 W45 2024 (print) |
LCC PS3616.R443 (ebook) | DDC 813/.6—dc23/eng/20231212
LC record available at https://lccn.loc.gov/2023056472
LC ebook record available at https://lccn.loc.gov/2023056473

Printed in the United States of America
1st Printing

Book design by Alison Cnockaert

For my father, Scott Preiss—the captain of the home team.

And for Larry Preiss, forever our MVP.

Maybe if I paid attention,
I could learn to love the landscape I was born to.

—*Nicole Atkins, "Neptune City"*

1

WHEN I GOT the call to come home to the Jersey Shore suburb Springsteen's always singing about, I was in the back of an Uber zipping across the Williamsburg Bridge with a stranger's hand down my pants. I vaguely remembered the guy's name being Ross, but I wasn't sure. In my attempt to ignore the incoming call, I accidentally answered it.

"Caroline, it's your father," my stepmother, Claudia, said, her voice steeped in melodrama, as if she were being ushered out of a failed soap opera audition. "We're at Shore Hospital. He told me to get you on the horn."

"Oh, God," I breathed into the phone. My anonymous suitor had his face buried so deep in my neck, he couldn't tell that I was in distress. He took the noise as a command to keep digging into me.

"He had a bad fall," Claudia continued, a different level of intensity affecting every line she delivered. In her purebred Ronkonkoma accent, she sounded like she was reciting a monologue about Humpty Dumpty. "About an hour ago. He flew down a whole set of stairs to the basement and landed in this horrible position. He just got out of the MRI . . ." She started to trail off. "We're waiting for results."

My heart raced. I needed to unlatch from my paramour. I peeled Ross off me, my neck and his hand both slick with anticipation. He was disoriented, still not understanding that I was on the phone and that the course of the night was being rerouted with every passing word. I shifted into an upright position, crossed one leg over the other, pointed to the black brick at my ear, and held a single finger to my mouth. He turned away from me and rested his head against the window.

"What do they think it is?" I murmured, chewing on a cuticle and bracing myself. Now I was the one affecting a phone persona. The character I chose was *concerned daughter who* did not *drink three filthy gin martinis and call it dinner "because of the olives."*

"Broken wrist, a couple of broken ribs. But they needed to check for internal bleeding and look at his ACL and his meniscus . . ." She dropped down to a whisper and got weepy. "And his . . . vertebrates." She started crying. I asked her to hand the phone to my father. She shuffled and muttered, "Leo, take this."

"Hello?" he said, his voice warm and familiar, albeit weak. I recognized then how much my chest had tightened, loosening only once he spoke.

"Sir," I said into the phone, "I'm so sorry to be the one to tell you this, but it says here on your chart you've got . . . *vertebrates*."

He laughed, and a racking cough chased the sound up his throat. "Lousy fuckin' spinal column," he muttered. "Now I'll never be a jellyfish."

"Or a Republican," I added. I glanced over at Ross, who discreetly sucked on a vape pen as he watched the city lights streak by out the window.

"Caro," my father said, and I could hear the starshine fading from his voice. It sobered me up. "You know I never want to be the one to ask, but it'd mean a lot if you came home."

The threat of tears stung my sinuses and plugged up my throat. My father always wore his endurance and immunity as badges of honor. Never took a sick day, never broke any bones. I was almost certain he'd never even had a cavity. Before I could answer, Claudia took the phone back. "The doctor's here now," she whispered. "I'll text with any news. Let me know which train you'll be on. I'll pick you up from the station in the morning."

A shuffle, a click. The flashy patina of the city went by in a smear outside my window. We were in the part of Brooklyn they'd turned into Disneyland—no more sugar factories and textile mills. A slice of pizza cost seven dollars. A single delicate earring from the boutique jeweler: $150. A one-bedroom apartment: $3,500 a month.

The dejected man sitting next to me in the Uber lived here. Earlier, I'd been eager enough to cross a bridge for Ross and see where the night led, but now I did not want to go upstairs with him and play pretend. I did not want to find out he was one of three roommates living in a two-bedroom. I did not want to wrap my panties around my wrist like a scrunchie to save myself the agony of feeling around for them in the post-coital dark, the next Uber driver waiting for me downstairs, messaging me, I'm here. Miss. Are you coming? while my heart searched for its natural rhythm.

But I also did not want to send him away forever, I decided then, examining his silhouette in the intermittent Bedford Avenue lamplight. He was an astute enough kisser to make me wonder what other skills he might possess. I wasn't ready to sacrifice the investment I'd made that night and send him to the island of lost Hinge dates. The old sunk cost conundrum. I'd have to put a pin in the family trauma if I wanted to save Ross for a rainy day.

"I can't come up tonight," I said, scooting over to recoup his affections, sliding a well-manicured hand over his black-denim-clad thigh. "But not for lack of wanting to."

"You came all the way out here just to go back downtown?"

he asked, gentle but incredulous. He blew a puff of nicotine vapor down the sleeve of his leather jacket. A hint of mint haunted the air between us. His face showed as much concern as four whiskeys on ice would allow. Ross looked like a young Alex Rodriguez, when he was just the rookie shortstop from my childhood whom I'd beg my dad to take me to see whenever the Mariners were in town. I pressed my lips to his jawline.

"Look, I'm not thrilled about it either. And this driver is going to be *even less* thrilled that I've taken up temporary residence in the back of his Impala. But it's a family emergency. I swear I wouldn't pull this shit if it wasn't serious. Scout's honor." I flashed him a double peace sign, like Richard Nixon with a mile of carefully displayed cleavage. My head buzzed as the martini fog receded, leaving me in a muzzy, in-between state of inebriation. Ross stayed quiet.

By the time the driver pulled up in front of his building, I'd kissed my way across his neck and crawled into his lap. *Not bad*, I thought, looking out the window and up at the facade. One of those modern structures with matte black banisters and semi-flush globe light fixtures. Inside I'd bet there were stainless steel appliances in every kitchen and a wheezing French bulldog on every floor.

"I think you should still come up. Make the trip worth it," he whispered, then stuck his tongue in my ear. I couldn't bring myself to recount the details of the phone call. Confiding in this stranger that I was legitimately worried about my dad felt too intimate and a little juvenile. I didn't want his pity.

"Listen, Ross," I said, pulling away. "Tonight's just not my night, but I really do want to see you again. And I'm not saying it in the obligatory you-just-gave-me-a-pelvic-exam-in-the-back-of-a-cab kind of way. I'm saying it because I just got out of a long-term relationship where no one spoke up about what they really wanted, and I think it's important for me—*for the universe*—that I tell you what I want."

Pivoting to the subject of Ben, my ex, was easier than that of my dad because I was still trying hard to tamp down the too-recent memory of him while I was out with other men. Both the parts of Ben that repulsed me (the relentless veneer, the cabal of New York City private school friends he never outgrew, the foggy intoxication-fueled fighting) and the good-on-paper parts that made me sure no one I could find on an app would ever measure up (the prospect of marrying into a family of Jewish doctors, the summer weekends in East Hampton, the sex that somehow stayed great and perhaps even got better when things between us were bad).

I searched Ross's expression for confirmation, but he just stared at me. Confusion masquerading as intensity, or perhaps the other way around. I clasped his tired face in my hands and looked at him without flinching.

"I'm looking for candor, Ross. Real life. I'm coming to you in a vulnerable moment and asking for your compassion. This is new terrain for me. I'm going to call you next week and we can pick this up where we left off. Are you with me? Can you be candid with me, too, Ross?"

He didn't break eye contact. Not to check and make sure we were stopped in front of the correct apartment, not to acknowledge the driver, who had begun wearily *ma'am*-ing me about my next destination. I thought maybe he had paused to appreciate the beauty in my humanity, or perhaps he had crossed his own liquor threshold and was calculating a vomit trajectory.

Then he broke his silence to ask me with utmost sincerity: "Who the fuck is 'Ross'?"

●   ●   ●

DON'T FALL.

In teetering heels, I climbed the stairs to my temporary sanctuary, the historic Greenwich Village gold mine where my best friend, Winnie, had graciously loaned me her couch after I found myself without a place to live. My eyelids felt like tiny anvils, and remnants of gin had alchemized to acetone in the back of my throat.

Inside the apartment, I knew I needed to make a plan but also that I wasn't in my right mind to process the chaotic tangle of information I'd been fed through the phone. After turning on the side table lamp, I tucked into the envelope-size kitchen and ran tap water into a Yankee Stadium souvenir cup littered with illustrated championship rings, peeling from age. I broke out what was left of the egg matzo and some rubbery non-dairy spread from the impromptu Passover seder we'd hosted a week earlier, willing myself sober.

Winnie heard me knocking around and emerged from her bedroom. "You're back early," she said, despite it being past three in the morning. She waggled her eyebrows with a sly smile. "I'm guessing Raphael was a bit of a quick draw?"

"Raphael!" I cried, slamming down my Yankees cup, sending a torrent of tap water onto the mint tiled floor. "*Raph! Fuck!*"

"You know what? I don't even want to know," she said, coming toward me, sidestepping the puddle to get to the sink. Winnie was the only person I knew who had one of those elegant little glass bedside carafes and actually used it.

I considered the modes of transportation ahead of me and tried not to think too much about the reason I had to go to New Jersey. I shooed away thoughts of my father, flattened and moving slowly through an MRI. Instead, I asked myself the age-old question: *Bus or train?* I held off looking at an Uber estimate after a phone notification informed me that my escapade from the Village to Williamsburg and back again had just set me back a cool eighty-seven dollars.

Winnie looked at me expectantly over the lip of her dainty glass as she took long pulls of water, her dark curls tucked back under a silk schmata. She looked pristine and angelic in the dim lighting, eager to absorb all my woe if I was prepared to unleash it. But even in my compromised state, I knew if I told her about the call from Claudia, I would dissolve into tears like a frightened child and lose my logistical focus.

Don't fall.

My father's spill down the steps was just the latest in a series of mishaps draining the consistency—and well-sought-after comfort—from my life. In the last two months, I'd championed, hired, and on-boarded the woman who would replace me as the events director at my dream marketing agency. I'd found someone to take over the remainder of the lease on my apartment. I said my teary goodbyes at the office where I had built my career. That same night, my boyfriend of three years informed me that the West Coast life we'd meticulously plotted was no longer happening. Ben explained it as though it were quite simple: *he* was still moving to Los Angeles, I was just no longer invited—despite having quit my job and gotten rid of my apartment to make the move. And of course this happened at the Minetta Tavern, where we'd planned a celebratory dinner of hamburgers and champagne. Foolish of him, really. While I don't enjoy crying in public, my aversion to it wouldn't keep me from making a scene.

"I don't understand," I said that night, understanding perfectly. "You're telling me I'm not *allowed* to come to California?"

"You can do whatever you'd like, Caroline," he said, tipping his glass over his nose and gulping. "If you still want to go to California, I think that's great. But I think it's best if we didn't go together."

I stared down at my hamburger, resenting its presence. I was already nostalgic, wistful to return to the naive ignorance I'd possessed when I'd ordered it. "How long have you been thinking about this?" I asked him without looking up from my plate.

He extended his arm across the table like he was going to grasp my hand, but instead he rested it a safe distance from mine. "Since our last trip to LA," he said finally. "It was such a disaster." I sank into my seat, still mortified thinking about what happened on that trip. "We deserve this chance to start over. You know, make a clean break."

But there could be no clean break for us, not when everything had already become such a mess.

I asked why he'd picked that moment and not, say, a few weeks prior, when I'd given notice and hired a replacement so scrappy and competent my employers actually seemed kind of glad to see me go. He said he hadn't been sure then, but he was now. That didn't stop me from trying to negotiate with him—the little bargaining measure desperate people do when they're being jilted. Trying to convince someone to love you back when they've already made up their mind is like reaching rock bottom and attempting, still, to gnaw through the subfloor.

It didn't work. Did it ever? In my head, I could hear my mother's voice—a sage divorcée—doling out the same kind of advice she'd given to me throughout my twenties. *You cannot cajole someone into loving you, Caroline. It doesn't work like that.* When Ben left, I knew what he was taking with him: my prospects of moving to a grand Hollywood apartment in the Cecil B. DeMille complex. The financial security I'd been relying on until I found a new job out west. The love and sense of stability I'd found with him. The assuredness that I'd never have to be back in the dating pool again. The Upper West Side doctor parents and their multiple vacation properties I could have been tethered to forever with the simple offer of an emerald-cut diamond ring.

When he walked out of the Minetta Tavern, I felt my future disintegrate. I sat alone at the table, fossilized meals and one empty glass in front of me. In an act of misguided pride, I'd waved away the patronizing stack of bills Ben tried to foist on me and was stuck with a check I no longer had the income to pay.

Don't fall.

"You good?" Winnie asked back in the kitchen, turning toward her bedroom but sensing there was more to the night than I was letting on. I was bad at keeping anything from her, especially after nearly two-and-a-half decades of friendship, but I was too exhausted to explain and too afraid saying it aloud would make me crumple into tears. I'd slip out at dawn,

I decided. Leave Winnie a note on the counter and head for Penn Station in a couple of hours, just as the sun was coming up. I closed my eyes, offered a weak smile, and flashed an insincere thumbs-up.

It occurred to me while putting on my bedtime uniform of an ancient knee-length Disney World twentieth-anniversary tee how serious the injuries must be for my father to call me home. How dire it sounded for me to actually cross the state line. I hadn't been back to Glen Brook in over a year, not even for the holidays. I'd spent Thanksgiving with Ben's family in Aspen; Chanukah and Christmas at their compound in Haleiwa.

The incident, as I imagined it, flickered on the tiny drive-in movie screen of my mind. A step miscalculated. The vibrato buzz of his spine against the stairs, like a child slamming a hand onto a grand piano and forcing their way up the scales. The crunch of a bone that stood up to greater impact throughout all his years playing softball—so why splinter now? The dizzying view forgotten in an instant, like looking out the porthole of the washing machine. The final thud. My oxlike father in a heap on the floor, limbs skewed like a Picasso portrait.

Don't fall was what my father's favorite uncle, Phil, said at his ninety-fourth birthday party when asked post–candle snuff what his key to longevity was. My father had jokingly parroted this warning ever since, but Phil's voice had no mirth to it that day. The men in my father's family had all lived well into their nineties. Phil had laced his hands with the graveside dirt of too many friends, of his own wife. He'd grown accustomed to saying goodbye. He was a faithful observer of exits; he kept diligent mental notes.

Even if a fall didn't kill Phil's peers, he found that falls marked seasons of decline. One thing would lead to another, and eventually Phil would shuffle into synagogue with the same burgundy knit kippah on his head. The key to a long life—he'd sworn until the day he finally took the spill that broke his hip and ushered him down the dark hallway to his own demise—was to stay with your feet planted on the goddamn ground.

Whatever you do, he'd warned, sitting at the head of the table like a Jewish mob boss in a paper party hat, *don't fall.*

2

THE NEXT MORNING, Claudia picked me up at the Glen Brook train station and rattled off Leo's ailments as we drove to the hospital. "Broken wrist, torn ACL, two broken ribs, and a bruised spine." She glanced at me. "I just want you to be prepared. None of us have ever seen him like this before."

When I followed her through the doors of Shore Hospital, I kept my head down and focused on the chalky blue floor tiles, letting Claudia guide me until we reached my father's room. Nestled in an inclined bed, Leo seemed small and pale. His graying hair was matted at his temples.

"Come here, Caro," he croaked when he spotted me lurking in the doorway. When I realized he probably sounded hoarse from screaming at the bottom of the stairs, I felt the color drain from my face, too. Sympathy pallor.

Claudia took a seat, and I walked over to stand next to his bed. "Pop," I whispered, gripping the knob of his hand.

"Caroline," he rasped. "What can I say? I'm devastated."

I pulled up a bedside chair next to Claudia's. "Well, rightfully so," I said. "You've never been down for the count like this before. It's natural to feel unmoored right now." He was more disheveled and weaker than I'd ever seen him, but I felt a twinge of relief to see him sitting upright and talking.

"Well, we did get some good news," Claudia interjected with some forced cheer, placing her hand on my father's hospital gown–draped knee. "Doctor says there's no internal bleeding. We'll take every silver lining we can get, right?"

"It's not supposed to be like this," Leo scoffed, ignoring Claudia's optimism. "It's springtime. Baseball season. I should be out on the field with my men." He sounded like he had been called home from war, tilting his chin to his chest, shaking his head softly. Leave it to my father to suffer a health setback and get lost in his decades-long preoccupation with the one true love of his life, the local men's softball league.

Claudia clicked her tongue and gave him an impatient look.

"Anyway," he said, refocusing on me. "Have you given any thought to what I said last night about coming home? I think with everything going on, it could be good for you. For both of us." He looked up at Claudia then. "For all of us."

"Pop, I'm right here," I laughed. I smiled at him and patted his hand. "You know I'd never refuse you in a time of need. I'm here all day." I tapped the dark face of my phone to check the time. My long-standing personal rule to never catch a train out of Jersey later than 5:45 p.m. was offset by my concern.

He shook his head, looking agitated. "No, I mean, I need you to come home. *Come home*, come home. I need you here for a while."

I turned to Claudia. She pursed her lips and gave a little eye roll. "I don't know what to tell you," she said. "This is all he's been talking about since last night."

"What am I missing here, Dad? I know you're in pain and this is all new to you, but there's no internal bleeding and it sounds like you're going to be okay? You'll be discharged soon, they'll send you to a physical therapist, Claudia's taking care of you . . ." I turned to my stepmother and asked, "Is that what this is about, help around the house? I can come down another weekend this month. Pitch in with groceries or chores?" But I could already sense they were angling for something I wouldn't see coming. Claudia's blood type was Scrubbing Bubbles. There was no housework my manicured hands could perform that would meet her standard.

"Claudia's gone at work all day, you know that," Leo said, a lilt of exasperation in his voice. "You're not moving to Los Angeles anymore. You're out of a job. You've been sleeping on Winnie's couch. I just thought you moving home for a bit could be a mutually beneficial arrangement."

My stepmother's eyebrows were cocked so high, they kissed her hairline. "Leo," she said, her voice firm. "Tell her what else."

He tossed his head back and forth, squinting, weighing whatever he was about to say. "I was thinking, also, you could take my place on the team."

I stared at my father in his hospital bed, pale and weak. "You really did hit your head on the way down," I said. "What team? The men's softball team?"

"It's our year, Caro. We're going to the show!"

"What show?!"

"The *show*! The Glen Brook Men's Softball League championships! The World Series!"

The World Series. Which was in September. It was barely April. I felt light-headed.

"My drafting strategy worked," he continued, animated for the first time since I'd arrived. I half expected him to pull a Willy Wonka and somersault out of bed. "I got Ryan Buckley and Billy the Kid on the team. One of those high risk/high reward situations. Sure, we got some duds thrown in the mix, but what team doesn't? I can feel it in my bones. We're finally gonna take it all this year."

My father had been a staple in the Glen Brook Men's

Softball League since before I was born. When my parents' cohort started moving out of Brooklyn thirty years ago, looking for starter homes on Long Island or in Westchester, Leo followed the friends who had decamped to New Jersey—in part because they'd all joined local men's sports teams. It was minor in the grand scheme of things, but the prospect of playing ball was part of what drew my family to Glen Brook in the first place. Real fields with real grass. No more concrete makeshift infields at Gerritsen Beach, where every slide and dive meant a serious injury.

In the 1990s, Leo held the town record for most consecutive World Series wins. It seemed anywhere he went, his team was gilded for success. But he hadn't been on a winning team since 2000. He spoke often about how desperate he was to break his streak—never blaming the drought on his age, and even more than once loosely implying that 9/11 had something to do with it, claiming his "mojo was never the same after that." At times, this team meant more to him than anything.

In the natural light of the hospital window, I studied the color of my father's eyes. Hazel, warm, like spun wool. The same as mine. It sent a little primordial zap through me, looking directly into them. This man, this insane person, had stitch for stitch the same eyes as mine. What did that mean for me? This lunatic. My father.

"I'm not sure I understand what you're asking me," I said slowly. "Or why."

"There's a long-standing league rumor," Claudia said, like a teenager divulging a secret at a slumber party. "The enrollment clause has some kind of loophole in it. Something about how if you're severely injured you can have a family member sub in for you on the roster."

"But a daughter? In a *men's* softball league?" The men who played in this league weren't just men. These were men who were obsessed with being men. They saw sport as an analogue for war, despite their collective physical and emotional shortcomings. They were poster boys for toxic masculinity, notorious in local lore, and devoted to my father—their champion of a bygone decade.

"Well," said Claudia, "Leo had me text the commissioner about it last night. We have reason to believe we'll be able to challenge the league rules and have a woman replace your father."

"Great," I laughed, incredulous. "Then you can replace him!"

"Don't be smart," my father said, summoning the terse tone he used to discipline my sister and me as children. "I just told you we have a killer team this year and we finally have a real shot at taking it all. We need someone who has hand-eye coordination above a third-grade level." I looked over at

Claudia, expecting a hurt reaction, but was instead met with a wide-eyed nod in confirmation: *Ain't that the truth*.

"Caro, you know how to do a lot more than field a ball." He softened. "Glen Brook Little League hasn't seen a third baseman with an arm like yours since. Not to mention, we haven't had any competent switch-hitters in a dog's day. You're the best natural hitter in the Kline family."

"Thanks, but I've been impervious to flattery since I was twenty-five."

"I'm not trying to flatter you—it's the truth. You're the only person who can take my place," he said. I had to stifle a laugh. Harper—my older, California-based sister and my father's unspoken favorite—was famously the better ballplayer of the two of us. But before I could remind him of that, he insisted: "You've got real ability, my Caroline. You've got this dormant talent, and it's about time you woke up, because we really need it right now."

I slunk down in my chair, pulled down the bill of the Yankees cap masking my slick scalp over my eyes, and remained quiet. I wanted to magically blink my ass back to Greenwich Village like *I Dream of Jeannie*. Things had become shitty there, sure, but they were predictably shitty. Even as I licked my wounds over getting dumped, mourned the future I'd been manifesting, and watched as my funds dwindled dangerously low, I could be anonymous in the city streets. I could feign the visage of someone who sort of had their shit together. I could distract myself from my father aging out of his right mind: his bones splintering, his vulnerability leaking at the seams. I could forget the insanity of his asking me to move home after a few personal setbacks—not even as a caretaker, but as the renegade replacement third baseman on his adult men's softball team.

"It's gonna break my heart not to be out there for the start of the season, and I've got no control over it. But you've got control over this. We can right a cosmic wrong! All you'd have to do is move home for a little while and claim New Jersey residency to be eligible for—"

He was asking me to surrender. Quit. After three decades of fatherly attempts at pep talking and refrains of "never give up," he'd appraised the ruins of my adult life as something I should simply walk away from. I stood up and turned to face him. My face got hot.

"I'm gonna stop you right there," I said. "I took one step back across the state line because you were hurt and I was worried, and now you expect me to *move back*?"

"You just told me you'd never deny me in my time of need—"

"But you don't want me home to help! You want me home to play baseball!" Even in this circumstance, it stung on some level to have him disregard the life I'd built and struggled to maintain away from home. He made me feel like a branch on his tree, but I was trying (and, alright, failing) to be my own tree.

He pulled the blanket from the foot of the bed onto his lap like FDR. He picked up a thick David McCullough book off the bedside table that held all his personal effects: tissues, ginger ale, a family of remotes.

"I wish you'd reconsider," he said, looking down at an arbitrary page, pantomiming reading. "Knowing you don't have much tethering you to the city at the moment. You need a big change right now. I thought this was a solution."

He waited for me to challenge him, but I couldn't. My moving home would be an infuriatingly apt solution for my problems—namely, the pressure to find a new apartment and make rent while being unemployed. But while it would temporarily take the pressure off my finances, it would also feel like an admission that everything I'd done so far had gone wrong. I couldn't bear it.

"I hate to disappoint you," I said snidely, "but I'm trying to fix things in my own way. If it were Harper sticking it out in the city after a series of unfortunate events, you'd call her tenacious and never stop saying how proud you are."

He removed his reading glasses, folded them calmly, and put them down beside him before he looked up at me. "Harper would never refuse to help me if I asked her for it," he said. "Especially if my asking for help came with a generous offer to help her in exchange. But you ought to go, get on with your plan to fix things. I wouldn't want you to miss your train."

I stood up and grasped for my purse, pivoted on the heel

of my Saint Laurent boot, and walked out without saying goodbye. My cheeks burned as I stomped down a long, salmon-walled hallway in search of an exit. It was barely noon. I didn't have a ride. I'd have to wait for an Uber to come collect me from the hospital parking lot. The driver would inevitably be some sad soul I went to grade school with, if not someone my father's age who couldn't find a new job after one of the big banks went belly-up.

"He didn't just fall out of nowhere, you know." I was waiting at the curb, pulling sharp hits off my tiny nicotine vape, and hadn't heard Claudia come up behind me. The click of her kitten heels usually gave her away, but she was wearing old Ugg boots this morning.

"What does that even mean? You pushed him?" I sneered.

"You know he's strong as an ox. He runs faster than half those twentysomething schmucks in that softball league. Something's wrong." She was calm as she spoke, which was unnervingly uncharacteristic. I removed my sunglasses and looked at her.

"There's *been* something wrong, but so far it's just been little things," she continued. "Small movements that weren't quite right. I couldn't put my finger on it. But with this fall, I'm finally able to get him to talk to some doctors . . ."

"What do they think it could be?" Claudia had experience with grim diagnoses: an aunt with Lewy body dementia and a sister who died of ALS a decade ago.

"We don't know yet. The tests so far are inconclusive. He's hesitant to keep digging because he's scared and he's stubborn and he doesn't want to admit to any sign of deterioration, and I get that," she said, still even-keeled. "But at least we're starting to have a conversation."

Looking at Claudia, at her steady demeanor and earnest request, I conceded: I'd stay the night and go home first thing tomorrow morning. I cancelled the Uber. I put my sunglasses back on. I tilted my head back until my ponytail touched the middle of my spine, and I took a deep breath. I was surprised to find I was already crying. When had I started crying?

"It was more than a fall," she said, hushed. "And it's more than a replacement in the lineup. It's not just an offer to put you up while you figure out your next move. He doesn't know how to tell you that he needs you. But I can tell you that he needs you. I need you, too."

* * *

I CALLED MY sister later that night from my childhood bedroom. It was midnight in New Jersey and I was taking inventory of sentimental items missing from my shelves and walls since I'd last been there. Harper was three hours behind and a quintillion miles away in Sausalito.

"I've been ransacked," I said when she picked up, instead of *hello*. "A bunch of my shit has disappeared."

"So, the rumors are true?" Harper responded, sounding

lighthearted in a way that felt foreign to me. "You're moving home to replace Dad in the league?"

I groaned. "Don't believe everything Claudia texts you. I agreed to stay here one night and they've already got me in the starting lineup."

"Calm down, it was just a passing comment made between doctor updates. And, sure, maybe she mentioned it to the league commissioner, too—who's to say?" I pictured her stretched out on a tufted bench beneath a bay window, wearing something breezy and cream colored with a mug of sustainably sourced tea in hand. I was in tattered old pinstripe pajamas, shuffling across the dingy blue carpet while gripping a scuffed mug of Claudia's preferred merlot. "Wait," Harper said. "What kind of stuff is missing from your bedroom?"

Above my dresser where there was once a photo of Ben and me, a bleached rectangular ghost of a picture frame now hovered in its place. A bouquet of dried anniversary roses was gone from its fluted vase on my nightstand. The Mike Wazowski plush he'd won me from a Long Beach Island claw machine when we first started dating was missing from its spot atop my bed.

"Anything remotely Ben-related, it appears," I said, studying each surface within my pink-butterfly-papered walls.

Harper laughed. "Glad to see Dad and Claudia have kept the tradition going."

"Tradition?"

"Don't act like you don't know," she chided. "You thought every time you went through a breakup, all the relationship memorabilia just magically disappeared from your room and reappeared in my bedroom closet?"

"You're joking," I said, eyes scanning my room for evidence to the contrary. My shelves still held my girlhood ephemera: Molly the American Girl doll, my purple Game Boy, Spice Girls CDs. But no past relationship detritus.

"Caroline," Harper said after a beat, adopting a serious tone. "How is Dad doing, really?"

I wanted to tell her it was all one big melodramatic event and that our father was probably fine. I wanted to be absolved and go back to the city without being gnawed by lingering guilt or concern. "It's hard to tell," I said with a sigh, skulking across the hall to her childhood bedroom, mug of wine still in hand. "You know how he is, never getting sick or hurt. Mushing field dirt into an open knee wound after sliding into a base too hard. Seeing him in the hospital made him seem . . . old in a way I'd never noticed before."

"Mr. I've Never Taken a Sick Day in My Entire Life," she said, soft into the receiver. "He hates being reminded he's human."

I turned on Harper's ancient pink bubble lamp and slid the mirrored door to her closet open slowly so it wouldn't get knocked off its track. Tucked into the back of Harper's closet, everything was just where she said it would be. The framed photo of Ben and me, the crumbling brown rose petals, a goofy plush eyeball glaring at me.

"So, it's just routine ACL surgery and a couple months' recovery?" Harper asked, pivoting back to brass tacks. "I'm trying to figure out if I should stay put or get to the airport tomorrow."

Harper was anxious about our father but unwilling to up-end her life in California. I, on the other hand, was desperate for a reason to pretend nothing was wrong and go back to the way things were before. Our concern and our selfishness had the same source but took the shape of different containers.

"I wouldn't book any flights yet, but I am kind of worried, Harp." I sat in the open doorway of Harper's closet, parsing through its contents. "Claudia seems to think the fall didn't just happen on its own. She's having the hospital run tests."

"What kind of *tests*?" she hissed.

"I don't know. Neurological tests, I guess? Anything to explain clumsiness, weakness, stuff like that."

As we spoke, I discovered Harper's closet contained things not just from the Ben era. It was everything. Bleached-ink ticket stubs from dates at Regal Cinemas and concerts at Continental Airlines Arena. Photo albums of mini Polaroids. *The Notebook* on DVD.

"What are we talking here?" she snapped. "Like he's got

vertigo, or is this some Lou Gehrig shit?" When Harper's anxiety spiked, the Jersey accent she trained herself to tamp down poked through.

"Jesus, Harp," I said, sucking in air. "I have no idea what they're looking for. I just know they're looking."

She got quiet. It was hard to give my sister bad news, but I was grateful not to be alone with it anymore. "Look, that's why I'm staying the night. I felt like I had to after Claudia insinuated something might really be wrong."

"Well, does he seem like something's really wrong?"

I thought about my last interaction with Leo before visiting hours ended. After a bedside dinner of canned peaches and meat loaf, he'd stared into the middle distance in quiet contemplation.

"You alright, Pop?" I asked, putting a hand to the curve of his back. "Whatcha thinkin' about?"

He held my gaze for ten long seconds, as though he were conjuring something profound. Something about being humbled after a lifetime of athleticism and maintenance and avoidance of infirmity. Instead, he broke into a wry smile and said, "You know, we talk a lot about vigor, but how come we never hear about vim? No vim on its own. Just vim and vigor. I want to know what *vim* is up to."

"Honestly, Harper, he's pretty much the same as usual. A couple of times today he seemed foggy and confused, but it ended up passing. Might just be the pain medication they've got him on."

I yanked a dusty, tuxedoed Build-A-Bear from the closet—a gift from a boy I'd barely dated, remarkable only in that he was the first to touch my bare breast. He'd presented the bear to me on Valentine's Day at a discount hibachi restaurant on Route 9, and it mortified me. It had a heart sewn onto its paw that, when squeezed, said: *I love you! I love you!* When I squeezed it now, it belched one tragic *I love youuuuu,* deep and slow.

When Harper didn't respond, I added, "I go back and forth, trying to believe it's nothing and then getting scared it's something. I can't accurately gauge how concerned to be."

"Concerned enough that you're seriously considering moving back and taking his place on the team," she said, her voice low but firm.

"How did you get 'seriously considering' from this conversation?"

"You'd never stay the night in that house if you weren't considering it," Harper nearly whispered.

She was right. We had a thing about being back in the house after our parents' divorce. Harper had her own radical means of dealing with it. She shocked us all by moving three thousand miles away, marrying a man none of us had met, and preparing to give birth less than a year after our parents had sat us down and told us they were splitting. I dealt with it by leaning into what I'd built in the city—*my real life*—and coming home less and less. I'd used Ben as an excuse. Brought him to one night of Chanukah then claimed every holiday forever after that was "his family's turn to host us," just to avoid crossing the river.

"For all the years I joked about hacking my way into the league," Harper mused, softer now, "I can't believe you're the one who actually might do it."

"Want to trade places?"

"You want to *Freaky Friday* my ass and come deal with the kids and Sil?"

"I'll pass, thank you," I said, snorting. "Besides, it'd be more fun if you came back and played on the team *with* me."

It was difficult to imagine the full breadth of Harper's life in Sausalito. I'd been to visit, but a visit was just a scenic amalgamation, not an accurate rendering of the day-to-day. We'd walked the misty footpath of the Golden Gate Bridge, drank chilly white wine at the yacht club, and bought overpriced mugs from Alice Waters's preferred ceramicist. But for most of the trip, I found myself fixated on the local Robin Williams memorials, feeling sad we'd lost him in such a gruesome way.

"I can't stop thinking about Robin Williams," I had confessed to Harper while we were eating on a dock, puncturing what was likely a lovelier moment for her—strawberry sunlight on her face, anchovies and salted butter and sliced watermelon radishes on thick toast, the kids under her husband's watch at home.

"Robin Williams didn't even live here, Caroline," she said, frowning beneath enormous sunglasses. "He was from Tiburon."

But it didn't matter. In Sausalito, they'd named a big rainbow-painted tunnel the Robin Williams Tunnel, and whenever I thought about my sister's new faraway hometown, I associated it with dead celebrities and fifty-two-dollar mugs.

"I hate to ask," Harper sighed, "but have you spoken to Ben? Does he know what's going on?"

I pulled down a shoebox from a high shelf, plastered with colorful tape and the words KEEP OUT scribbled across the top. Inside were the trappings of my first unrequited love. A Nokia phone with a pink leopard-print faceplate. A wad of photos from an eighth-grade pool party printed off a disposable camera. An ancient tube of Dr Pepper lip balm. A green guitar pick strung on a chain. I unfolded a torn sheet of notebook paper and examined its contents. In childlike scrawl, it read: *I (Crispin Davis) promise to teach public school's finest (Caroline Kline) to SHRED THE AXE (if she ever gets one). This offer expires: NEVER!*

"I hate to ask," I parroted in response, slugging the rest of my wine and ignoring Harper's question about Ben, "but was I really this obsessed with Crispin Davis growing up? I have, like, thirty blurry photos of him in swim trunks stashed in a shoebox." I thumbed through the photos, staring into the printed green eyes of my defining teenage crush. Eyes I last saw fifteen years ago, flashing across a dark gymnasium. My chest still fluttered at the thought.

"You certainly don't need me to remind you how obsessed you were with Crispin Davis," Harper said into the phone. "You're being a bad baby."

She would know about bad babies. She had two of them. A four-year-old boy named Tolon and a two-year-old girl, Nina. It wasn't that they were bad, exactly, but they were loud. How could the quiet sister bear such loud children?

"So everyone just picks through my stuff and hides it from me? Dad thinks I'm that much of a delicate flower?" I asked, refilling the box and setting it aside. "Also, some liberties were taken. Only in my wildest dreams was Crispin Davis my ex-boyfriend."

"We were just looking out for you, Caro," Harper laughed. "I love how you're only noticing the Hall of Exes now that you're thinking about moving back."

"I'm not thinking about moving back," I repeated by rote as I uncovered yet another box of old photos that made my breath catch. Kelly Quinn stared back at me.

"Uh, why is there Kelly Quinn memorabilia in my mausoleum of exes?"

"Oh, you mean, the worst breakup of them all?" Harper said, incredulous.

Kelly was the sort of best friend you formed an intense bond with at eleven years old, then looked back and wondered if you weren't a little bit in love with each other. There were photos of Kelly and me, dressed in our softball uniforms at the Little League World Series, cartoonishly flexing our biceps. Kelly and me, in matching seafoam sleep shirts at a slumber party, arms wrapped around each other. Kelly was a head taller than me in every shot—some cosmic joke, maybe, to keep me gazing up at her in quiet awe. I knew what these photographs smelled like: Kelly's sweet, floral Tommy Girl perfume and pink Herbal Essences conditioner. I'd use her bath products whenever I slept at her house, and when I'd return home the next day, I'd keep sniffing myself, trying to conjure her.

"I bet your old war crony would support you hijacking a men's league. You two, with your back-to-back girls' softball World Series championships."

I winced. "Actually, only Kelly had back-to-back wins," I corrected her, sliding shut the closet door on my past, save the couple of shoeboxes I kept in the crook of my arm. "I was only on her team for the first of the two."

"Look," Harper said, in the resigned tone she'd take when she remembered she had crafted a life to retreat to, "please keep me posted on Dad. Let me know what you decide to do."

"Dad's not getting discharged for another few days," I said, a little dazed from the wine and the nostalgia. I went back to my own room, closed the door behind me, and sat on the floor beside my bed. "I'm heading back in the morning. Claudia's driving me to the train."

"To pack your things?" she teased.

I rolled my eyes. "To think things over." I didn't want to explain to her what I suspected she already knew: that I'd spent years inside this very bedroom, dreaming up ways to leave Glen Brook behind me forever. Plotting a map of my life that led to a metropolitan existence and looked like success as I'd always defined it. Coming home would crumple that map. It would feel like an admission of defeat.

I spread the artifacts I'd taken from Harper's closet out in front of me. The great ghosts of my hometown. Evidence of dissolved relationships I still dreamed about sometimes into adulthood. I touched Crispin Davis's signature, then Kelly Quinn's glossy face. I imagined the younger version of me, the last time I'd sat in this room, with this ephemera. Who I had been and what I had aspired to. Everything that was still ahead of me. Every disappointment I didn't know to fear yet.

3

WHEN I GOT back to the city, Winnie and I met at our regular hole-in-the-wall, installed ourselves at the bar, and ordered our usual: chips and guac and four margaritas. Above our heads, a flat-screen television wreathed in string lights played a hit movie from the 1980s. It was where everybody knew our names, if only so they could ask us to quiet down.

"Alright, pitch it to me again," Winnie said, pinching loose cilantro off our guacamole and sprinkling it onto the bar top without a care. She'd gotten there first and was a margarita ahead of me, loose and warm. "Leo's at death's door and you have to take his place on the team and protect your family's honor?"

"God, no." I wasn't yet anesthetized enough for *death's door*. "It's not that dramatic. He fell. He's hurt. He's asking me to come home for a couple of months to help around the house while he recovers."

She cocked a skeptical eyebrow at me. "And yes," I sighed, "one aspect of helping out happens to be filling in as third baseman in his barbaric men's softball league that I'm almost positive they're not going to let me play in."

"Got it," she said, grabbing the last tortilla chip. "It's giving *Mulan*, but make it baseball."

I gave the bartender a pleading look, which he knew meant I needed another drink. *Purple Rain* played on mute against the shelves of glinting liquor behind him. Last time it had been *The Outsiders*, and Winnie and I had been shushed after rattling off our cast rankings in order of fuckability. ("Honestly, I don't even think it was me being loud that offended them," she insisted. "I think it was you forgetting to rank Diane Lane and then including Leif Garrett at all.")

"So, what's the new plan, Stan? You're really thinking about going?" she asked while flagging down another bowl of chips.

Winnie was so married to the idea that she would never leave New York that, on some level, she believed everyone close to her should also stay forever. And I understood it, because if I was Winnie, I would never leave either. She was part of a cool community of leftist Mizrahi Jews who hosted weekly Shabbat dinners, was verified on Instagram, and had dated at least two professional sports stars and one Booker Prize nominee in the last three years.

Winnie hated any conversation around leaving the city. A book of essays about "escaping" New York came out years ago while we were still trying to climb the ladder, and it made her indignant. "Why brag about throwing in the towel?" she'd said. "How mortifying. And don't get me started on those people who move to Phoenicia and call themselves *expats*." When my abandonment of the Los Angeles plan came at the expense of my long-term boyfriend, job, and daydream future, Winnie seemed pleased because I was, at the very least, staying in Manhattan. And after I had discovered that my replacement at the agency had outpaced me so spectacularly in just her first month—already bringing in a new seven-figure retainer client and ruining any chance I had of asking for my old job back—she insisted I crash at her place while I figured things out. Better sharing a one-bedroom for a few weeks than giving up on New York.

"There is no real plan. I only told them I'd think about it. Also, this league loophole is just speculation right now," I explained, flicking my tongue at the salt rim of my margarita glass. "But I guess giving a probationary go of it would entail leaving the city until Dad is healed up enough to play, or at least not require constant companionship."

I looked up at her, expecting her to balk, but she just sat sucking on her cocktail straw, nodding, twirling the pink paper umbrella between her thumb and forefinger.

"I guess I'd . . . see if they actually let me step in to play?

Then I could apply to jobs from the confines of my childhood bedroom? The whole prospect feels so grim to me. I just hate to abandon—"

"Abandon what?" she said, half laughing. "Caroline, you're down to the dregs of your savings account. You hired your own too-competent successor, and it's going to take a minute before you find another job like that one. I don't think going home for a little while and saving some money is an unreasonable option."

I stared at her, stunned she wasn't trying to pressure me into staying. She had berated me for weeks for wanting to move to Los Angeles with Ben. I realized then that I'd been counting on her to talk me out of giving in and going home. I hadn't considered how I'd react to her encouraging it.

"Look, obviously I want you here, but in the long term this might actually work out to your benefit. You'd have some buffer time to find a new gig. You'd be doing a good deed for your dad. It's more than just a chance to save money; I think it'd be a good distraction from this whole mess." *This whole mess* had become shorthand for Ben's leaving me.

Winnie was the effervescent kind of friend I felt lucky to have, which made me grateful I'd known her for most of my life. She grew up in Glen Brook just three blocks from me, and we spent the last two decades walking in lockstep with each other. When we were fifteen, we started cutting class, taking the bus to Manhattan and scheming about moving to the city for college and becoming our own fictional ideals. She wanted to be a playwright, continuing the long tradition of alchemizing the tragedy of the Jewish experience into comedic fodder. I wanted to be a rock journalist—a femme Chuck Klosterman—and live on tour buses for months out of the year.

We both ended up going to NYU, but she came closer to our dreams than I did to mine. I ended up in marketing as an event producer with a penchant for spending beyond my means on designer clothing and restaurant hopping. She was a staff writer for *The New Yorker*, which she'd joke just meant being verified on social media and having a tolerance for long elevator rides inside the Freedom Tower.

"It's not a bad option," Winnie nudged. "Could be a good chance to recalibrate, you know? Give yourself some time and space to think about where you want to be next. What you actually want to be doing."

The concrete around my reality began to harden. I knew I wasn't losing Winnie, but I was losing what I shared with her. No matter how depressed we'd been at any point of our lives in New York City—failed relationships, professional disappointments, the wide gulf between what we dreamed for ourselves and the actuality we crafted—we were buoyed by the petty belief that we still had one up on our Glen Brook High School peers. The ones who stayed in the suburbs and posted little keyhole peeks into their lives on Facebook. I believed if you left your hometown and failed, you didn't *really* fail, because at least you left. I'd spent a decade clinging to this essential truth.

Convincing myself otherwise was the part of the plan I hadn't yet come up with.

4

I WAS BACK in Glen Brook less than a week later, riding shotgun in my stepmother's car and staring down a pair of baseball-shaped Mylar balloons that read HAPPY BIRTHDAY tethered to the mailbox. Claudia paused before pulling all the way into the driveway and looked at me expectantly. "Well, they didn't have any 'Welcome Home' balloons," she said. I pursed my lips together in a weak, insincere smile.

Inside was no better: glossy streamers hung down from the foyer's high ceilings (how had she even gotten up there?), and a banner of gold letters with thick joints spelled out WELCOME HOME, CAROLINE! over the railing of the staircase. It all had big family birthday party vibes. I half expected trays of once-frozen jalapeño poppers from Costco to be arranged on the kitchen countertop.

I followed Claudia as we shuttled my bags to the room

where I slept for the first eighteen years of my life. In the short span of time since I'd last been there, Claudia had crafted a makeshift pied-à-terre, complete with a mini fridge and microwave like a freshman dorm room. A card table with a sheet over it had been placed in the corner by the window, bearing a platter with a small single-serve coffee maker, a basket of coffee pods, and a speckled camping mug that had ROOK COFFEE emblazoned across it.

Claudia requested I join her and Leo downstairs after I'd had a moment to settle. "He's not really up to doing the stairs more than once a day," she whispered. I chased away the thought of him feebly attempting to climb the Cinderella staircase—his favorite feature of the house—as I descended it, following the nostalgic sound of John Sterling's booming commentator voice into the great room, where it echoed off the slanted ceiling.

Leo was propped up in his favorite spot, the corner of our buttery brown leather sectional. Every surface surrounding him—the side tables, the long console behind the couch—was littered with greeting cards and flowers.

"All from his teammates," Claudia said, stepping into the kitchen, where there were arrangements of chocolate-covered pineapple chunks cut into butterfly shapes and smoked-fish platters from Ringer's Bialys. "And some from his rivals," she added, pointing at a box of fat pears wrapped in gold foil, allegedly soft enough to eat with a spoon. "It's been a nice reminder for him, to remember how the league reveres him."

"Are you sure they don't think he died?" I asked, eyeing the trays of pastrami and rye bread from my favorite kosher deli over on Pond Road. It was at least a week's worth of food. "I just hope no one shows up to pay a shiva call."

Back in the great room, the glow of the Yankees flashed on the enormous screen, reflecting in my dad's big wire-rimmed glasses straight out of the 1980s. He always hated the network announcers, so the television was muted and the mildewed plastic shower radio at his side was turned all the way up, the sounds of the game tinny and waterlogged. It was enough to make me want to look past the circumstances, if only for a split second, and slip down next to him on the couch, letting the game wash over me like warm water. The sound of the broadcast alone could lower my blood pressure.

"What we have here," my father said, clapping and rubbing his hands together as soon as the game cut to a commercial break, "is a real case of tikkun olam."

"Please hold the hyperbole. I'm having sincere doubts about my ability to still swing a bat. We don't even know if the petition to let me play is going to pass."

"Oh, it passed alright," Claudia said, back with a collection of my father's medications in one hand—pill bottles clustered into the salmon-pink shower caddy I used my freshman year of college (where on earth had she found that thing?)—and a printed stack of papers in the other hand. "We waited to deliver the good news in person. Meeting minutes," she added as she dropped the stack into my lap. "Read 'em and weep."

After a day of snooping in the municipal complex cellar, Claudia found a register from an August 1977 game with a stipulation to the lineup. On the ledger, they listed a woman named Ruby Winnick batting cleanup and playing right field. A note in the margins indicated she'd substituted for a guy named Donnie Winnick, who played in every other game that season.

In the case that the player becomes injured or infirm during the regular season and cannot perform for a spell that cannot be immediately determined, the handbook noted, *the player may designate a family member as an alternate. Family member must meet league selection criteria.*

"It doesn't say *shit* about being a woman! We're calling it 'The Ruby Winnick Loophole.' The board voted, and we won by a narrow margin. Your father had to recuse himself and everything."

My father waved a hand across his face, as though shooing a fly. "That's not what I'm talking about. I'm talking about Caroline's homecoming. The pursuit of victory." He turned to me, lowered his glasses to look at me. "What you're doing right now is a real mitzvah."

Something I loved about my father was his willingness to consider any act of kindness—no matter if it was as noncommittal as putting a spare dollar into a paper cup or as grandiose as, say, moving home at a parent's behest—a mitzvah. "What can I say?" I shrugged. "My mitzvah count was low." More urgently, so was my bank account.

The caddy of medicines made me nauseous the longer I looked at it. The sickening cadence of Claudia removing each bottle, one by one, and examining the label through readers perched at the end of her nose. Unscrewing each cap and counting out a precise number of pills to place on the card table in front of my dad among the remotes and sections of newspaper. Trying to digest this tableau in front of me made me feel like gravity was loosening its grip. I wanted to run back to the city, stay out all night with Winnie, drain margaritas and lick the salt off the rim and shimmer with sex and possibility until the bruise of the night sky healed into dawn. If I'd stayed in the city with her, I could have avoided all this to some degree. I could have kept running around and finding ways to anesthetize and distract myself. Coming home meant a halt to the party. Grief would inevitably seep into the void. It was already starting to.

"Caro, this is more than a mitzvah, really," my father said, pulling my attention back to the great room. "I spoke to the rabbi this morning, and he agreed. This could be your tikkun olam. I'm not being hyperbolic; I'm being serious."

Tikkun olam was a concept that preoccupied and enchanted me in Hebrew school as a kid. *A Jewish person's life mission to heal the world.* I remember the day we learned the phrase, how I held it close to my chest. It was one of those things that seemed steeped in magic and promise, like *manna* or *beshert*. It made me feel excited to be alive: To believe I was here for a reason. To believe I existed to fulfill a mission and do my part to heal the world.

I hadn't thought about tikkun olam in years. As the Yankees resumed gameplay, I tried to tell my father the stakes were not quite high enough to qualify this as an act of global healing, but he wouldn't hear it.

"That's how I know you've been stuck among schmucks for too long, doubting yourself like that." I imagined him summoning the image of Ben's tanned, grinning face to the forefront of his mind, cursing him and the next three generations of his family. "You're a superstar, Caro," he said, leaning over to pat my head with the arm that wasn't in a sling before settling back into his seat. "Deal with it."

After a few innings of watching the Yankees waver, I started to think of reasons to excuse myself. To unpack, to pee, to cry from the privacy of Harper's closet. In the hallway, I stood at the bottom of the staircase for a moment like I had as a kid. The view was similar, but everything else was different: the people inside, the scents emanating from Claudia's candles and aromatic sachets tucked into every corner, instead of my mother's perfume. I stared at my banner: WELCOME HOME, CAROLINE! The sticky tack holding it in place had given way, and my name drooped and hung at a dismal angle, kissing the walnut-stained stairs.

· · ·

I DECIDED UPON returning to New Jersey that if I didn't carve out a daily routine for myself, the magnitude of my situation would hit me and I'd opt into sleeping all day and slip into a depression—the caliber of which I'd never known. Instead, I had a plan. Wake up every morning at sunrise. Go for a run down the long road that abutted my father's house. After my run, I'd shower, dress for the day in a matching black athleisure set, and install myself in Leo's office to keep my finger on the pulse of experiential marketing job posts. Leo would be on the couch, limbs propped up at whatever angle they needed to be in order to facilitate healing. I would be within earshot, prepared to leap up and grab meals or newspapers for him on command.

I managed this routine two days in a row before abandoning it. After that, I stayed up late watching video tours of celebrities' homes on YouTube and stalking Ben's friends' Instagram stories from a private burner account. I siphoned Claudia's mediocre wine supply. I stopped setting an alarm and let myself be roused from the weighted burgundy velvet of my hangover only by Leo shouting for help retrieving the remote or more coffee. When I'd arrive at his side, hair matted to my head and a white, crusty flourish of dried drool on my cheek, he'd tsk and say, "Ugh, Caroline, again with these green sweatpants?"

Not that my father ever let me rest too long. Around three most afternoons, Leo requested transport to the local park—not to enjoy sunlight and fresh suburban air on his face but to ready me for the rapidly approaching season, which was set to start in just two weeks. Shuffling him off the couch, into the car, out of the car, and onto the field was a workout in itself, but then the real training began.

After situating him outside the batter's box in his canvas camping chair, I'd start "batting practice," which was just me taking softballs out of an old chlorine tablet bucket, tossing them high in the air, and swinging at them in hopes of hitting a reasonable number into the outfield. Then he'd have me run drills around the baselines and practice sliding until a strawberry bruise bloomed on my right hip.

If Leo was disappointed in my performance, he let me know. If I did something praiseworthy, he conceded only a smug smile. He held my ability to impress him, still, just out of reach. "When you walk off that field after a game," he instructed in a near-bark from his post off to the side, "you are to remain dignified, win or lose. Confident, not cocky. Think of Whitey Ford. He wasn't a tall man, but he kept his shoulders up and his head down."

After a week of training alone, he decided to assemble the rest of the team for a late-afternoon practice. He was eager to observe our new dynamic and have us get acclimated to one another. Despite it being a team of twelve, only two other players showed up: Timmy "The Tortoise" Moriarty and baby-faced Robbie Walker.

Timmy Moriarty was one of the old-timers. An outfielder around Leo's age with a hint of a hump to his back, he wore big plastic goggles he called his "Rec Specs," which offered zero perceptible improvement to his gameplay. The last time his bat made meaningful contact with the ball was probably sometime in 1994. I knew from my years as a spectator how he liked to mutter little affirmations to himself while he was at bat ("Come on, Timbo, you've got this, buddy . . .") before hitting a pop-up to the infield, at which point he'd scream *FUCK* and trudge toward first base, knowing he was an easy out. He arrived to practice first, mistakenly called me "Carol," and hugged Leo too tight in his camp chair, making him wince. "This'll all be over soon, buddy," he said, patting Leo's bad shoulder gruffly. "We need you to heal up and get back out there with us."

I'd gone to high school with Robbie Walker and was fond of him, though not as fond as he was of me. As teenagers, I'd admired how he contained multitudes: batting cleanup on the varsity team and starring as Tony in the sophomore production of *West Side Story*. As adults, I fucked him in a bathroom stall at a Belmar bar one Thanksgiving Eve after four gin and tonics. That was the year we'd graduated college, and I could tell by the way he still got all pink and breathless whenever I ran into him in the years following that he'd been waiting for a repeat performance ever since. When he arrived to practice, he greeted me with a flushed, awkward embrace.

After twenty-five minutes of guided stretches, Leo gave up hope that the rest of the team would show and sunk into a scowling anger. "This was not a casual lunch invitation," he growled, unable to swallow the absentees' disrespect. "Leo Kline's practices are mandatory!"

I wondered if the men on the team were trying to slight him. Maybe the no-shows were meant to send a message that Leo hadn't chosen a suitable replacement? Or perhaps preseason practices were so few and far between, they had forgotten in earnest. Was this a simple act of negligence, or was it a protest?

"I'm sure a few of the guys just got caught in commuter traffic or something," Robbie offered with a nervous grin. "There's still time for them to show."

"What the fuck are we supposed to do with only three players?" Leo yelled, but he wasn't really asking the question.

"We can do lots, Mr. Kline!" Robbie answered anyway, springing to his feet and jogging to grab the batting equipment.

Leo instructed Timmy to toss me orange Ping-Pong balls while Robbie chased the ones I hit, collecting them as they dotted the field. The Ping-Pong balls were a Little League practice tactic my dad used when I was ten to "make the game ball look as big as a watermelon" in comparison. It seemed ridiculous, but his instinct wasn't wrong; I had one of the best batting averages in the girls' division. "If my coaching legacy in this town is tiny balls, so be it," he said once while driving home from Little League after I pulled a game-winning sizzler to left field. The resolution in his voice made me spray pink Powerade out my nose and all over his windshield.

Now all he could do was watch from his post, critiquing my form while Timmy Moriarty failed to throw even a single Ping-Pong ball in the strike zone and Robbie ran around like a golden retriever in the background.

"This is like watching clowns play," Leo barked after I chased and missed another ball.

By then I was sweating and achy and angry. Leo was mad none of his men had shown up—no one who'd have made it a worthwhile practice, anyway—and he was taking it out on me. I threw my bat down and whipped around to face him. "Who are you calling a fucking clown?" I yelled. "How about some of that constructive criticism for Igor on the mound over there?" I pointed at Timmy, who looked like he was going to cry, then proceeded to rip his Rec Specs off and throw them in the dirt at his feet.

"Watch your language, Caroline! And pick up that fucking bat!" my father yelled back. But he knew I had a point. "Timbo, buddy," he said, attempting to yell softer. "Why don't you take center field for a while? Robbie, you're on the mound. Give her some real balls now." Timmy trudged to the outfield, and Robbie, red as a beet, started throwing actual softballs to me, slow and underhand. Following each pitch, Leo continued his running commentary about my form, but I got better with each swing. My perception narrowed into a cone of focus.

"Faster now, Robbie," my father commanded. "Same speed they'd throw at during a game. Caroline, you're gonna run on the first real hit. Don't look at it, just go. Take some practice swings first."

I touched the tip of my bat to the far corner at the top of home plate, approximating where the handle reached and standing in that spot. Right foot aligned with the closest corner. A few practice swings: my weight shifted to the back of my body, power compressed then released in my right leg, rising up my sides like heat, through my biceps, into the bat. The force of cutting through the air. The ache for contact, for resistance. The audible whoosh like a caped superhero springing into action.

If you stepped away from it long enough, you might forget. But baseball lurked in unsuspecting talismans. The slick sheen of the grass after a downpour could trigger decades of dormant physical devotion. The sticky rubber grip of the bat in your hands. The soft leather palm of a well-worn mitt. Every scent was a memory. Every pitch was a storm. That bat was a lightning rod. I was a house, ready to see if I'd catch fire.

· · ·

WHAT SEEMED LIKE an impossible change just weeks before had become my reality. Claudia lent me the old green Saab she kept in the driveway under a sheet, a vestige from her youth she couldn't bear to part with. I caught myself sometimes— driving the Saab to run errands, wearing the old neighborhood like a second skin—and realized some undertow from within was trying to carry me toward acceptance and assimilation. *You are really here, and this is really happening.* It startled me. Sometimes I'd flinch, alone and unprovoked.

I took Leo to his weekly physical therapy appointments, where I stood guard in the corner of the room and tried not to wince as I watched him grimace in time with the practitioner's bending of his limbs.

"So, this is the baseball star!" the physical therapist exclaimed on my first trip in, and I blushed reflexively. "It's so good to finally meet you, Harper! Leo never stops talking about you."

My father attempted to recover: "Actually, this is Caroline, Harper's little sister. She's come home to stay with me for a while and take my spot on the team." He glanced over at my sunken face and turned back to the therapist. "She was a bit of a baseball star in her youth, too," he offered. "Harper had that golden arm, but Caro's a great natural hitter."

It didn't matter. The therapist still called me Harper every week, and by the third visit, I'd stopped correcting him. I wished I was Harper, too. I longed for the insulation and security of her life; the distance that shielded her from watching our father in decline as he hobbled around in his sling and crutches, too proud to use a walker or, God forbid, a wheelchair.

Occasionally, I'd have lunch with my mother, Bobbi, who lived only twenty minutes away and was in the middle of a personal renaissance: the new era of her life she could not accomplish while still being tethered to my dad. Once they divorced, she started dressing in long, drapey layers and scarves (like Stevie Nicks without the top hat) and took a chairwoman's seat with the Glen Brook Players. Within the year, the local theatre staged my mother's original musical, *Hannie*. A prequel to *Annie*, the show was a sympathetic portrait of Miss Hannigan exploring the tumultuous life and Midwestern upbringing that, ultimately, led her to her fate as the dismal, disturbed matron of a New York City orphanage. It was lauded for being humanizing, humorous, and wholly original. "*Wicked* walked so *Hannie* could run," she liked to say.

"Now I'm casting for *Guys and Dolls*, but gender roles reversed," she told me over brunch in her neighborhood, crisscrossing her fingers to indicate the swap. When she moved out, she bought an old candy-colored Victorian house in Ocean Grove—the historic Methodist community that abutted Asbury Park—and turned it into a boardinghouse for Jewish divorcées in a state of transition. The wooden sign out front read *Agunot by the Sea*. She wanted to be close to the beach and to give other women a soft place to land. The coasters on her coffee tables read: *Saltwater cures everything*.

"I'm in the market for a choreographer and a musical director. So, if you know anyone."

"*Know anyone?*" I was careful not to let food fly out of my mouth, my fingers flying up to gate my lips. "Ma, I'm here to play baseball and keep an eye on Dad." The fewer people I came in contact with, the better. I already felt a prickle of shame walking into the restaurant we were in, recognizing at least one member of the waitstaff as someone I'd known in high school.

I worried she'd think my moving home meant I was doing exactly what she wanted to avoid: sacrificing the *self* for a *man*. More specifically, a man named Leo Kline. But instead, when I told her what I was doing, she seemed thrilled at the prospect of seeing me more often and, frankly, too preoccupied with getting *Dolls and Guys* off the ground to care.

"That's good," she said, dusting crumbs off her sweater onto the pale blue Formica tabletop. "Stay focused. Keep your head down and that mitzvah count up."

Preseason days mostly ended the same way: Claudia came

55

home from work and enlisted my help in making a dinner that looked straight out of a grease-stained 1970s *Good Housekeeping* cookbook, complete with a side dish of medications for Leo. I'd open a bottle of wine "to split" and end up draining it myself—something I wouldn't have clocked back in the city. Later, we'd watch the Yankees game to see what "lessons in tenacity" I could glean, usually against my volition. I longed to unwind in the ways I was capable of only from behind a closed bedroom door: getting lost in a novel I'd never be seen with on the subway, curling next to the warmth of my laptop as I watched a TV show I'd seen ten times already on Netflix, attempting to masturbate to the thought of someone who wasn't my ex. But according to Leo, I was not to forget that this journey home—this mitzvah—was, above all, about baseball.

"I thought it was about honoring my family," I'd respond, turning to my father, nestled in his corner of the couch whenever he said something like this.

"Baseball is your family," he'd say back without breaking eye contact from the screen.

If I asked how he was feeling, he always said, "Good," with an exhale and zero eye contact. It felt as though we were all part of a carefully orchestrated performance around the house—my father insisting he was fine, and Claudia following his lead between rounds of administering his medication. The dance of denial continued each time I asked how he was really doing. But if I pushed, he would retaliate and ask me questions he knew I didn't want to answer either: how much longer I'd be covered by my old company's COBRA health insurance, or if Ben had unblocked me on Instagram yet.

Sometimes he asked about my friends or if I'd spoken to Harper or what music I'd been listening to. But mostly he asked, *Holy fuckoly, did you just see that play?* And: *Did I ever tell you about the time I got Joe Pepitone to show up at your uncle's bachelor party?* And we watched the game, the ancestral tie that bound us. Our love for that diamond steeped in our blood like tea.

5

MY FIRST GAME was on an idle Wednesday night. Everything on me was new: new cleats, new bat, new glove. Everything was a little stiff, and nothing had a story attached to it yet. Our team was sponsored by Ringer's Bialys on Main Street, and my crisp yellow shirt featured an anthropomorphic bagel. I wore fitted black pants, thick at the knees for sliding reinforcement. Across my back in white vinyl letters: C. KLINE.

We were assigned the visitors, which, in a league where we played only other Glen Brook teams, just dictated who batted first and which side of the field was ours. The bare visitors bench made me long for the Little League dugouts of my youth: the painted blue cinder block clubhouses where gruff girlhood reigned supreme, all spitting and chants and spraying Gatorade into the dirt so we could write expletives on the walls in mud with our tiny fingers.

There would be no slumber party–style camaraderie here. As I clipped my bag on the fence, I spotted Ryan Buckley and Billy the Kid ambling over from the parking lot. I'd known them since I was a teenager: they were both a few years ahead of me at the high school, and whispers of their bad boy reputations haunted the halls even after they'd graduated. I'd also seen them get ejected from multiple games when I'd watched my father play against them. I'd have recognized their signature swaggering gait and too-loud cackling from across a major league stadium, but there they were—the reigning champion brothers of the league—sidling up to me on the bench. The problematic favorites. My teammates.

Billy was the younger of the two—both the best hitter and the true enfant terrible of the league. He looked the part: gangly arms covered in loud tattoos; a cigarette always sticking out of his stubbly mouth; sweaty, unkempt ringlets poking from beneath his ballcap. Ryan was maybe two years older than him, the star pitcher and regarded as the more reasonable of the pair. He had long, dishwater-colored hair he kept in a low-slung bun but was otherwise clean-cut to Billy's scruff: no tattoos, no nicotine dependency, a big toothy grin. Even with Ryan's all-American-boy charm, I knew he could get just as wild as Billy on and off the field.

They ignored me as they carried on about the captain of the team we were about to face, their perennial rival who'd been drafted to the Door Crusaders—a just-okay team sponsored by the local garage door repair company.

"And if he even looks at me funny," boomed Billy the Kid, "I'll break his other fuckin' ankle this time."

Ryan cackled in reply, then, when an uncomfortable amount of time in silence had passed, turned around and finally acknowledged me. "Hey! Ruth Bader Ginsburg!" he said, clapping me on the back. "She has arrived!"

"Sandra Day O'Connor would be more apt, no?" I asked as I pulled my ponytail through the hole in the back of my Bialys cap. He went back to ignoring me.

As the rest of the Bialys shuffled into the dugout, my greetings ranged from lukewarm to nonexistent. A couple of the old-timers—league veterans and Leo's peers who'd known me as a child—gave small, genial waves accompanied with rhetorical *hi-how-are-ya*s. Timmy Moriarty, still peeved about my name-calling at the practice, narrowed his eyes and turned his hump on me.

As expected, I got a quick, sweaty embrace from Robbie Walker. Also as expected, I got an outright sneer from Pete Peretti, a buff late-thirties power hitter who looked like a *Jersey Shore* casting reject with his dark, slicked-back hair and thick, manicured eyebrows. I'd never met him in person but knew from a social media search that he owned a local vitamin shop and at least one garment with the words *Hillary for Prison* printed on it. Even though his on-base percentage was among the highest in the league, he was better known for an incident during a playoff game a few years back. After striking out, Pete had pulled his pants down to his ankles, turned to face the mound, and told the pitcher to suck his cock. The cops had to come to the field.

"Since an unacceptable number of you opted out of last week's team practice, I realize not all of you have been formally introduced yet," Leo said from his spot on the bench, waving his sling around as the rest of the team filed in, passing a roll of duct tape and a marker around to denote where their bag hung, which water bottle was theirs, and to write "EAT ME" across Timmy's ass. "This is my replacement, my daughter Caroline. She's taking over at third base until further notice."

I raised a simultaneous eyebrow and hand to wave hello. The men stayed quiet and looked at me as though they'd been saddled with Betty Boop to lead their battalion into battle. Part of me wanted to shrink away, and the other part of me thought: *You don't like it? Too damn bad. I don't like it either.*

"Time to receive communion," Ryan called out, clapping and rubbing his hands together. I looked over at my father, who rolled his eyes as if to say: *Not this again.* Pete Peretti pulled a Ziploc baggie filled with a dozen blue gummies out of his back pocket and waggled them in front of everyone's faces as they circled around him, holding their hands out. After he'd deposited one into every palm except for mine, they huddled in close and yelled, "*GIMME THE JUICE!*" in one another's faces, then exaggeratedly popped the blue gummies into their mouths.

"Uh, sir?" I muttered from outside the scrum, turning to Leo. "Any other pregame rituals or other forms of communion you'd like to brief me on? I have no aptitude for steroids or Catholicism."

Leo waved me off, incredulous. "It's just B_{12} vitamins. Something Peretti's hawking at his little supplement shop and doling out to his teammates the last couple seasons. I don't like it, but if they think it's gonna help with their bats, they can go right ahead." I let myself wonder for a moment if Pete had run out of gummies or if he just didn't want to include me in the ritual, but I already knew the answer.

The umpire cried out a few minutes later—indicating the ball was in play—and the game unfurled around me. I watched my teammates strike out, field a couple of simple plays, and shout staccato little messages about the pitch count: *Two down, two away!* I felt less like part of the team and more like a spectator with uncanny access to the field until the second inning, when I had my inaugural at bat. I hit a long line drive deep to center field, but Anthony Scolari—the Door Crusaders' crew-cut, loudmouthed outfielder and sworn rival of the

Buckley brothers—made a dramatic show of intercepting the ball. He pumped his fists in the sky like he'd pulled off a Willie Mays–caliber upset.

Hungry to return the favor, I got my chance when Scolari hit a pop fly right to me in the third inning with two outs. "I got it!" I called, tilting my head all the way back to trace the ball's trajectory into my glove. But before it landed, a brute force came at my side, knocking the wind out of my chest and knocking my body down into the dirt before landing on top of me. It was Timmy Moriarty, who had ignored my call and ran to catch the ball himself, which landed with a dull thud beside us. Two runs scored, and Scolari made it to second base easily.

"What the fuck, Timmy?" I shouted, dusting myself off. "You don't believe me when I say, 'I got it'?"

"I didn't hear you!" he yelled, adjusting his Rec Specs, but we both knew that was a lie.

"Yes, you fucking did!" left my mouth, but I wasn't looking at Timmy, I was looking over at my father—planted in the dugout with his eyes narrowed to pits—waiting for him to defend me.

Instead, Ryan Buckley, Robbie, and the umpire approached us, halting gameplay. Ryan clapped Timmy on the curve of his back and walked him back out to left field. I heard him in the distance: "You're not the problem here, Timbo. Remember this is only temporary; don't let her bitchin' get to you." Robbie pulled me over the baseline for an aside, but the umpire wanted me first.

"Little lady," he said, removing the tiny cage from his sweaty red face, "we adhere to a strict code of conduct in this league. There'll be no swearing. There are families watching the game. I know you're new here, but you need to know there'll be no special treatment for you."

I faced Robbie with my back to the umpire, holding up my hand and calling over my shoulder, "If there's no special treatment, then I expect you'll be calling my teammates *little ladies* as well. But got it, no cursing, cool."

I knew these wholesome families had previously been subjected to Billy the Kid's threats, Tony Scolari's toilet mouth, and—on at least one occasion—a sobering glimpse of Pete Peretti's testicles.

"Don't cry to Leo about Timmy the Tortoise," Robbie murmured as the umpire retreated, like he was delivering classified information in a spy movie.

"God, I hate this revival of *Evita*."

"I'm serious. They'll never let you hear the end of it."

I knew I should take Robbie at his word. He was on the inside and therefore privy to whatever the team's true sentiment surrounding me was. I understood I couldn't use my father to curry favor with them—their loyalty to him clearly didn't translate to affection for me—but I was literally getting knocked down by their distrust. I was dreaming of quippier comebacks for my hostile teammates when the opposing batter popped the ball right back to Ryan on the pitcher's mound—an easy third out—and broke up the fantasy in my head.

Scolari jogged past me from second base to fetch his glove from the rival dugout, clapping his hand hard between my shoulder blades as he passed me. "Hear that, little lady?" he called out, his high-pitched laughter trailing him. "No special treatment for you!" If it had been anyone else, I'd have felt like I was in on the joke—laughing along at the ludicrous notion that these men had some honor to uphold, or that I ever stood a chance of unbiased treatment. But with Scolari—who was, by all accounts, a middle school bully in a thirty-five-year-old's body—I knew I was being laughed at.

The laughing continued. Every time I jogged off the field or pivoted my stance on third base, the Door Crusaders' dugout erupted. I thought I'd aged into the sort of person who wouldn't get rattled by such a juvenile thing as laughter, but each time it happened I felt heat creep from my collarbones to my scalp.

It took two innings for someone on our bench to point out the strip of duct tape to Robbie, who called time so he could rip it off my shirt. But the damage had been done. Above my number, Tony Scolari had stuck a Sharpie-d *UNT* where KLINE had been—a premeditated act, requiring him to wear the roll of tape on his wrist like a discreet bangle while he ran the bases—so that c.unt was emblazoned across my back.

Instead of calling out, *Cunt joke—real original!* I tried to focus on what mattered: I was doing a mitzvah for my father. I balled my slick hands into tight fists, digging my fingernails into the soft meat of my palms, willing myself not to get visibly upset. I took a deep breath and tried to focus on the scent of the clean grass and sooty field dirt. My mother always said the skin around my eyebrows would redden when I was about to cry—my "tell" when I'd get upset as a child. I pulled the brim of my cap down to my eyes. There were no red eyebrows in baseball.

In the ninth, we were down two runs. The dugout was quiet and tense as it became apparent that my turn at bat was also potentially the last out. I wondered what it was like in the dugout when I wasn't around. Perhaps the men believed silence and awkward refusal to make eye contact were effective ways to encourage one another. More likely, the quiet cruelty was reserved just for me. When I struck out swinging, no one looked surprised. Just exhausted.

6

IN THE DAYS after I blew the season opener, the energy around the house was both tense and tender. At first, my father and Claudia did their best to comfort me about the lackluster performance. My father told me stories about the Yankees coming back from an eight-run deficit to defeat the White Sox in 1933. Claudia took to sending screenshots of motivational quotes she'd pulled off Pinterest. But quickly enough, that gentle encouragement evaporated into my father's refusal to let me sulk.

"I'm warning you, Caroline," he boomed on my second day of unwashed hair and despondency, "if you don't get back up now, you're just going to stay down. Now's the moment to commit to betterment, if not excellence. We need to keep the momentum going." Where was this energy, I wondered, when I had wanted to stick it out in the city and rebuild my life?

I was still in bed around noon that Friday when Claudia sent a graphic that read: *There may be people who have more talent than you, but there's no excuse for anyone to work harder than you do.* The quote was written in bridesmaid script, bordered in flowers and baseballs, and attributed to Derek Jeter. I scowled at it, pulling on my vape and releasing a puff of smoke at the screen. The only other message I received was from Bobbi, who sent over a photo of her handmade audition flyer that read "Luck be a Lady (or Man!)" in blocky letters and asked again if any of my "local network" might be interested in joining Central Jersey's hotly anticipated run of *Dolls and Guys*.

That's it, I texted Winnie. I'm moving back. If you won't have me on the couch, I'll sleep in the bathtub.

Might I suggest playing a game of Hometown Tinder to liven things up? Winnie responded to my empty threat. And if you do, I request you send screenshots of everyone we knew in our past life.

That afternoon, men we'd known as boys in elementary school flew across my screen. They each shared arbitrary details of their lives, hoping to ignite conversation with women on the other end of the app. They were lawyers at tiny firms or salesmen at car dealerships or nothing at all, it seemed—no title, no education. Where a college or university was meant to show up in their bios, one had entered "School of Hard

Knocks" into the field. No matter who they were or what they did, they were all looking for the "Pam" to their "Jim."

In the photos, there was facial hair, army fatigues, cigar smoking, bloat on the beach, tiny nieces in flower girl dresses, dogs on walks at Manasquan Reservoir, firing ranges, tiger cages, Bob Marley tapestries tacked to drywall, misty trail summits, squads of groomsmen, and fishing—so much fishing. Who knew that every man in New Jersey loved to fish like this? I had an unbidden flash of waking in the cornflower light of early dawn, curled against Ben's bare back in his cool, silky sheets, kissing the constellations of freckles between his shoulders before drifting back to sleep. At full force, I felt the failure I'd been warding off from the moment I boarded the bus home to New Jersey. In only a couple of months' time, I had gone from three-year-long intimacy to swiping through an anonymous roster of suburban fare.

I took screengrabs of the men Winnie and I knew, cataloging each before swiping left. As the hours ticked by, I was fueled by an intense desire to lose myself in the hands of someone willing. I swiped right when Robbie Walker's sweet face beamed back at me, only because I knew we would match instantly and I needed the attention. When we did match, I deleted the app and considered giving my phone a warm bath.

I spent Saturday curled up in my bed thinking about all the ways my life in New York was going on without me and watching ASMR videos on my phone. Amateur clips of teen-age girls with straight hair and thin eyebrows whispering and fluttering their fingers and dragging soft makeup brushes across a microphone. Footage of hydraulic presses crushing things that weren't meant to be crushed, like car batteries, or ponies made of clay, or a gang of burning candles. When the press came down, the silvery innards spilled, the pony eyes bugged, and the candles got snuffed out. Tiny plumes of smoke rose before streams of wax shot everywhere like a celebration at the end of a world war.

Around dusk, I re-downloaded the dating app and opened a message from Robbie (which only read: hey!—an indicator of hopeless blandness and likely why he was still single) and wrote back: want to fill me in on all the inner workings of this softball league over an adult beverage or several?

We agreed to meet at the Mexican restaurant behind the mall within the hour. I dragged my carcass—dirty to the point of waxiness—into the shower, where I took special care to make myself immaculate in case my need for attention trans-lated into sex later. I shaved off every patch of prickling hair and soaped up my crotch twice.

I got to the restaurant early and perched in the corner booth to drain a margarita before he arrived so I could be properly anesthetized. In the background, a high-top of Mets fans watched a mounted screen in disappointment while the house musician strummed his acoustic guitar. My phone buzzed with more inspirational quotes from Claudia. This time, it was a dancing GIF of a Wayne Gretzky quote. I glanced at it and thought: *Maybe by the time I get home she'll have summoned the ghost of Vince Lombardi to perform cunnilingus on me.*

When Robbie arrived, I was two margaritas in and chanting at the guitar player, begging him over his clumsy rendition of the Beatles' "And I Love Her" to "play something that really rips" as I shoveled tortilla chips into my mouth. Robbie nervously smoothed his hair as he walked into the cantina, scanning each booth for my face. When he registered my location and the empty glasses in my midst, he couldn't mask his disappointment that I'd gotten started without him.

"Does your dad know we're out together right now?" he asked, after ordering a plate of cheese enchiladas and a Modelo.

"My dad is probably sitting at the dinner table yelling my name and wondering why I'm not coming down from my room," I said, poking the innards of my mahi taco around my plate. "Being home is like reverting to my fifteen-year-old self in the worst possible way. You must know what I mean."

Robbie had followed a common path for many Glen Brook residents in my age group. He'd graduated from a state college, gotten an entry-level job at an accounting firm in Midtown, moved to Murray Hill or Hoboken, did the happy hours and hookups and brunches and day drinks, got a little older, got a little tired, moved back in with his parents, and started commuting. This, under the auspice of saving money for an eventual house to impress the wife he hadn't yet met and shelter the kids he didn't yet have.

"Like, here's one for you," I offered, lobbying hard for some commiseration. "What do you do when you run into people you know? I literally popped the lapels on my trench coat up last week so I wouldn't be recognized at Wawa. I'm about to start carrying around those Groucho Marx novelty glasses."

He looked down at his hands, which were rolling his straw wrapper and bits of place mat into tiny cylinders. "When I run into people I know," he chuckled, "I say hi to them. Ask them how they are and what they've been up to. Sometimes I get Mexican food with them."

"Cute," I said flatly as my hand found my drink and my mouth found my straw.

When I asked him to dish about the league, he talked about how he had been playing only since he moved back a couple of years ago but was proud of the fact that they'd given him control of the website and newsletter. He used it to track players' stats and team victory updates each week, with his full commentary making its way to every subscriber's inbox (all forty-seven dedicated readers) every month. Despite our poor showing at the first game, he was excited to be on Leo's team because of all the buzz that we were favored for the championship. He admitted the high of Ryan Buckley and Billy the Kid's promise to lead Ringer's Bialys to glory had been dampened by the news of Leo's injuries and my subsequent arrival.

"So, people *have* been talking about it?" I asked. "They think I'm going to shake things up?"

"That's a diplomatic way of putting it," he said, rubbing the back of his neck, trying not to meet my eyes. After thirty seconds of silence, and my increasing side-eye, he relented. "Come on, Caroline. You've been around some of these guys practically your whole life. You know how they can get."

I held my finger up to indicate to our weary server another round was needed. "That's the thing: I *have* known some of them my whole life. Timmy Moriarty bought me a Polly Pocket for my fifth birthday and I never forgot it! Now he can't even look at me. I guess I'm just a little surprised at how annoyed they are by my simply existing in their vicinity. They've been so devoted to my dad all these years, but now I'm some kind of pariah?"

"Sure, I mean, to the old-timers your dad is still the best thing that ever happened but—" Robbie stopped himself. He looked embarrassed and lowered his voice. "Don't get me wrong, I love Leo. He's a living legend. It's just that he was the league's big star thirty years ago and now it's a whole new generation of players. There's a lack of trust and respect, I think."

The recruits had been getting younger, Robbie explained.

It was harder to ignore the fact that the league staples were getting older. Their judgment and ability were subject to scrutiny now in a way they had never been before.

Leo's foray into his golden years had been an anomaly before his accident—he could still hit, and he was still fast. But he was the only one of his cohort truly left in the league. The rest of them had aged out; a few moved away to Florida or North Carolina. Still, he didn't see himself as the old guy. He remembered the league's old guys from when he first got there. He was nothing like them. He refused to believe he was now the age that they were back then. In a few cases, he was even older than they had been.

"Anyway, even the guys who love your dad still want to preserve what they've got on the field," Robbie added, taking a polite little sip from his beer bottle. "It's their boys' club. They hate having to watch what they say or how they act."

"This is the censored version?" I snorted, thinking about the word *CUNT* stuck to my back.

"I think they'll ease up; they just feel a little invaded right now. Very few people were at that board meeting that voted on you, so it's tough to tell what's real and what's hearsay, but your stepmother apparently tore the chairman to shreds. She refused to leave without a verdict in your favor. You can see how that rubbed some people the wrong way."

"Of course," I scoffed. "I mean, it's bad enough I'm threatening to join the team, but now a woman with an advanced degree wants to tell them what's what? What kind of tampon commercial is this, right?"

"That's not what I'm saying."

Sensing he should change the subject before I went on some feminist tear about the league he loved, Robbie pivoted to a series of banal topics to keep this suburban night alive. Inquiring if I'd seen the latest Marvel movie. Explaining the improvement of his daily train commute since New Jersey Transit had updated its rolling stock. Asking how my own commute was going now that I didn't live in the city anymore, perhaps angling to find out if he had a chance of running into me on the platform one of these mornings.

"Oh, I don't commute," I said, fighting at that point to keep my eyes open. "I quit my job to move out west with my boyfriend and then he discarded me like a piece of trash." After what had felt like an endless ramble, Robbie didn't have a response to that tidbit. He looked past me, nostrils slightly flared, and finished the rest of his beer.

When the bill came, I insisted on paying it.

"Caroline," he whispered, inching closer to me around the curve of the plush booth. "Let me take you home."

I suddenly pictured what it might be like to go to the split-level house Robbie grew up in and straddle his hips in his old twin-size bed, both of us trying not to emit any moans or creaks loud enough to wake his parents. I imagined dodging calls from Leo and Claudia, slinking back home in the twilight. Being pressed to explain where I'd been. Looking over at Robbie at the next game and for the rest of the season and flashing back to what we did in his childhood bedroom. His boyish mop of sandy blond hair, the big puppyish eyes, how his long limbs fell in repose. When I matched with him on the app, I knew I didn't want to date Robbie Walker; I just wanted to know what my options were.

I kept my face close to his jawline, my chin tilted down, eyes looking up. "Not tonight," I said, watching as his face gently fell. "But I'm open to fooling around in your car for a little while."

"No, Caroline, that's not what I—"

"Yeah, I know what you want, but look, *I* don't exactly want to go back to your parents' house and fuck you in a twin bed and sweat all over your Superman sheets, all right?" I'd said the last part louder than intended, and everyone in the cantina—the guitar player included—stared at me.

Robbie winced. "What I mean is I'd like to drive you home because I don't think you should be driving right now," he clarified, looking not at me but at the small garden of empty glasses, rings of water, and discarded cocktail umbrellas surrounding the table. "You don't need to hide the bill from me just so I don't see the extent of the damage. I'm happy to give you a ride home."

"I'm fine," I insisted, lowering my head as I scribbled my name across the bottom half of the check. He was right, I had been holding the bill half in my lap. "I'm better than fine, I just need to get the fuck out of here." I took a quick slug of water—hot with embarrassment over his sincere concern for my well-being and his sincere lack of interest in fucking me—and bolted from the booth to the parking lot, eager to get home and put the whole night behind me.

Robbie chased me to my car, calling my name. "Look, I'm good, see?" I said, whirling around to face him. I started pinching the thin skin of my temples to demonstrate that I hadn't had so much to drink that I'd lost physical sensation, which made sense to me at the time but in retrospect must have made me look insane.

He stood outside the driver's-side window of the Saab, looking pitiful as I clicked my seat belt into place and turned on the stereo. The car was so old it only played cassettes, with a standby already lodged in the player: a best of Lionel Richie tape, but just the ballads. I turned the volume all the way up on "Say You, Say Me," muttering at Robbie from behind my closed windows to *fuck off forever* as I peeled out of the parking lot in the dark and navigated toward the house.

Near the end of the song and about midway through my drive home, my pantomiming a fight with Robbie morphed into a hypothetical freak-out at Ben, complete with big, heaving sobs. I was daring him to find someone better suited to him in Los Angeles when a Chevy Trailblazer came up from behind me and passed in the shoulder while sitting on their horn. The sound rattled in my brain like a pinball against flippers, spooking me so much I blew through a stop sign, then swerved a little bit as I tried to see if I really did just blow through a stop sign. I was only three minutes from home when I got pulled over. The red-and-blue strobing lights coupled with "Endless Love" blaring from the stereo turned my car into the smallest, saddest discotheque in the history of New Jersey.

7

THE REINSTATEMENT OF my license was contingent on my attending a court-ordered DUI program called Monmouth Alcohol Programming and Services, or MAPS for short. My suspension would lift after the inaugural session, but I'd have to abide by a curfew and get an ignition interlock Breathalyzer installed into the Saab. My full driving privileges would be restored only after I attended the county-sanctioned sessions for the next six weeks. About a week after my incident, my mother dropped me off at the big brick building where MAPS was held, parroting Eckhart Tolle quotes about acceptance and action to me the entire drive over.

Dad and Claudia weren't giving me the silent treatment, per se, but I felt too shitty to ask them for a ride to the facility. Frankly, my father seemed more embarrassed than truly angry. The night I got pulled over, I wanted to avoid rousing Leo at all costs and tried calling my mother first instead. But she'd been at a late off-off-Broadway show and her phone was silenced. I could tell by the way my father refused to meet my eyes when he had to come limping in on his crutches to retrieve me from the drunk tank, which was surprisingly well lit and comfortably outfitted with armchairs. "Is this vinyl?" I'd asked a mean-mugged cop while I waited to be released. "So soft," I whispered, petting its arm like a cat when he didn't answer.

Now, inside the county building, I saw that my cohort was a mixed bag of first offenders, ranging in age and visible shame. Men in too-big suits wearing too-small wedding bands and fortysomething-year-olds in tie-dyed shirts and nervous mom types with tourmaline necklaces. I was the best dressed in the small, sterile amphitheater—positively Keatonian in my large sunglasses, smooth hair, and belted wide-legged trousers—but not the youngest. A girl even younger than me sat just a few rows below, shiny and skinny and agitated. Her phone case read *I'M ALWAYS BUSY* in bold letters. I stared at the back of her head and tried to remember a not-so-distant past when I, too, was always busy.

A woman a few years older than me with thick tortoise-rimmed glasses over ice-blue eyes stood at the front of the room. "Welcome to MAPS," she called out to the crowd. "Let's get down to it, now, shall we? I'm Colleen, I'm an alcoholic.

I'll be your tour guide this evening for your introductory meeting."

I was immediately compelled by her. She was self-assured in a way I recognized. It was the way I had been when I thought I had it all—the man, the promising career, the Celine bag. Colleen demonstrated an uncanny proprioception and total ownership of her body—narrow hips, round cheeks, sparse eyebrows. It all looked good on her as she moved around the lecture space with gentle authority, holding the marker like a fat cigarette as she described her rock bottom: her girlfriend moving out after pleading with her to curb the drinking, the friend group picking sides, the screaming match she got into with a diplomat while photographing a United Nations summit that resulted in her getting fired from *The New York Times*. Even while describing personal atrocity, she spoke with such command that I felt like I'd trust her with my life.

"So, what then? Everything gone in a flash. No way to pay rent. I had family in Jersey, but do you know how demoralizing *that* seemed? To spend all that time bragging about getting out and making it to the big show just to have to go back from whence you came?" My face prickled with heat, and sweat sprung to my palms. "I always try to honor who I used to be, at every phase of my life, but when I look back on the girl I was in that moment? All I see is ego, baby."

New Jersey saved her life, she said. She found her recovery

community and got back to doing things she'd forgotten she'd loved: growing vegetables and perennials, biking around the reservoir, seeing live music. She got a job at a café in Red Bank where she'd since become the manager. She started photographing weddings for young couples instead of political turmoil for newspapers. She claimed, without shame, it was the best season of her life.

She explained how this would go: We were to attend MAPS weekly. We were also welcome to join another arm of the program—an optional set of parallel meetings focused on the social and community aspects of living an alcohol-free lifestyle. It was called the Jersey Alcohol Monitoring System, colloquially known as JAMS, and they met every Tuesday. There were also, of course, several local Alcoholics Anonymous chapters, which anyone was free to pursue for sustained recovery support, if needed.

"I have a great lineup for you here tonight," Colleen said, clapping her hands together like a *Saturday Night Live* host, just as I was on the precipice of being lulled into a total meditative state by her fairy tale of suburban acceptance. "A vet and a rookie, and y'all are gonna love them." She was, apparently, the kind of girl who said *y'all* despite being from Middletown.

She introduced her first speaker, a burly man in his seventies wearing a US Air Force cap, to walk us through the course expectations—paying fines, reinstating our licenses, and the like. Clutching a slim tome in his paw, he approached the podium, lowered his sunglasses, and cleared his throat. "But first I'd like to start off by reading this poem by Sharon Olds," he said, and I immediately turned my attention to the back of Colleen's head. She sat in the front row, rapt, as the old man read about vessels and desire and obliteration. I wondered about her, if she really meant what she said about loving New Jersey or if she was just trying to put on a happy face and spin a personal failure into a triumph. I had a strong compulsion to corner and question her when the class was over.

Did she ever get embarrassed about being home? Did she, too, have the ignition lock system installed in her car that made her blow a zero BAC to start the engine? Did someone show her how to tend a garden, or did she have to teach herself? Had her ex blocked her on all social media platforms, or were they civil adults? What did other *New York Times* staffers really think of the Opinion editors? Had she ever read *The Four Agreements*? Did she have the Molly American Girl doll as a kid, too?

My inquiries ran through my brain like ticker tape, taking me somewhere else until the veteran's time was up. My classmates offered scattered applause as Colleen returned to the lectern and announced the next guest, who was going to share his story with us and tell us more about JAMS and the ways we could get involved.

I braced for another gnarled old man to take his place at the lectern and bore us with sad stories of suburban woe.

Instead, the rookie Colleen welcomed was not only around my age, but *exactly* my age. A veritable ghost of my past. He was a man now but had the same unmistakable heartthrob face as he did all those years ago: the sparkling evergreen eyes, a sharply angled jaw, that easy boyish grin. He dropped his folded arms and took three long strides toward the center of the room. Crispin Davis—the great love of my youth.

• • •

THE FIRST TIME I saw Crispin Davis, I was thirteen years old. He was wandering the halls of Glen Brook Middle School with quiet confidence and a face that looked like a teen idol's from a bygone era. Winnie and I decided that, although he was short, he'd be a bona fide contender once his braces came off.

He and I didn't speak until the very end of eighth grade, when the music teacher decided to merge band groups of all levels to orchestrate a special send-off at graduation. Crispin was lead guitar in the jazz band, hot off their recent national competition in Orlando. Winnie and I were, respectively, the ninth and tenth clarinets in regular band. At rehearsal, Crispin caught my eyes as we took our seats. I knew I held my stare too long only after he laughed a little to himself and looked away. It was a good-natured chuckle, but I felt the embers beneath my cheeks burn.

I'd just gotten my first cell phone—a Nokia brick with changeable patterned faceplates—and the first text message I ever sent was to Crispin, inviting him to Winnie's grad party on the last day of school. When he actually showed, it sent me into a mini frenzy. He could have chosen any other person in that backyard to make the rounds with, but he stuck by me the whole time—plucking sweating soda cans out of a blue plastic cooler, making fun of the mix CDs being played.

"I could get down with some Pantera," he said, sitting on the stamped concrete with his feet in the pool, swigging out of the can with his head tilted back and his eyes closed, as though he were guzzling something more exciting than an icy wild cherry Pepsi.

"You have the strangest taste in music," I said, trying hard not to sound like I was fawning. "Tons of metal, but you also have a sort of punk thing going on . . . and you love the Grateful Dead?"

"Eclectic recognize eclectic," he said, gesturing two pointed fingers back and forth between his eyes and mine. "What sort of shit are you into? Aside from being a clarinet maestro."

Winnie swam up between our legs then, pressing her palms into the pool siding and lifting herself up out of the water. "If you're impressed with her clarinet skills, you should see this girl play the skin flute!" she cried. Before I had a chance to drown her, she pulled us both in by our ankles.

After that, Crispin skateboarded to my house every week. We talked about concerts we wanted to go to, bands that sucked, people who sucked who liked bands that sucked. After dusk, we'd sprawl in low-clearance beach chairs on his driveway with a bag of mini marshmallows between us, heads tilted back toward the sky, misidentifying constellations and wondering aloud what high school would be like. He was going to Catholic school, and I'd continue with my public school education. He told me if I got a guitar for my birthday, he'd teach me how to play. At night I'd lie in bed and think about his hands pushing my fingertips into the frets.

The ease of our dynamic surprised and thrilled me. I'd had trouble talking to boys when prompted. I couldn't pay attention to what they said because I was busy conjuring what I would say next. But conversation with Crispin was seamless. We could talk for hours and still have plenty to discuss by the time we met up again. When he would disappear to his family's summer rental in Point Pleasant on weekends, we'd send texts until we hit our monthly mobile plan limits.

I hoped we were pulling off a slow burn and he would become my boyfriend by the start of school. Instead, the impending rigors of Catholic school depleted him of energy and interest. After weeks of not seeing him once classes started, we made plans to ironically attend Glen Brook Day at the fairgrounds together. I had some fuzzy old-fashioned fantasy of balmy September night air and crackling fireworks and sticky cotton candy lips meeting in some spot tucked away from the flashing lights and childish cacophony.

I'm out front, I texted Crispin from the back seat of my mother's Volvo when we pulled up to collect him. I called twice, but he didn't pick up. His mother answered the door, surprised I was looking for him. He was out with his brothers, she didn't know where, and didn't expect them back until late. When he texted me hours later, it was inane and unmemorable: sorry, got caught up. My mother had taken me for consolation hamburgers, and when we got home, I curled into a white-hot little ball on my bed and sobbed.

He texted less, never first, then not at all. He'd sign into AIM and back out without saying anything, the slammed-door sound effect marking his uneventful exit. I got a guitar for my birthday and baffled my parents by refusing lessons. I had wanted only him to teach me. Every time I looked in the mirror, I tugged on my face, my hips, wondering what about me had made him want to disappear.

By early spring I'd begun to lose hope of ever seeing Crispin Davis again, but I'd also semiconsciously started dressing and behaving in homage to him. It felt like a way to pay tribute—as if he really were a missing person and I was honoring his memory with every meticulously curated detail. Black glitter nail polish. A bedazzled red tank top that read *ROCK*

ROYALTY across my tiny chest. I'd drilled a hole into an emerald guitar pick so I could wear it around my neck. This veneer, my existence, was a silent attempt to summon him. In unrequited love, I built an altar out of myself.

Winnie and I had been active on the Catholic school dance circuit all year. She found it liberating to socialize among kids we didn't see every day. I was always hopeful we would run into Crispin. We had a ritual at these dances of trying to goad the DJ into playing songs that would horrify the nuns. We once slipped a rookie with a prickling chinstrap of acne five bucks to play "Like a Virgin." Winnie rolled around on the linoleum-tiled cafeteria floor like Madonna at the 1984 MTV Video Music Awards and got us banned from all future Saint Aloysius events.

But the dances at Saint Christopher's were different. Saint Christopher's was a boys' school. There were no nuns to pull us out of the dance by a flailing limb or chunk of hair. Theirs was the most well-attended dance we'd ever been to, and the raunchiest. Everyone was ready for the thaw of springtime and arrived stripped down to almost nothing, even though it was barely fifty degrees outside.

There was grinding. The undulating mass of bodies in the room trapped the air between us until we were all humid and sticky. The painted white cinder block walls of the gymnasium dripped with sweat. The DJ didn't need any coercing. He played songs about sweat dripping down walls and balls and everyone screamed along because we were living it.

Our plan that evening had been to get the DJ to play "Paradise by the Dashboard Light"—Meat Loaf's sprawling ode to teen horniness, and a time-honored, albeit unofficial, tradition among the B'nai B'rith Youth Organization that we belonged to. It always moved me how every person at the Jewish youth group dances would follow suit: boys to one side of the gym, girls to the other, screaming every pleading, dripping word across the chasm. That night, Andrew Rosen—our favorite member of the local boys' BBYO chapter—enticed the Catholic-school DJ with two crumpled singles, a loosely rolled joint, and a big, charming grin.

Despite my attendance being a testament to my yearning, by the time the Saint Christopher's dance had rolled around, I had all but declared Crispin Davis dead. He had not appeared at any of the dances prior, regardless of where they were held. The closest I'd come to confirming his existence was when I met a group of freshmen girls at the mall one Friday night who also went to his school—Our Lady of Perpetual Help. I tried to be slick and scrape some intel. One girl sat behind him in American History and told me, "He's super quiet, like, I've never heard him speak before. He's fallen asleep in class twice and always reeks of weed."

That was why, when he walked through the double doors

to the damp, dark gymnasium that night—lit from behind by the fluorescent beams of a sterile hallway—I felt like I was looking at a ghost. I scanned the crowd for Winnie, but she and Andrew were still hounding the DJ for a chance to re-create our Jewish youth group glory.

Crispin made his way toward me, visible only in flashes as he moved across the linoleum against the strobe lights. In no time at all, he was ten feet away from me. The blinking neon ferried me into each subsequent moment without mercy. He was four feet away. Then close enough that I could smell the drugstore cologne emanating off his collarbone.

I had bought that cologne once, as part of a sampler pack with five other mini bottles. Winnie told me to just open the box and pocket the one I wanted, but I felt guilty enough just trying to get closer to him. I dripped it on everything in the months after he disappeared. My shirtsleeves. My bathrobe. My pillowcases.

In the dark, his eyes lit up green, like the cologne bottle. My heart throttled against my ribs. I couldn't bring myself to speak, so I just blinked three long, dramatic blinks. *He's really here*, I remember thinking. *His face is really on the other side of these eyelashes.*

I'd sailed through seven hundred dreams on a vision of his mouth. He parted those perfect pink lips: *Hey, it's you.*

The parts of that night I wish I remembered with clarity—the brief conversation I had with Crispin, for instance—are out of focus. Meanwhile, I can remember I wore Raspberry Starburst Lip Smacker. I remember how I felt breathless and noodle-legged standing that close to him in the dark. I remember he touched the guitar pick on my neck and asked if I'd learned to play. But mostly I remember Winnie and Andrew swooping over, microphones in hand, to announce over the din: *Bitch, it's time!*

Winnie saw what was going on—that I'd found him, that my throbbing heart was perhaps about to fall out of my ass—but she was guided by her *show must go on* ethos. "Here's your microphone," she said, shoving it into my hand and ignoring the ghost of Crispin. "You know what to do."

Well, I remember every little thing as if it happened only yesterday.

I gave Crispin a pleading look as a crowd formed around us. "It's a routine!" I called out as he broke away from me, shrugging and backing up to let more people into the middle of the basketball court. I looked at him across a deepening divide, pulsing lights providing some protection against the intensity of my stare. He looked different. Harder. I couldn't tell if he was imperiled or feigning disaffection or sincerely bored. I watched him lift a plastic water bottle to his lips and drain the clear liquid from it in seconds.

Winnie and Andrew faced each other in the jump circle and launched into the first of the song's three acts: Andrew crooning to Winnie, trying to sell her on the idea of sex in a parked car as she vamped around him with big, melodramatic flips of her hair and convincing looks of longing. I had assumed Catholic school kids might be slow on the uptake given their aversion to anything that wasn't on top forty radio, but they impressed me with their assimilation. Like animals following a biological impulse, they ferried themselves into our ritual. Attention was a commodity, and we knew how to get rich quick. Winnie cocked her eyebrow at me mid–body roll: *They're catching on.*

As they approached the second act, the moment had come to do "my part": the interlude where Phil Rizzuto narrates a hookup as though he were calling a Yankees game. At the BBYO dances, I relished the chance to provide comedic relief with my rubber-faced portrayal of the old-timey radio announcer while the crowd separated into gender-specific sides of the room. But that night, I was nervous.

I'd half expected the authority figures of Saint Christopher's to shut down our raunchfest by then. Instead, a spotlight appeared, egging us on. As I stepped into the light, I shot one last look at Crispin. Some boys like a goofball, but I knew he was looking for someone more like him: cool and unassuming. He was a quiet backyard chat at the raucous pool party. The text message sent from the screened-in porch of the beach house. He didn't like a big show. He didn't appreciate the spectacle.

Sorry, I tried to say with my eyes and a shrug as I leaned in and became the booming caricature I was born to play with a nasal, mid-Atlantic accent. Jaunty, loose-limbed little jigs, rolling my eyes around in my skull, tilting my head back to hoot toward the ceiling. My voice took on a dramatic, jagged rise and fall as the narration escalated—Andrew's character just on the precipice of coaxing what he wanted out of Winnie's character.

With laughter and applause following my bit, I knew I'd amused my peers, but I scanned the crowd to find the only one who mattered. Crispin had produced a tiny handblown glass bowl in the palm of his hand. He brought a lighter to the small indentation of weed and the stem to his mouth. Then, perhaps suspecting eyes were on him, he backed out of the gym. Sucked back into the fluorescent-lit ether from whence he'd come. Maybe it was an apparition all along. He went back to having disappeared.

I remember leaving before the third act of "Paradise by the Dashboard Light," pushing open the double doors from the back of the gym, and the shock of how cold it was outside. The smell of the frigid, sweet air as it descended upon my skin and hair and clothes, all still damp from the sweatbox of the gymnasium. I didn't go back in to collect the denim jacket I'd left beneath the bleachers. I remember thinking the agony of rejection would make me impervious to pain. I thought, *Maybe I'll never be cold again.*

Reliving that night was a subconscious but relentless phenomenon for years to come, even when I began to date in earnest. It played in my head just as faithfully as "Bat Out of Hell" played on rock radio.

8

"I WISH YOU'D held on to that guitar pick necklace," Winnie laughed from over her tray of gleaming Wellfleet oysters. "Imagine if you were wearing *that* thing all these years later?"

When I told Winnie I had a story for her that was over a decade in the making, she insisted I meet her for lunch at our favorite spot on Second Avenue. When Leo and Claudia asked what I had to go into the city for, I lied and told them I had a job interview; I felt a pinch of guilt but needed some distance from caretaking and Ping-Pong balling, even if just for one day. When I arrived, Winnie and I ordered our usual: lobster rolls and Old Bay fries and as many oysters as we could handle.

"You're such a bitch," I said, smiling and sucking a lemony iced tea through the dam of my front teeth. "I wasn't wearing any jewelry, in fact. I was dressed down!" I clarified: "In head-to-toe Saint Laurent."

"Sir?" Winnie said then, gently resting her fingertips on the elbow of a passing waiter. "I'm so sorry, we're going to need some Veuve."

He bowed ever so slightly and glided off to gather glasses. I started to lift my arm in objection, knowing Claudia's Saab was waiting for me back at the train station with a newly installed ignition Breathalyzer device, but he was gone too soon. I hadn't planned on letting my mandated MAPS attendance turn me into a nun, but I also knew I had to blow into a tube and get a clean reading to start the car.

"Start from the beginning. Fuck what you were wearing, what was *he* wearing? What did he say? How did you leave things?"

"I'll tell you everything I remember, but you should know I was mostly trying to keep myself from slipping into one of those hazy *Wayne's World* vignette sequences the entire interaction."

Winnie started howling "Dream Weaver" by Gary Wright across the table as the server came back with a bottle and two flutes. "So sorry, *mes amis*," Winnie said, rebuffing his offering. I thought she'd remembered that I was in a probationary period and wanted to switch to soda water, but instead she clutched her hands together and said, "We're actually going to need a coupe situation—I'm allergic to long glass. Thanks so much."

"You're demonstrating serial-killer levels of specificity

lately, I hope you know," I told her. She squeezed her eyes shut and beamed, accepting the comment as a compliment. "Anyway. He was wearing a rugby shirt of some sort, dark colors. Jeans maybe? He definitely wore Adidas Sambas. I stared at the floor long enough to remember those." The server came back with a diminished look and started pouring champagne into shallow little glasses.

"Let's talk smell," Winnie said, tilting the rim to her mouth and pulling the gold liquid across her tongue. "I *know* he's graduated from that green-bottle drugstore cologne."

"Okay, now you're only feeding into the serial-killer vibe more," I warned. "No overwhelming scent, but pleasant. Clean. Warm. Like when you walk by an apartment building with laundry exhaust."

"And his reaction to seeing you?"

It was difficult to gauge. About midway through his spiel about his experience with MAPS and working the twelve-step program through AA, he'd finally caught my eyes. I was frozen all the way in the back of the amphitheater, staring at him as I did all those years ago in the gymnasium: like I had seen an apparition. I saw the flash of recognition in his eyes, but he didn't change his tone, never stumbled as he touted the benefits of ongoing education and community work. Just before class was dismissed, he'd waved around a JAMS sign-up clipboard, reminding us it was not a mandatory program but highly recommended. I was the first one down to the lectern, wondering if he would pretend not to know my name or insist he couldn't place me.

"You interested in JAMS, ma'am?" he said with a wry smile as I approached him. Before I could string together a sentence, he extended his sinewy arms and pulled me in, whispering, "I don't know why you're here, but it sure is good to see you, Caroline Kline."

I focused all my energy into remaining upright as Colleen herded the emptying class over to Crispin and his clipboard, courting commitment. Seeing how immediately I'd beelined over to Crispin, she clapped her hand on my shoulder and exclaimed, "This is what I'm talking about! See ya in JAMS, sister! Now, who else is gonna join us?"

Back at the oyster bar, I reached out for the server as he passed our table. "Sorry, one more thing," I whispered. "I'm actually going to have some ginger ale instead."

He looked disapprovingly at Winnie, who shrugged at him and said, "I forgot, we're celebrating the fact that she's having twins. More for me.

"God," she continued, pouring herself another glass from the personal bottle. "I want to, like, send a postcard back through time right now. Wouldn't teenage you just *plotz*? Don't you feel *avenged* somehow?"

Avenged was the wrong word for what I felt after seeing Crispin Davis for the first time in fifteen years. I felt unmoored. I felt like I'd followed the whims of my father down a dark life path that left me without the neat logline I had spent my twenties honing and perfecting.

I usually took great pride in feeding people from my past the elevator-pitch version of a life update. *I'm the experiential director at a small but mighty agency in Midtown. We deal mostly with luxury brands.* It paid the bills, and the Cannes Lions and Clio Awards weren't bad to look at either. A couple of months prior, I could tout the tall Jewish boyfriend or the singular majesty of my old Greenwich Village apartment. But at this point, what did I have? A DUI, a municipal men's softball uniform, and a seat at my childhood dinner table. A father whose infirmity made me anxious. Dark circles beneath my eyes because I could hear him stumble for the bathroom at 3:00 a.m., taking an eternity to complete even the most mundane tasks.

Fast-forward to being arm's length from the first person I had ever felt compelled by, the prototype of my obsession. I didn't have a story worth telling. How could I explain where I had been, why I was in that amphitheater at that moment—exhausted, incognito in the back of an alcohol education program, blowing a discreet trail of nicotine vapor down a billowing sleeve?

I struggled to keep my composure in the amphitheater while cobbling together a story in my head about why I was back in New Jersey. *My dad is going through a really hard time right now,* I imagined myself saying with cool confidence before breaking and babbling: *And I'm having a hard time, too. In my effort to heal us both, I've come here to take his place in the men's softball league, lead the team to glory, and bring honor to my family name.*

But Crispin didn't ask what I was doing back in New Jersey. He had no way of knowing I had left in the first place. For years I'd searched for evidence of him on social media, this great ghost of my past lingering in the corners of my mind. If I had to guess, I'd say on average I'd looked for him two to three times a year every year since the advent of Facebook. But no trace of him. No profile on any platform and therefore no way of knowing where I was or whom I had become in return.

Time had softened him. I could see it in the skin around his eyes, which was starting to crease. His face was marred with gentle imperfections: A small crest of acne scars blooming over his left eyebrow. A tiny hole where there used to be a nose ring. But his eyes were still like I remembered: kaleidoscopic. Looking into them, even briefly, felt like some coveted view at a national park—the kind you had to climb for, the kind you had to earn.

"But where has he been hiding?" Winnie asked. "What's the motherfucker been up to?"

"Getting and staying sober, I guess," I said, shrugging. "At least for the last few months. He said he rededicated his life to playing music and he's been teaching guitar at his grandfather's music store in Asbury Park, right on Bangs Avenue."

"Hiding in plain sight down the shore," Winnie said, tsking.

"I mean, he wasn't giving me a play-by-play of the last decade and a half. We had a crowd of drunk drivers surrounding us." As our conversation went on, recounting the run-in was deflating me a bit. What had I expected? For him to break into song and explain where he'd run off to one night at a forgettable dance fifteen years ago?

I spooned mignonette onto an oyster. "I hate to disappoint you and tell you it was anticlimactic," I told Winnie, who had been eager to re-create the fervor of our youth. The energy that made us collapse on each other's twin beds, screaming, *Just* wait *until you get a load of this!* Then unleashing some exchange with an oversize crush that was benign but seemed axis-shifting. But we were not fourteen anymore.

"It was a net positive experience," I insisted, "but it was brief. He was in the middle of enrolling people in this program, and he said we should catch up. And look, I have to keep going to these MAPS meetings to satisfy this court order, so maybe I'll run into him again. Otherwise, it was just a warm chance encounter. A little bow at the end of a very long saga. Case of the missing Jewish Catholic school boy hath drawn to a close."

Winnie cocked an eyebrow. "I hate when you're blasé about these things," she said.

"You just miss the excitement of being young and forlorn," I told her. "It's okay. I miss it, too."

When our lobster rolls came, we changed the subject. She

asked if I could hook her up with a press pass to Bobbi's *Dolls and Guys* premiere, and I asked what she was working on. "That's a hostile question," she moaned. Lately, she'd been in hot pursuit of an oral history of Elaine's, tracking down the restaurant's regulars and grilling them about sordid tales of the 1980s. "But I have a feeling my editor is about to put the kibosh on it," she said.

"You're being hard on yourself," I told her. This was what best friends were good at: insisting the other should be kinder to herself while continuing to let their own cruel interior monologue stream without mercy.

The server dropped the check, and Winnie raised her final glass of champagne to him and winked. He rolled his eyes and deposited a small ramekin of chocolate pot de crème and a fortune-teller fish made of thin red cellophane. I put it in my palm, and it curled up on both sides. The key printed on the wrapper the fish came in claimed this meant I was in love.

As I readied myself to launch into a Fiona Apple–esque *I am not in love* protest, I received a text message from an unsaved number. It had a 732 area code like mine, and the text preview on my lock screen read: **Crazy seeing you again after all this time. Sorry I—** It took me a moment of staring at it to get my bearings, like I was waking up from a couch nap that had gone on too long.

Winnie, meanwhile, consulted the fish key and muttered, "Curled on both sides . . . let's see here . . ."

I opened the message to read the rest: Sorry I had to run the other night. I forgot to get your number, but luckily you signed up for my silly JAMS update list. Any interest in coming to a show in Asbury with me next Tuesday after the meeting?

I slid the phone across the table to Winnie, who read the message and promptly screamed, "She's in love, folks! Let's give it up for love!" She then knocked over the last of her champagne, hurling the phone back to me while bouncing up and down in the booth. I did the same, tossing empty oyster shells at her across the table, sending ice chips everywhere.

A text from Crispin Davis sent us back fifteen years and got us banned from the oyster bar for the next twenty.

9

I LONGED FOR a Sunday morning that didn't feel like wartime; one where I could wake up and my guts didn't feel like a clenched fist. I wanted a Sunday where I could make pour-over coffee and read the *Times Book Review*. But Sunday morning in Glen Brook became a breeding ground for combat, and I had something to prove. I had to gird myself for battle. There was no time, and no *Times*.

It was my third game with Ringer's Bialys, and I was coming off two consecutive losses. We were set to face Tavoularis Brothers Disposal that morning—colloquially known as the Garbagemen, much to their chagrin. The owner of the waste management company was one man with no brother and only nine fingers. The missing digit and the line of work implied some nose-bending mafia gesture, but the last name was pure spanakopita, so it was tough to tell what the deal was there.

According to my father, John Tavoularis seemed person-ally invested in the game, which was unheard of for a sponsor. He often showed up on Sunday mornings with one of those shareable boxes of coffee and a single cup just for himself, ready to weigh in on important matters that shouldn't concern him. Changes to the lineup, pitching staff, pinch runners. "Like Steinbrenner, but even more flagrant overstepping, if you can believe it," said Leo, who upon arrival crutched him-self over to Tavoularis on the cold metal slab of bleacher and gave his good hand a brusque shake.

The duct tape on our piece of fence read VISITOR in the child's scrawl so many mortgage-paying men somehow got away with calling proper penmanship. My teammates had been talking about Tavoularis's wife—holding out their hands in front of their chests and flinging the word *bitch* around—but got quiet as I approached the dugout. I noticed Ryan make a gesture as if to say, *not in front of Caroline.* "Oh, don't hold back on my account," I said, clipping my bag up onto the fence. "It's not like I'm the only bitch on this field right now. Hell, even in this dugout."

It had recently occurred to me it wasn't me as a person they despised; it was me in this context. Some of them had been regular fixtures of my youth—genial, just-shy-of-uncle figures at Sunday-morning games and backyard barbecues. But these men fully believed they had so precious little that was just theirs. They had wives who dictated their home interiors and wardrobes. They had jobs where they had to sit through mandatory harassment webinars twice a year. The ballfield was supposed to be where they could really let loose. The place where they were free from dusty rose walls, unflattering slim-cut button-downs, and "worrying about being PC." When they saw me on the field, I wasn't Caroline Kline, daughter of their beloved Leo. I was Caroline Kline—disruptor, intruder, interloper.

When the B_{12} vitamins were doled out, my open hand was skipped. I was buried at the end of the lineup again but did my best to ignore that fact, shooing away the implications as I did the feelings of failure I'd let crowd my brain throughout the previous week. I tried to focus on what had promise. In the batter's box there was no running away from my problems in the city, no DUI classes, no parental mystery ailments, no Ben. In my uniform, I didn't have to be the person I was becoming: on the cusp of thirty and starting over—if you could call watching your savings dwindle and crying in the shower at your father's house "starting over." None of that existed when my gloved hands were wrapped around the gummy neck of the too-heavy composite bat I'd inherited from the garage graveyard of sporting equipment. With my cleats planted in the orange dirt of Glen Brook's finest field, watching the ball leave the pitcher's callused fingertips and speed toward me, I could be someone else.

"Strike," the umpire called as the ball landed in the slice of dirt between the catcher and home plate.

"That was *literally* in the dirt," I said, whipping around fast enough for my ponytail to chase my shoulders.

"*Caroline*," Leo barked from the dugout. I looked back at him, his eyes like a wild dog's, warning me not to dig deeper. *Head in the game.* Fine. I assumed my position, gently shaking out my arms as I returned to the soft stare-down I had going with the pitcher. I started to ask myself how it was that this man could get away with such a mediocre pitch, but I realized I already knew the answer.

That time, the ball came close enough to me that I had to step back on my right leg and lean outside the box to avoid getting my elbow grazed.

"Strike," the umpire called as the catcher fell out of his crouched position to chase the errant softball.

"Come the fuck on, blue," I said, releasing my arms down to my sides, ignoring the Bialys' shared wish that I magically demure myself onto first base. "That pitch was in my armpit."

He removed the tiny cage from his creased, sagging visage and narrowed his eyes at me. "We don't take kindly to the overdramatics here, missy. And I'll issue you a formal warning next time I hear you swear on my field."

I swung at the next one—a ball so high and outside I couldn't have hit it with a pool skimmer—to hear the umpire's reprise, sending me to the dugout fearful of the passive-aggressive wrath I was about to endure from the other Bialys. But by the time I took off my helmet and laid it down on the bench, I noticed their rage was not directed toward me. In fact, no one was even looking at me—I may as well have not even been there—because they were too busy fuming over Tavoularis, who was trying to make a pitching change. The men glowered, watching him out on the pitcher's mound, slouching and dragging on a cigarette nearly smoked down to the filter. Pointing and making demands and sending exasperated players to different positions as though he were a child playing with a bucket of plastic Starting Lineup figurines.

Ours wasn't the only team getting flustered over the constant time-outs for staffing changes. The Garbagemen bore the brunt of the commands and got increasingly annoyed as each inning went on. By the sixth, their rookie shouted they were running out of pitchers. When Billy the Kid stepped up to bat, Tavoularis once again called time to chat with the pitcher. Once gameplay resumed, the pitcher stood on the mound with a stony look and proceeded to intentionally walk Billy.

As the pitches collided with the backdrop, Billy turned around and shouted something none of us could quite make out at Tavoularis, who sat on the bleachers with his coffee cup and crinkled the wedge of his nose as though he were wafting the scent of his own truck contents.

"*Den mas gamas!*" Billy shouted again over his shoulder as

he trotted down the first base line following the fourth errant pitch. *"Den mas xezeis!"*

"Is Billy trying to speak Greek?" I asked his brother, who looked alarmed.

"All right, which one of you assholes showed him how to use Google Translate?" Ryan asked the rest of the bench without waiting for an answer before running out to meet his brother on first base. He spoke to Billy in hushed tones. Something about *not getting into this again* and *remember last time*—hinting at a seasons-old feud with Tavoularis. The inning ended before any runs on our end could score, putting us in a deficit that would grow slowly but significantly for the remainder of the game.

Which was how I found myself, once again, in a position to make the last out. Top of the ninth, two out, two on. I braced for the sting of the loss but felt confident this time around it didn't rest entirely on my tiny shoulders, but on those of the man sitting behind me on the bleachers, blowing a clumsy, unending stream of smoke through the fence. As I lined up the tip of my bat against the corner of the plate, Tavoularis stepped onto the field to call time, gesturing over to the dugout to summon another pitcher.

"John," the home team's mild-mannered captain said, emerging from behind the fence with the scorebook in his hands, extended in a gesture of peacemaking or exasperation, "we've got two outs, just let him finish this."

"Two outs, but they've got two on," Tavoularis said, pointing four fingers and a stump toward the infield and blowing a plume of smoke into the captain's face. "I can't take any chances. We need someone else to pitch to her." He then gestured over to me, pointing out my left-handed stance.

They brought out one of the best left-handed pitchers in the league—according to the constant fawning in Robbie's newsletter—and no doubt a talent the team was saving to open their next game. But a lefty pitcher against a lefty batter was more likely to yield the final out. As I stood back with the bat slung over my shoulder to let him pitch a few practice balls, I heard Leo behind me trying to get my attention. I ignored him because I already knew what to do.

When the pitcher was ready, I stepped into the batter's box and assumed my usual lefty stance. Then, just as he began his windup, I stepped back and called for a time-out. "*TIME!*" the umpire cried, looking at me with incredulity through the slats of his mask as I took a wide, dramatic step over to the other side of the plate and assumed my righty stance. At once, the Bialys in the dugout erupted into cheers for me and jeers for the adversarial sponsor. I heard sharp, defeated mutters from the home bench. My only regret was that I couldn't see Tavoularis on the cold metal bleacher behind me, where I imagined the color had drained from his face and the cigarette had fallen from his slackened jaw.

The pitcher looked rattled, which made me feel powerful.

The Bialys took notice and got louder when his first pitch hit the dirt, far too low and outside for even a toddler to swing at. But in trying to course correct, his second pitch was perfect. I hadn't batted righty in years, save a couple of Ping-Pong practice swings at Leo's request. But the ball was too squarely in my sweet spot to miss or squibble. Contact with the bat rang out, the sound suffocated by the immediate wave of whooping coming from the visitors' side, as I drove the ball deep into the outfield. It landed with a thud several feet behind where the left fielder had inadequately positioned himself.

As the ball crawled toward the corner of the fence and he scurried after it, I knew I could handily make it to second base while the other two on-base Bialys made it home. I rounded first with my hand thrust into the air, one finger sticking out. But the umpire wouldn't be able to nab me for flipping the bird, because it wasn't my middle finger. It was my ring finger. The finger Tavoularis was missing. When the Bialys noticed what I was doing, they cheered even louder.

The deficit was too wide to close, and we still lost the game. But watching Tavoularis skulk back to his car, quiet and livid and trailed by a tail of gray smoke, as the Bialys took turns drumming on my batter's helmet with glee didn't feel much like losing to me.

10

KEY PARTS STAYED the same, but so much of Asbury Park had changed in the decade since I'd been back, I barely recognized the landscape. Before we left for college, Winnie and I used to haunt Asbury for the rock shows—whoever was headlining at the Stone Pony or the Lanes—and it always looked dreary and half-abandoned. Now gentrification had a Disneyland effect on the town. Storefronts teemed with antique upsells and vegan ice cream. Men in vests crafted bespoke cocktails for a premium.

But amid the town's breakneck transformation, this was what had not changed: Literally everything about the Stone Pony. The look of it from the outside. The sweet, semi-filthy smell of it on the inside (like tonic water comingling with sweat). The types of bands that played there. The crowd that smoked cigarettes between sets out back. When I approached, Crispin was one of the cigarette smokers by the stage entrance. I spotted him before he spotted me, giving me a minute to really take him in.

An idle Tuesday night with Crispin Davis. He'd offered me a ride after the JAMS meeting, but I drove myself, in need of the privacy and respite of the Saab to quiet my nerves before our outing.

He had no way of knowing about my low-grade Serene Jackson obsession, making it even more shocking he'd invited me to her show that week. *Of all the rock clubs in all the world.* An Asbury native, Serene had booked *Letterman* about a decade ago, and watching her howl on a national stage had ignited the community like nothing I had seen before. She was just ten years my senior and raised in the same county I grew up in, which gave her hometown hero status. People billed her as Fiona Apple meets Bruce Springsteen, and Springsteen himself even endorsed her—showing up sometimes at the Pony to close out a show with her.

But despite the hope and superlatives, her record company dropped her a year or so later, blaming "sagging sales" of her sophomore album. She ended up in Nashville, writing songs for younger girls to sing. Sometimes she would head back up to Jersey and give everyone a thrill by playing some surprise shows down the shore. I tried to imagine how it must feel for her to return to the place where the crowd loved her best. Like a movie star from a bygone era remembering a small, still-devoted fan club. Or maybe she felt like a soldier trudging home after a lost war.

As I got close enough to catch Crispin's eyes, he squinted and waved, cigarette still in his mouth. I smiled and waved back. I saw then, with a bit more clarity, who stood beside him. They were leaned back against the venue's iconic white facade, embracing the calm before the storm. Serene Jackson's unmistakable long jet-black shag, sapphire eyes in a nest of kohl, cheekbones that could julienne vegetables. My heart pirouetted in my chest, and I couldn't be sure if it was in response to seeing Crispin or Serene in the flesh.

I strode up tentatively, self-conscious in the shadow of the woman who had soundtracked whole eras of my life. I had dressed the way I believed one should be dressed at a rock show: dark-wash jeans cut raw at the bottom, silk top, my father's leather jacket, the boots that could eclipse the cost of a month's rent in a moderately sized city. But Serene was dressed like she knew something I didn't: paper-bag-waist trousers, pointy-toed creepers, a cape that seemed functional without sacrificing its Stevie Nicks whimsy, and a little T-shirt that said *ZAPPA SAVES*. I stood in sharp contrast with her, my flaxen hair cropped at my collarbone, painstakingly rendered a precise shade of ash-blond. Her long locks flowed down past her shoulders, making it difficult to see where her hair ended and her cape began. It could have been, for all I knew, a cape of hair.

"Hey, girl," Crispin laughed, perhaps catching me taking the sartorial temperature a little too intently. He extended the crook of his elbow and pulled me into a quick, familiar hug, careful to hold his cigarette away from my hair. He gripped a lowball glass of brown liquid with mostly melted ice clinking softly on the sides. "Don't worry, it's Dr Pepper," he whispered mid-hug.

I flashed my eyes wide, giving him a smile to match. "Hi!" I chimed too eagerly. This was a handicap of my career in events: my propensity to launch into greeter mode in situations that might call better for something low-key. I wanted to thank him for inviting me, to tell him how excited I was to hear Serene croon after all these years, but it felt impossible with her stamping out a Camel Silver two feet in front of us.

"I gotta head in, Crisp," she said, with one final twist of her toe into the pavement, picking up a matching lowball glass that had been sitting at her feet. She tilted her chin at me in welcome acknowledgment, squeezed his shoulder, took a swig, and vanished through a set of private doors with the stringy, coughing keyboardist who had been keeping them company.

A heated flash of panic crept up my neck. I wondered if Crispin Davis was dating Serene Jackson. If maybe he'd invited me to this cathedral of Jersey rock to see the woman he was pining over. Maybe she wrote her new songs for Crispin—a boy with eyes so big and green I'd have written all my songs about him, too.

"How do you know Serene Jackson?" I asked.

He smiled, gesturing vaguely at the open Asbury landscape with his cigarette. "From around. We, uh, share a community. You know what I mean?"

I didn't know what he meant, but I nodded. He neared the filter on his cigarette as I pulled on my tiny vaporizer that looked like one of those USB drives. They had become so ubiquitous in my circle that I'd forgotten to feel ashamed about sucking on a tiny robot dick. New Jersey was in retrograde. Everyone still smoked actual cigarettes, and the thick tobacco musk surrounding us smelled anachronistic.

"I couldn't show her how uncool I am while she was out here, but I'm obsessed with Serene Jackson," I confessed, exhaling a neat plume of fruit-scented vapor past his ear. "Her *Shark River Blues* album basically saved my life the summer after freshman year of college."

"That's one of my favorite albums, too." He beamed, nursing his Dr Pepper. "I'm so glad you came. You're gonna love her show."

Crispin was still cool. He was still kind. He seemed tired, yet more clear-eyed and emotive than he ever was when we were teenagers. Earnest in the ways we tried to tamp down in our youth to project a disaffected image.

When we walked through the double doors, I felt a hint of the same rush I'd felt at sixteen—waltzing in like I owned the place, eager to see one of the local bands I so diligently followed. The left wall was still covered in merch I would recognize anywhere: the Stone Pony logo emblazoned on dad caps, T-shirts, sweatshirts, tote bags, and the crotch of a pair of thong panties.

"Hot!" Crispin yelled over the din, waggling his eyebrows suggestively when I pointed up at them and laughed.

We found a spot we both felt properly nestled into—two or three rows of bodies back from the stage, just left of center. I realized only then, when the sound was ramping up around us, that a rock concert was not the ideal forum for me to reintroduce myself to Crispin Davis nor for him to catch me up on his life. I wanted to know, for the satisfaction of my younger self, what he had been doing all that time. I wondered why he picked this venue, knowing our exchange would be limited.

I wanted my body to relax, but I was too self-conscious in my stone-cold sobriety. Too awake beneath the wave of cold brew I had inhaled on the drive over. When was the last time I'd let a date begin without downing my customary two drinks first? I couldn't remember. And those were all low-stakes dates, mostly. Anonymous people I'd found on an app who could disappear just as fast as I'd summoned them. None of them were the long-lost architect of my nascent desire.

I needed to procure a drink, but I wanted to do so without his noticing. I looked over at the back bar to calculate the distance, taking account of the surrounding area to ascertain where I could hide. My yearning—or my neck craning—must have been obvious, as Crispin leaned in and said, "Do what you've gotta do. I know not everyone in MAPS is in active recovery."

"I—I'm not sure how this all works," I said weakly, not knowing entirely what I was referring to. *How what works?* MAPS? Hanging out with someone actually committed to sobriety? Being a person who couldn't handle a social interaction without a drink but also needed a clean Breathalyzer blow to start her car? Tears of frustration plugged up the back of my throat.

"It's fine, Caroline." He stood a little taller and crossed his arms in front of him, calm as a stone Buddha. "I'll hold your spot if you want to get a drink."

Without looking at him, I jettisoned myself over to the bar. *Fuck, fuck, fuck.* I blinked hard, but I couldn't shake the feeling that I was doing the wrong thing. How quickly could a drink make its way out of my system before I had to get back in the Saab?

"Missy," the bartender grunted at me. *Now what?* I didn't know how to navigate this moment without anesthetizing my every zing of doubt and discomfort. But I also wanted to remain on the same cognitive plane as Crispin. I didn't want to sprint ahead of him in a race he wasn't running. I wanted to take in the evening. I wanted to know what he was really like. I wanted to know what *I* was really like.

"Two club sodas, extra lemons," I said just as the bartender was about to get testy. I detected a slight eye roll—maybe they didn't charge for club soda—which made me indignant, already defensive of Crispin. *How are people who don't drink supposed to navigate this hostile landscape?* When the bartender plunked down the glasses in front of me, I slipped him a ten and charged back to my place, fizz dribbling off the rims and down my forearms.

"Just soda," I offered with a sheepish grin, handing one glass to Crispin with caution. "Promise."

He took a few quick sips and nudged his shoulder into mine. I could feel my face grow hot, and I was grateful for the Pony's dim interior. Leo always told me that embarrassment was a waste of emotion—shame was the enemy, and you had to move on as quickly as you could. I concentrated on trying to melt down my lingering shame like butter.

"How often do you come down here to see shows?" I asked over the buzzing crowd. "If I lived in Asbury I'd be tempted to take up residency at will call."

Before he could answer, the lights took a final dip. This was my favorite moment at every concert: the inverse proportion of light to noise, the palpable anticipation. When I went into a career doing events, it was this sensation that acted as my guide. Producing live music events had been my ultimate goal, even if I had only made it up to brand launch parties and press dinners by now. The band took the stage with Serene following them, cape trailing behind her, a laughing empress in the spotlight of the land that loved her. "Asbury Park!" she cried into the microphone. "Thanks for makin' the time to welcome me home!"

A Serene Jackson show was more of a séance than a concert. Her dusky voice reverberated off the walls of the Stone Pony and drew her rapt audience into her. It was as though she had summoned the ghosts of the greats who preceded her; like she was courting a cavalcade of old loves, old dreams, old idols. Candles on wrought iron pedestals lined the stage, a romantic fire hazard. The songs on her set list alternated between sorrow and celebration, teeming with an emotional heft that could not be concealed, rattling the floorboards with mourning for a bygone era.

The stage narrowed my field of vision: Serene crooning at the end of a tunnel. As much as I wanted to pay attention to Crispin—watch him watch the show, see what he reacted to—I couldn't help but be pulled back into her. The songs that defined my nascent adulthood: the frustrations, the heartbreaks, the longing to leave home.

There in the candlelight, I wished, again, for my body to relent. To sink into the sensuality of the sound and set aside the weight of inhibition. Around the fourth or fifth song, Crispin sensed my discomfort, or else he saw I was stiff as a board. He set his glass at his feet, positioned himself behind me, and dug his thumbs into the soft place where my shoulders met—like a trainer loosening up their boxer, preparing them for another round. We both laughed as he returned next to me. I rolled my shoulders, bent my knees, and gave an animated little wave of my arms to show him I was a good sport.

From there, we slipped into a feat of nonverbal communication—our bodies swaying in the dark, intuitively positioning ourselves as the crowd took new shapes between songs, communing with Serene. I didn't say anything when I started to feel thirsty again, but Crispin—in an act of extrasensory perception—slipped off and returned with two water bottles.

The last song: her biggest hit from back during my freshman year of college. It had placed moderately high on the Billboard Hot 100, and the Gap used it in a television commercial, commissioning bony models to skip around to it to usher in a khaki revival. Now, Crispin and I danced like hipsters in khakis, for old times' sake.

"Serene Jackson and the Hot Rollers!" an emcee announced to a sea of cheering fans as the lights came up. Crispin and I clutched each other's forearms in silent agreement. *Holy fuckoly, how great is she?* "And if you haven't heard yet, Asbury's sweetheart will be returning to the Stone Pony later this year for a weeklong residency. Special guests to be announced. Tickets available through her website and ours."

I pointed to the restrooms, and Crispin nodded. We forked in our respective directions, though I knew he'd be in and out in a matter of minutes while the line for the women's room snaked back to the bar. The disappointment that had threatened to descend on me an hour prior had dissipated: somehow not being able to speak had fostered something intimate between us. I still needed to know more—about him, about the state of his life, about why the universe crossed our paths at this precise moment—but I came away from the set feeling like I knew more than I did earlier that night. Or ever before.

Diner? he texted while I was still in line. And because the evening of forlorn songs had bound us so that we were beyond words, I sent back only a pair of praying-hand emojis in response. *Yes.*

• • •

A RELENTLESS PURSUIT of rigorous honesty. That was how Crispin Davis defined the path he was on the night we saw Serene Jackson and holed up at a diner in the morning's earliest hours. We chose the Manalapan Diner on Route 9 because the food was reliable and it had integrity: old but clean, charming but not cutesy. Desserts nestled behind lit glass in perfect wedge and dollop shapes. Jukeboxes lined the window tables and would still play "This Magic Moment" by the Drifters if you fed them spare change. Two coffees and a little cream. Hamburger deluxe with a side of disco fries for him. Corned beef hash and two eggs over medium for me. Breakfast at a dark hour came with a quiet thrill of intimacy.

"Telling the truth even when it's easier to lie has been one of the biggest game changers for me," he said, sitting across from me in a plush old booth, flicking then ripping a pinched stack of sugar packets and pouring them into his coffee. "It was one of the earliest lessons of my recovery and, it's weird, but I'm always thinking about it in the back of my mind now. I feel like it's become the foundation of my life. The guiding force in every interaction."

He told his story so methodically, it was clear he'd done it many times before. There was the depression and anxiety that had started at the onset of high school. He knew no one at Our Lady of Perpetual Help except his brothers, who, in taking Crispin under their wing, had gotten him into drinking and getting high. This escape route was helpful both at the harsh and unfamiliar institution of the Catholic school and at home, where their parents' relationship grew increasingly volatile.

The depression and unease and social withdrawal increased through the years. There was a car accident and a shoulder surgery when he was seventeen. The prescription they gave him did more than alleviate the shoulder pain: it blotted out the low-grade agony he had been schlepping around since he was younger. But it obliterated the good bits that remained, too.

I'd heard about the painkiller crackdowns on the news. Restrictions that came too little, too late. The pills that were already difficult for Crispin to stockpile became impossible to acquire. Not with the kind of money he was making, working at a bike shop in Belmar that was dead during the winter months. "I couldn't sustain a habit like that; no one could." When he moved on to heroin, which he could get cheap, that was when it got ugly.

For Crispin, that ugliness manifested in the alienation of his family, getting kicked out of Berklee College of Music after a few semesters, watching his best friend die doing the same shit, then getting blamed for aiding and abetting the situation. I recognized the name when he mentioned it: *Mikey Rosenthal*. Not someone I knew intimately, but a path I'd crossed in our youth for sure. Quintessential upper-middle-class nice Jewish boy who had parents who loved him and an in-ground pool.

Mikey was always so charismatic and energized that his family had trouble believing he'd fallen into a habit in the first place. Crispin was an easy scapegoat, the sullen friend struggling with his own downward spiral. "To his parents and his girlfriend and the whole neighborhood, I was nothing but the lowlife who dragged him down with me." At Crispin's lowest point, he believed them, even though it was Mikey's dealer who sold Mikey the bad batch that killed him.

There were a few narratives common to the area, Crispin explained. If you didn't go the way of Mikey, there was jail. Drug court. Detox down by Princeton. Rehab out past Philly. Sober-living communities down the shore or way down in Delray Beach. Meetings in the church at the peak of the hill in that old Revolutionary War–era graveyard where we used to roll spliffs on Halloween and try to freak ourselves out.

After rehab, Crispin did his step work, made amends to his family, and got a job teaching guitar lessons at his uncle's music store on Bangs Avenue in Asbury Park. He hoped to get involved with more of the local scene. He got a sponsor and a big blue book with his name on the spine. He clung to his commitment to sobriety and went to AA meetings five days a week, which he described as his "life rafts." He fulfilled the service aspect of the program with speaking engagements (where he packaged and perfected his harrowing origin story) and JAMS volunteering. If he kept it up, by the end of the summer he'd have a year under his belt.

He'd made an about-face so severe it would be easy to chalk it up as a miracle. But he wasn't supposed to think in those terms. He credited his success to his rigid adherence to the program. "'Rarely have we seen a person fail who has thoroughly followed our path,'" he said, quoting the big book.

"It's really just all about treating the program like your life depends on it, because right now mine does." His method was formulaic, upheld by decades of success and engraved on big flat coins jangling in millions of pockets: *one day at a time*.

"I don't know the ins and outs of whatever brought you to that municipal building, but I know how it can feel to find yourself in a room like that. Looking back at every mistake that's been made like one cigarette lit off another before it."

I looked down at my hands and realized I'd been stockpiling lemon seeds rescued from my ice water next to my plate, halving them with a fingernail and pulverizing the insides. A nervous, unbecoming restaurant habit.

"I know a lot of people say they're an open book," he said, with a soft smile sloping to one side of his tired face. "But I really mean it, Caroline, you can ask me anything."

I was always insecure about being a bad question-asker, feeling put on the spot when clients asked, *Do you have any questions for me?* But I smiled when I realized I had a sincere one for him.

"What are you tired of people asking you?"

I knew he hadn't heard that one yet because he laughed. His wide smile reminded me of when we were teenagers.

"Honestly? I couldn't be more grateful for all the support my family's given me, especially after those years when we fell out of contact. And I'm grateful to the people I run into who are excited about my recovery and shocked by this new trajectory . . ." He trailed off.

"But?"

He laughed again, swiping his big hand over his face with a soft tug. "But if one more person asks me 'what's next' or 'what now' I think I'm going to lose it."

I flicked a lemon seed across the table and thought, *Thank God I didn't ask him anything about his grand plans.*

"It just took so much for me to get here. It's been a lot of painful work, but I feel like I'm starting to hit my stride," he explained. "Last month I moved into this place in Asbury on my own. I'm building my credit and going to as many meetings as I can and trying to take any music opportunity that comes my way. Sometimes I still feel fragile and scared and new to it all, but lately I just want to enjoy where I'm at for a second. I don't necessarily want to think about what's next so much as I want to focus on right now."

I thought about how I used to stand in the shadow of this fashion ad–cum–art wall that stood over Lafayette Street a few years back that read in big, black scrawl: *What are we going to do with all this future?* Every time I passed by, en route to dinner or the bookstore, I'd spot it and find myself embarrassed that the notion overwhelmed me rather than inspiring me to purchase loafers with snakes on them.

"I admire your candor," I told him, not quite knowing

what to say or how to practice the same truthfulness. "I've been dreading running into anyone who might ask what I've been up to because I can never figure out a good answer for them. And you're just—I don't know. So forthcoming."

His good-natured smile seemed different then: hard won. A smile could so easily be ascribed as an afterthought, casual as a handshake, but his was a triumph. "I lived this secret life in sickness for so long," he said. "And I managed to get sober. So now I just have to throw myself into the program as much as possible and try to approach every situation I'm in with the truth."

∙ ∙ ∙

IF I'D BEEN capable of practicing rigorous honesty, I could have told Crispin about what the last fifteen years looked like for me. It might have gone something like this:

After the night at Saint Christopher's, I had to let go of my fantasy of him. Winnie thought a message in a bottle would heal me somehow and made me write a goodbye letter by hand. With no access to a proper bottle with a cork, she drained a Mountain Dew Code Red from the school vending machine, and we threw it into the reservoir.

"Can't we get fined for that?" I asked her. "This is the state's drinking water."

"Can't put a price on catharsis," she said, staring stoically out at the water like a retired sea captain.

I had it in my head that fifteen was an appropriate age to lose one's virginity. If pressed for a reason why, I would have demurred, or claimed a woman's instinct: *It just feels right.* But in the spirit of honesty, it was because I once watched an episode of *Pop-Up Video* on VH1 and in the annotations on Madonna's "Like a Virgin" clip—the one where she's spread-eagle on a gondola in Venice with a live lion—it noted she'd first had sex at fifteen. It also noted that she was menstruating during the video's filming, which posed a threat because lions were inherently attracted to the blood. *Noted,* I thought. *Sex at fifteen, stay away from lions.*

I lost it to some Catholic school sociopath I hung around with sophomore year. A junior whom I badly wanted a prom invite from. It was a quick, painful, passionless romp in a guest room at some after-party in a Rumson mansion. I bled all over a stranger's floral quilt.

I would explain to Crispin that I'd spent college and my early twenties dating a wild assortment of people to see whose personality fit me best. Mitch McConnell—a plucky Tisch grad with a liberal heart and an unfortunate name—practically lived at the improv theatre on Twenty-Fourth Street. During my senior year at NYU, I followed him around like the Beatles. When we finally slept together, I thought it was the start of a long, bountiful relationship. I envisioned myself smugly telling my friends over a picnic in Prospect Park, *When you know, you know.* In this fantasy, I was always tall and lean and wearing some long, gauzy dress that tied at the waist with a wide-brimmed sun hat—both articles of clothing I did not own.

But I wouldn't get to don my fantasy picnic attire or brag to my friends about Mitch, because I was too busy bawling to them about how he had stopped returning my texts after sleeping with me three times. "He can't ghost me if I know where he hangs out all the time, right?" I remember sobbing in Madison Square Park, pitiful, over a calcifying hamburger nestled in a cardboard box.

"Not if you hang out there all the time, too!" Winnie insisted, indignant. "You can haunt him all you like. I'll go with you. We'll march up onto that improv stage wrapped in sheets and say, 'You can't ghost me, I'm the fuckin' ghost! And I'm haunting you!' What's the worst he can say? 'Yes, and . . . '?"

We proceeded to sleep together on and off for years. It was a profoundly humorless experience.

I met Jackie Meyerson at one of my own events, a big launch party for Tiffany's holiday campaign. She had recently completed a Series A funding round for her beauty startup— a vegan powdered adaptogen brand called Poshun, custom blended to fit every femme person's wellness needs. The product was GOOP-sanctioned, and the packaging was designed by someone Jackie had poached from Glossier. Without knowing Jackie personally, I still knew who she was because of social media and a feature *Domino* had done on her enviable

Ettore Sottsass–inspired workspace. It startled me when she seized me by the elbow and led me to a quiet corner of the venue.

"No one was making the intro, so I just had to kidnap you," she mewled, just inches from my face, Moët on her tongue, pores so tiny they were worthy of a sleek editorial. "I heard you're responsible for all this, and I think I need your services for our upcoming launch."

This was during an era when I was equal parts naive and reckless, believing she so urgently needed to show me some master plan back at her pastel-hued office later that evening. In no time at all I was sitting on her sleek, white desk with my heels propped up on the arms of her plush, green velvet chair, where she sat eye level with my La Perla–clad labia. When she hooked the crotch of the silk thong with two fingers and moved it to the side, looking up at me with the excitement of a teeny-bopper about to be pulled onstage at a rock concert, I shuffled the Rolodex of my mind: *No longer a prospective client.*

We were together for a year, and there was not one minute I could relinquish my certainty that I would never catch up with her. She was only three years older than me, but leaps and bounds ahead professionally, personally, and from a skin-care perspective. My parents were in the middle of their di-vorce, and her intimidating family of lawyers with their big house in Larchmont overwhelmed me. We spent Passover there, and I was stricken with envy and inadequacy. We fought on the Metro-North en route back to the city, broke up at Grand Central Terminal, and reconciled within the hour over a slice of strawberry cheesecake from the Junior's outpost. A week later, a spread in *New York* magazine named her among the city's most eligible single New Yorkers—complete with a photo shoot she had done in secret months prior—and then we broke up for good.

I matched with Steven Schwartz on a dating app he maintained for one night only, one long weekend. "My girls cajoled me into this," he typed to me from his perch in East Hampton on the third of July, referring to his teenage daughters.

His profile said he was a truth seeker, a bon vivant, and fifty-four years old. His photos indicated he was a kayak enthusiast with toned arms and a graying but full head of hair and frameless glasses. He was a Pulitzer Prize–winning journalist. Corruption was his beat. He had a robust body of work in prestigious publications, a famous book editor ex-wife, and a stipple of his face in *The Wall Street Journal*.

That weekend, I asked him to describe his surroundings via text message. He detailed the salinity of the oysters, the sugar rim of his watermelon margarita glass, and the fecund bloom of yellow hibiscus threatening to spill over the pots lining the pool. I looked around at my apartment, at every sentimental possession lining my shelves, thinking about every aspect of my hard-won independent life, and decided I would be willing to part with it all for a chance to inhabit his world.

In his SoHo apartment, he took painstaking care to craft cocktails in matching Waterford crystal lowball glasses while Wynton Marsalis played over the Sonos. In his house out east, he went through the trouble of making buttermilk biscuits from scratch and serving them to me with thick slabs of butter with flaky salt and four-fruits jam. *This is my life now*, I would tell myself, clutching the bottom of the Bonne Maman jar in my hand. *A man who investigates and cooks and buys. A house with a skylight and a two-hundred-dollar pool float. Stepdaughters a few years younger than me who have the same auto-renew Glossier orders and Lorde albums that I have.*

But that was not my life. It never would be. I couldn't be sure what made Steven come to his senses by the end of the summer. Maybe it was the fact that I looked young for twenty-six while he looked fifty-four in earnest. After he broke things off, I called my father. "What was your endgame, Caroline?" Leo asked, trying to be gentle but genuinely baffled that I'd been dating someone close to his age. "Did you think you were going to run off and have babies with a sixty-year-old?" Then I started sobbing. If I was being honest, for a few smug moments that fancy, jam-smeared summer, I was certain this was the case.

If I'd been *rigorously* honest, I could have told Crispin that night over breakfast for dinner that every time I had my heart broken, I convinced myself: *This time, it's for real. This time is the deepest cut. No one will ever get to me like this again because I'll never love anyone like that again. And I'll never let anyone get that close.* I meant it, too. But soon after Steven left, I met Ben.

Rigorous honesty felt like too tall an order for me, and I wished it didn't. It felt impossible to talk about where I was at because my life in that moment seemed so temporary and situational. But if I were practicing true honesty, I'd have to admit my life had been falling apart before I ever quit my job and got that call from Claudia and shimmied into my softball uniform.

Where I found myself was tricky to tease out into a story that made sense. It was hard to talk about where I had been, too—what essential forces had ferried me into that moment. How could I explain to Crispin what had shaped me in the fifteen years since we last sat across from each other at a diner like this one: pristine at two in the morning and interchangeable with any other chrome-coated Monmouth County establishment?

I longed for the impulse Crispin had so I could be honest with him, too. But instead, I narrowed in on his aforementioned desire to get involved with new music opportunities and asked, "Would you happen to have any interest in being the musical director in a gender-bending production of *Guys and Dolls* at a local but highly acclaimed theatre?"

11

AFTER THE TAVOULARIS incident, the Bialys warmed to me. They didn't look at me with disdain when an errant ball pulled deep up the left side went right through the wickets of my legs. They didn't sneer when I swung at a pitch too high to be worthy of my efforts. Derogatory synonyms for *woman* seemed to fade from their lexicon. Even Pete Peretti, the coldest among them, seemed neutral toward me. During the pregame ritual, he started handing me my own gummy vitamin, and in return I participated in their *GIMME THE JUICE* rally cry, despite my wish to chant literally anything else.

I became more comfortable with them, too. I felt freer to celebrate and cheer and even admonish them if their newly minted enthusiasm for me crossed a line.

One game, after I hit the cutoff and facilitated the out at home plate, Ryan Buckley crowed: "This bitch has got an arm like a rocket!" He beamed, then performatively took his hand out of his mitt and shook it like the force of my throw had stung his palm.

I approached the mound with a soft jog, mirroring his big grin. Up close, I murmured through closed teeth: "Call me a bitch again and I'll use my rocket arm to rip that man bun off your head, fuckbag."

He cocked a playful eyebrow and nodded—*point taken*. I smiled in earnest then.

"Two down!" I called to the rest, waggling a hand to the sky, pointer and pinky fingers out like a heavy metal concertgoer, as I pivoted on the ball of my cleat and returned to my post at third base.

Per league rules, we all tried our best not to curse, but barely a month into the season, half the team had at least one warning. I got one after popping up to first and muttering, *Oh, you motherless cunt bastard* while I was still watching it from the plate. Even Timmy "The Tortoise" Moriarty got one for *fuck*ing too loud after he failed to beat the tag at home. I slapped him gently on the curve of his back and said, "It happens to the best of us, Timbo."

Billy the Kid—notorious for his scuffles with various umpires over the years—already had two citations and was facing suspension. We had a particularly rowdy outing where Billy got into a verbal altercation with the sidelined wife of the visiting team's catcher. After that, Leo had me print and distribute to the whole team remedial meditation techniques he'd compiled in a Microsoft Word document.

"Everyone needs a little anger management from time to time, now don't we?" Leo said, clutching the paper in his slung arm and trying not to be patronizing. The rest of the team turned their eyes to Billy, tattooed, scruffy, and sullen. He sat on his own batting helmet, smoking a cigarette while he stared at a patch of dirt between his knees. "Don't you look at him," Leo reprimanded us. "Need I remind you that the fuzz was ready to handcuff Peretti's cock a few seasons back?" Pete nodded in concession. "That's right. No one's immune to overreaction."

For a while, the meditation techniques seemed to work. With our collective anger, hot heads, and filthy mouths in momentary check, we rose to the occasion and seized some of the reputation my father had predicted for us back when he first called me home in early April. As we hit the stride of spring, all green lawns and allergy medication, I could imagine the team being capable of going to the show—even if I was hoping I'd be back in Manhattan by then.

Everyone did their best to make up for their shortcomings. The vets on the team were, by turns, slow but powerful. Aging but strategic. Pete Peretti, nearing forty, was obnoxious but a reliable hitter. Timmy Moriarty, pushing sixty, lived up to his turtle moniker when he wasn't sidelined with minor injuries but was an enthusiastic and encouraging presence. We had a hot streak that lasted six games, including two doubleheaders. Robbie Walker hit a walk-off grand slam, and we started chanting *MVP* every time he got up to bat for weeks after. I made a Derek Jeter–esque jump throw—backhand catching a hit over third base and leaping as I sent it sailing toward first—to end a perilous fourth inning, and Pete called out, "It's all those vitamins we've been feeding her!"

By the big Memorial Day marathon tournament, we were neck and neck with the team to beat: the Moby Dicks— sponsored by a local seafood restaurant, and colloquially known in the Kline household as the Dicks. This year's Moby Dicks lineup was packed with great players, no duds, and re- garded as one of the greatest draft upsets since the league's inception. While the Bialys could barely convince our families into showing up as spectators, the bleachers overflowed for the Moby Dicks on a weekly basis. At their games, the lawns were crowded with other players from the league, off duty in their canvas camping chairs, slurping iced coffees and breath- ing in the crisp scent of the wet grass underfoot.

Leo and I did a drive-by one Wednesday night on our way home from grocery shopping, just to see who was playing be- neath the lights. The Dicks lined the infield, and most of our roster was hanging back to take it all in.

"It's educational!" cried Timmy the Tortoise defensively to a disappointed Leo, who hung his shaking head.

"What, you think that talent comes to you by osmosis?" Leo said, almost yelling.

Timmy shrugged. "So, sue me. Maybe I just like watchin' 'em play."

The Dicks had enough chutzpah and pure power to inspire even a league of rivals, but I had a tough time summoning the same level of adoration the rest of the town had for them. For one, I didn't think it was all that impressive for a team of young bucks to whoop the asses of, sure, some peers, but mostly the town's scrappiest, paunchiest dads. It was hard for me to admire a bunch of men I recognized from my high school yearbook who had stuck around town. But the exception—and the most notable of them all—was Thomas Mills.

Corporal Tommy Mills lived down the block from us growing up and was a couple of grades ahead of me in school. After making a name for himself as a track star and ROTC standout, he turned down a full ride to UNC Chapel Hill and joined the Marines. He had already completed a tour in Iraq and was close to finishing his second when he was injured on a food distribution mission in Baghdad. Three of the other men accompanying him—including his closest friend, a young captain from Ocean County—were killed by an improvised explosive device.

Tommy took shrapnel to his arms, legs, and chest, but survived. After the initial flurry of press surrounding the incident and his return, I would only hear about him occasionally, usually from my mother after she ran into him at the market or the post office. How her heart just broke for him, and she hoped the girls were nice to him—*so handsome, but so quiet.*

The post-traumatic aura he'd returned with a decade ago had since lifted and shifted, making him town golden boy once again. He spent years completing different forms of physical rehabilitation, restoring himself to the athlete he'd been back as a teenager. His joining the league ushered in a new generation of softball recruits—if Tommy was in, other guys our age were in, too. They called him Captain America, which played into the one-dimensional brand of patriotism everyone in the tristate area adopted after September 11.

I couldn't tell if playing a Memorial Day weekend tournament game against a local war hero was a bad omen for the Bialys, or maybe expecting Tommy to play that day was in poor taste all around. *Maybe he won't even show*, I thought. Maybe he would sit out for his fallen brothers, whose names and faces were immortalized in black ink on his scarred pitching arm.

But that Sunday at noon, he arrived right on time to a sea of applause. Tommy waved to his fans but beelined for my father, placed a gentle hand on his shoulder, and asked how he was doing. "Hope to see you back out there soon, Mr. Kline," he said before joining his teammates.

I could tell from the look on my father's face that this was exactly the sort of optimism he wanted to hear. He wasn't getting much of it from Claudia and me, who had worrying up-close-and-personal views into his stumbling attempts to regain mobility around the house. Two months in physical therapy had yielded marginal results: the doctor said his sling was finally ready to come off, but he'd need crutches for a little while longer—which was a relief because it had been nearly impossible for him to manage both at once. Still, Leo felt certain that he would return to the field in a month. As much as I'd have loved to believe his progress would get him back in the game—and get me back to Manhattan—I felt skeptical that would happen by Fourth of July weekend. Claudia, too, suspected he might be disappointed with the slow reality of his recovery. But he was right about one thing: his men missed him on the field. Even as I got some wins under my belt and our team dynamic became less hostile, their longing for his return to the diamond was palpable. "Heal up, buddy," Timmy Moriarty liked to say to my dad at some point during every game, clapping him on the back a little too hard. "We're nothin' without ya." At which point Leo would squint, give him a closed-mouth smile, then turn to me and whisper, "He's not much *with* me either."

At the Memorial Day tournament, Tommy's fan base had shown up early and in full scale. They arranged a sea of camping chairs, erected a white pop-up tent with two charcoal grills going, and summoned the best ice cream truck in town—the one that was owned by an Elvis impersonator. The chain-link fence was adorned with tiny American flags, and little girls with red, white, and blue ribbons braided through their hair held up homemade signs that read, *THANK YOU, CAPTAIN AMERICA!*

Perhaps then it was a demonstration of patriotism when the Bialys essentially handed the game over to the Dicks. There was a messy cavalcade of missed opportunities: dropped pop-ups, botched bunts, steal attempts made with poor judgment. I got caught in a rundown between second and third that made me look like the Road Runner cartoon and ended with me screaming, "Cock! Cock! Cock! Fuck!" after their shortstop finally tagged me out.

"A poet and a lady," he muttered before he trotted back to his post.

"*That's* a warning," the umpire grunted, pointing at me, as I trudged back to the bench, kicking up clods of dirt as I went.

The game ended earlier than anticipated, as the Dicks were up by ten in the seventh inning, kicking the mercy rule into effect. After we lined up for our obligatory *good game* hand-shakes across the pitcher's mound, Timmy Moriarty turned back and said, "Hey, Cap," loud enough for all to hear, hold-ing his hand to his eyebrow in salute. "Thank you for your service." Cheers erupted, and other arms followed suit, a wave of salutes around the ballfield and in the crowd. I awarded myself an honorary Nobel Prize in the field of restraint for not rolling my eyes and even throwing in a light golf clap. Pete Peretti waited until we were back by our bench packing up our equipment to hiss, "What's the matter, Timbo, you don't wanna go over and cup his balls while you're at it?"

As I hoisted my bag across my shoulder and made my way over to the bleachers, bracing to endure Leo's full annotation of disappointments, I watched as Tommy Mills was greeted by two tiny girls—one barely a toddler, one about four years old—with Elvis ice cream all over their little faces and matching white dresses, running up to him and hugging his knees. With no effort, he hoisted them into the crooks of his muscled, tanned arms and walked them over to their mother. She mirrored his smile for a moment before drawing him in for a kiss. When they fell away, she looked over at me. I felt a hot flash of embarrassment for having been caught in a stare, bearing witness to an intimate moment.

I took about twenty seconds to register that she wasn't looking at me because she was concerned I'd been staring, or even because I was the only woman on a field drenched in testosterone and hostility. She was looking at me because I was Caroline Kline and she was Kelly Quinn, my childhood rival and onetime best friend.

• • •

KELLY QUINN MOVED to Glen Brook from Princeton in fifth grade—the same year girls' softball came to the Little

League. Her father, Big Steve Quinn, was brawny with a big handlebar mustache and pale blue eyes. He was the coach of the Tar Heels, the team I was drafted to by pure chance.

When Kelly invited me over to her house after softball practice one day, it took everything in me to keep it together. With her, there was no shy new girl shit. She blew into town with a signature haircut and a mean windmill pitch at just eleven years old. She had no trouble plopping herself down at the most coveted table in the lunchroom with zero regard for pre-established social hierarchy. She had so much ready-made confidence, I felt like she could immortalize me or level me with just a look.

At her house, I demonstrated the tucked-in species of politeness I trotted out for teachers and parents who weren't mine. "You sure you're not hungry?" her sweet mother asked the first time I went over, holding a cold, wiggling square of icebox cake out to me on a spatula. I was starving. My salivary glands ached at the sight of the Cool Whip. "No thank you," I nearly whispered, misunderstanding—as so many young girls do—the difference between being polite and denying oneself. Kelly—a head taller than me, with long legs and straight hips—handily put away two pieces of cake before grabbing a bag of Bugles and my hand and tearing upstairs to the sanctuary of her bedroom.

I didn't know another eleven-year-old with a room like the one Kelly had, but then, I didn't know another eleven-year-old like Kelly. She had a pink iMac computer, a translucent purple phone, and her own phone number—which I impressed her by memorizing the instant she recited it. She had a culture unto herself. If she loved something, it was *her thing*, an emblem she wore. One was expected to think of her when these things came up outside of her purview. She was "addicted" to MTV, never missed an episode of *TRL*, and persuaded me to adopt her *NSYNC obsession. She had already picked Justin Timberlake to be hers. I went with Lance, convinced I was smart to pick the unassuming one: in case we ever met the band, I'd have a better chance.

Of all the *things* that belonged to Kelly, though, the biggest was baseball. Looking back now, it was likely the reason she was drawn to me despite my meek first impression. The other girls in our grade could swap racy Carson Daly fantasies or sports bra recommendations, but none of them came from a baseball family like mine. No one at Glen Brook Elementary except me could monologue about Chuck Knoblauch's batting stance or quote the entirety of *A League of Their Own*. That was exactly what Kelly Quinn—whose bedroom was wallpapered in photographs of Andy Pettite the way mine was wallpapered with Derek Jeter—needed in a best friend.

"I just feel so lucky you were drafted to our team," she said in the dark the first time I slept over, one Saturday night after our first game. We shut out the Lady Hawks 7–0. Her dad had taken the whole team for pizza after, but only I had gotten the invite to spend the night. "So far the best part about leaving Princeton is finding you."

"It's kismet," I said without thinking, giddy and unselfconscious. The word wasn't in her Presbyterian lexicon, so I explained what I meant: *It was something like fate.* She agreed.

We went on like this until the fall of seventh grade, when our foray into middle school meant more friends for her, fewer friends for me, and barely any classes overlapping between our schedules. For Halloween that year, she bought five laminated backstage passes and insisted we dress up as *NSYNC. She was, of course, Justin—clad in a curly blond wig, blue bandana, and matching denim jacket and jeans. I wasn't allowed to be Lance because her cousin from Trenton wanted to be Lance, and she happened to have the platinum hair for the role. I was Chris Kirkpatrick. The braids sprouting out of my head weren't authentic enough to satisfy her, and she moved fast to draw a crude eyeliner goatee on my face without my consent before we started ringing doorbells.

In the spring, there were enough girls interested in Little League for a proper draft, complete with tryouts. I was confused when I ended up on the Sand Gnats, a team of misfit duds coached by a local dad who didn't know the first thing about baseball. Kelly was one of three blond Amazonian pitchers on the Flyers, Big Steve's monopoly of a team. At first, I didn't perceive it as a slight—I knew shuffling Little League teams was inevitable once we ascended to our new preteen age bracket. But eventually I realized that nearly every other girl from our old winning team had been reassembled under the Flyers. I imagined Kelly begging Steve not to draft me, needing his help to put some distance between us. I knew in the pit of my stomach she had somehow grown bored and was done with me, over my childish reindeer games and on to middle school maturity.

When I summoned the courage to confront her at her locker one day, shakily asking why I'd been relegated to a losing team, she brushed me off with a cruel laugh. Her unaffected response to my draft-induced devastation (*Don't take it so personally, Caroline*) inspired me to chuck my backstage pass, which I had foolishly held on to since Halloween, into my father's shredder. It would be many years before I ever felt rattled in a way that reminded me of this incident with Kelly—that stomach-turning, numb-handed ache—and it'd come only when I'd get unceremoniously dumped by someone who had just recently claimed to love me.

The Gnats didn't have as much to work with as the better teams in the league, but we were scrappy. We eventually found our groove and eked into the playoffs that year. After being so smug on Big Steve's team the year prior, so handily making it to the softball World Series on the jet stream of Kelly's windmill pitch, I was proud to make it there on my own accord.

With no clear star among us, I took a vocal position on the roster—leading the squad in chants and ballsy taunts I'd picked up on the bench from last year's girls, who liked to supplement their talent with arrogance.

We reached our second round of playoff games—making it further than anyone, even our own parents, thought we would—before we had to face the Flyers. Leo spent long evenings psyching me up for that game: running drills in the backyard, tossing Ping-Pong balls to test my precision. "That's right, hit that little Ping-Pong ball, Caro," he said, crouching a safe distance to the right of me and tossing them into my line of vision. "Then when Kelly what's-her-fuck lobs her little signature spins at you it's gonna look like you're swinging at a watermelon!"

We held a small lead into the third inning before it all started to fall apart. The Gnats looked to me to help amp them up after the Flyers pulled ahead, but I got distracted staring into the void of the visitors' dugout. The white flash of Kelly Quinn's teeth in the dark as she laughed, the spray of sunflower seeds through the chain-link fence, the familiar choruses used to rally one another and rattle the likes of me. I let myself feel dejected and worthless for two innings before I pulled myself up by the cleats and announced: "We're the home team, we have last licks, and we're going to beat these bitches," loud enough so Kelly could hear me from the mound.

We rallied some; they rallied back. In the bottom of the ninth, I got up with two outs. We were down by two, but we had two on. The girls on first and second looked at me with big, pleading eyes. Not that they had done much to earn their spots on base. Kelly nipped one of them in the elbow on an 0-2 count, and the incident shook her enough that she walked the next girl. What about me? I wondered if I would stir her nerves more, the prospect of facing off against a girl who had once been her best friend in the not-so-distant past. A girl who was the Kelly Quinn of her own team now, teaching the other girls new comeback songs to sing. Or did she know better? Perhaps she knew not to fear me because ours was a power dynamic that was well established and would remain through the end of that game, and maybe even forever. The concrete had hardened on our relationship. She was Kelly Quinn of Princeton, with a beach house and a lofted bed and amber eyes and a killer laugh. I was just me.

The Sand Gnats' better-than-fine season ended when Kelly Quinn struck me out. We lined up like we always did, in neat parallel lines to say a customary "good game" to each girl on the opposing team. But no one's heart was in it. It all blended into one monotone amorphous sound: *googamegoogamegoo-gamegoogame.* Kelly looked straight ahead and didn't meet my eyes when her hand quickly brushed past mine. *Good game* were the last words Kelly Quinn ever spoke to me until the day she spotted me exiting the field after being defeated by her husband and said, "Caroline Kline. I thought that was you out there."

· · ·

KELLY QUINN BECAME Kelly Quinn-Mills. She sported a cushion-cut diamond on her ring finger, given to her on Christmas Eve six years prior by Corporal Thomas Mills, who joked he went through hell in physical therapy just to get down on bended knee for her. Her wedge sandals exaggerated her already considerable height, so that twenty years later I still had to look up to her. She wore white denim cut-offs to let everyone know she still had great legs, despite having two kids under five whom she pushed around in an inexpensive dupe of an UPPAbaby double stroller.

"I actually ran into your mom at the grocery store about a month ago, I don't know if she told you," Kelly chirped, like we were picking up a recent conversation. "She is such a riot! Nothing about her has changed since we were kids, I swear."

I volleyed back a tight smile. "Yep, still a firecracker. How are your parents these days? Still local?"

"They're great," she said, like she had rehearsed for a pageant. "Mom retired from teaching, and I actually went into business with my dad a while back. We started our own hybrid real estate agency specializing in fixer-upper shore homes. He fixes, I sell. We've made a killing with all the Sandy properties. I don't know if you remember this, but we have a house down on LBI, so we're familiar with the market."

Don't know if I'd remember? I could still recite the code to her garage.

"Yeah, of course I remember," I said, refusing to feign distance. "I was always so fond of your dad. Please tell him I say hi whenever you see him next."

"Oh, he'd love that. And how about you?" she asked, head cocked. "Your mom mentioned you're a . . . party planner, was it? But that you'd recently moved into your dad's house?"

If her husband and children hadn't been standing beside her, I'd have considered taking a swipe at her. I let out a laugh—a long, low *HA*.

"Uh, no. I'm not a party planner," I said, incredulous. It didn't matter how I spun it; Kelly already thought I was pathetic. "I was the experiential director at a luxury marketing agency, and now I'm—"

"Mom!" the older of the two little girls cried out, yanking on the hem of Kelly's shorts. "You said it was time to go so long ago now!"

Kelly bent down and hoisted her up with little effort, positioning the child to sit against one hip and propping her tan, muscled arm up onto the other.

"Okay, girl boss!" she said to her daughter, all smiles. She turned back to me and shot me an eye-rolling look like, *Kids, right?* "I so envy you, Caroline. One day you'll know what this is like," she added, gesturing to the whining kids with a jutted chin. "So just enjoy being alone now while you still can!"

I seethed as she turned her back and clomped toward the parking lot. How had two decades gone by and I still let myself feel belittled by her small-town confidence? She had ascended to a social stratum of young moms who went to college in-state, got married at twenty-four, and wanted to live in Glen Brook. Women I'd gone to high school with who now had children they posted photos of on Facebook. I'd been conditioned to consider these women my enemies, and for all I knew, they considered me theirs. We were the antithesis to each other's desires and visions of success. I knew the longer I stayed in Glen Brook, the longer I ran the risk of bumping into them wherever I went, their pitying looks directed at my ringless finger. I thought I'd be prepared to ward off their quiet smugness with my city-honed, albeit snobbish, approach. (*Don't feel bad for me! I feel bad for you!*) Sometimes I was able to trick myself into believing I was superior to them.

But I couldn't get there after seeing Kelly Quinn. Even if she had become a suburban mom, nothing could inoculate me against feeling minimized in front of her all these years later. I felt myself shrink beneath her gaze, some quiet part of me devastated that I still couldn't impress her.

12

FOLLOWING SUNDAY'S GAME, Claudia tried to perform some Memorial Day normalcy with a backyard barbecue. I carefully installed Leo onto a lounge chair beside the pool then dove in and practiced my butterfly stroke. As I swam, I stewed over my brief exchange with Kelly and my wooden, polite delivery. I could never come up with the right words in the moment. Between laps, while I was dreaming up better comebacks I'd missed the chance to deploy, I heard Leo start to shift around and get agitated. Then, I heard him mutter Harper's name. I looked up to find him swatting at the air, sunglasses knocked to the ground, yelling to no one, "Get out of here with that nonsense!"

"Dad?" I called, but he didn't acknowledge me. He'd gotten up and was stumbling, crutch-less, on the hot pavers surrounding the deep end of the pool, squinting at the sun. "Dad!" I called again, louder, when he took a step too close to the edge, but it was too late. One foot awkwardly crossed in front of the other and the back ankle rolled beneath him. He fell into the pool—both in a flash and in slow motion—sideways and headfirst.

Claudia still had grill tongs in her hand when she ran down to the pool area, both of us screaming, hauling him out by any grabbable limb, ignoring his previous injuries we'd so delicately managed as we yanked and pushed.

"Well, I don't know what the fuck *that* was," he said afterward with the tone of a businessman having just watched a jam band set, perched on the edge of his lounge chair, wrapped in a towel. Claudia and I stared at each other, panting and soaked, for a long minute before she announced she was calling the doctor. A new doctor, a specialist in Manhattan she'd scouted. That sudden drunken disorientation, she claimed, mimicked his conditions from the night he fell down the stairs.

Claudia offered to cancel her work meetings and take Leo to the city to get an MRI and meet the specialist on Tuesday morning, but I insisted she let me do it. "Is this not what I'm here for?" I asked, knowing it was true but wishing that wasn't the case.

I wouldn't blame my father if he preferred Claudia's or even Harper's company in those moments. Like him, I had a strong aversion to bodily deterioration and a low tolerance for beholding it. My weak constitution had only increased with my time at home: I'd wince in tandem with Leo if he was visibly in pain; my stomach lurched at the sight of his little dish of horse pills served alongside each meal. At appointments, Claudia was ironclad and asked a lot of questions; a natural advocate. Harper was similar—marching through the hallway of any hospital like the star of a medical procedural. She was not easily nauseated. But my father's golden child wasn't there. That Tuesday morning, I had to be the advocate, holding Leo steady with one arm as we walked through the airy threshold of the sliding glass doors of the uptown hospital, gag-belching into the crook of my other arm at the first waft of clinical soap and rubbered supplies.

When it was time to take him to imaging, a nurse swung around with a wheelchair to assist him. He bristled at the sight of it. "Is that really necessary?" he asked, growing pale. Falling into the pool had set him back on much of the progress he'd made since the initial fall: his sling returned, and he was even less graceful on his crutches than before. Watching him lower himself into the chair made me feel raw and exposed by proxy. I couldn't help letting a small squeak of a sob escape me. He turned to me and yelled, "Is *that* really necessary?" While he was away, I attempted to distract myself by burying my head in old, sticky issues of magazines left in a pile on the vinyl chair next to me. I crinkled my nose at the sun-bleached covers that claimed to hold the key to *what he's* really *thinking*, "family fun," and how to dress if your body has the sort of pear shape that wasn't valued on Instagram. None of it held my interest, and instead I caught myself staring at the framed pastel beachscapes hanging on the walls, thinking about how my father and I—both so squeamish in the face of infirmity, possibly the two worst patients in the tristate area—were a uniquely bad fit for the day's itinerary. We hadn't even seen the doctor yet.

On another floor, we met the specialist, who seemed warm and calm, with a full head of hair and a thick broom of a mustache. He was a ballplayer back in the day, too, he said. A softball league that played in Central Park every week for many years. This put my father somewhat at ease. Being in the care of someone who knew the injustices of being stuck on the injured list. Someone who could have a vested interest in getting him back on the field.

"Miss Kline," the doctor said politely, turning to me after greeting his patient. "Your stepmother mentioned you'd taken your father's place on the team in the interim." He clasped my hand in a short shake. "You're riling up the old-timers, from what I hear. Well done."

He lulled us into a false sense of placidity as I camped out in a chair in the corner of the room and my father sat atop an examination table, the sanitary paper rustling every time he shifted his ass. The doctor oscillated between inquiring about symptoms and gameplay. Leo rattled off lists of maladies—stiffness in his legs, loss of balance, dizziness, compromised vision, momentary disorientation—punctuated with commentary about the league he was itching to get back to. "I put together a great team this year, really. I haven't seen this much chutzpah in a lineup since the early nineties."

The doctor nodded along to the baseball anecdotes but turned his attention to Leo's scans—pulling them out of a wide white envelope and holding them against the buzzing ceiling fluorescents, staring hard through the skinny frameless readers positioned at the end of his nose. As he walked over to the light box attached to the wall, his mouth clipped into a soft, tight-lipped expression one might trade with a stranger passing on the street.

"This, Mr. Kline," he said softly, as he attached the scans to the light box, turned it on, and pointed to what looked like an arbitrary piece of the image, "is what I don't want to see."

Leo and I both squinted at the scan and then turned to each other—our faces affixed in the same rubber-faced frown of tentative concern. "All right, Doc," Leo started, trying to tamp down the agitation rising in his voice. "Whatever you don't want to see, I *can't* see. Help me out here." I stepped closer to the light box because I could, leaving Leo at a distance on the table.

"See here," the doctor said to me conspiratorially, pulling a pencil out of his breast pocket and poking the eraser at the scan. "These white spots," he noted. I could see them when he pointed to them. Faint but visible. A couple of them lurked around the map of Leo's brain.

"Again, I ask you," Leo boomed, feeling ignored, "what are we looking at? What does this mean? Help me out here, for chrissakes!" I kept my hand over my mouth and my wide eyes on the image. I didn't want to look at my dad for whatever the doctor was going to say next.

"Lesions, Leo. These are lesions," he replied, solemn. "I took a look at your old scans from after that fall a few months back. These marks weren't present on those scans. What that means, I don't quite know yet."

"Well, take a wild guess," I said, the sharpness in my voice catching them both off guard. "If you could put money on it, what would you say this is?" I pecked my fingernail at a white splotch on the screen.

"Caroline," my father growled at me.

"I can't say definitively without more tests," the doctor responded, even-keeled as ever. He walked back over to the scans, pointed again with his pencil eraser. "I've seen multiple sclerosis present itself this way in other patients, but, admittedly, it's rare for multiple sclerosis to just show up in someone your father's age. We need to glean a bit more about what's going on."

"You think it's MS?" I asked, fighting to flatten the tremble in my voice.

He scribbled notes onto a pad while Leo sat stone-faced on the edge of the table, hands clasped, jaw locked.

"I'm just talking through some possibilities, Miss Kline.

You said this most recent incident was triggered by heat?" the doctor asked, looking up from his notes. "Out by the pool? Lots of sun?"

Leo blinked and swallowed in lieu of a response.

"Yes," I broke in. "Midday, lots of sun, eighty-something degrees." My voice shook as I spoke.

The doctor handed me a slip of paper covered in scrawl, mostly words I couldn't make out or phrases I didn't understand—*McDonald criteria*, *Uhthoff's sign*, *possible PPMS*—and instructed me to give it to the receptionist up front for follow-up scheduling. I snapped a quick photo of it with my phone, planning to send it to Claudia and Harper whenever my father inevitably refused to tell them how the appointment went. The woman at the front desk, fluent in chicken scratch, squinted down at the sheet and then gave me a pinched, sympathetic smile as she slid a business card with the time and date of the next appointment beneath a protective glass barrier. Leo didn't wait for this transaction to be complete—he maneuvered his way toward the elevator, poking the down button with one free elbow. He waited for me in the lobby of the hospital like a reluctantly obedient dog.

After I retrieved the Saab from the parking garage and exhausted myself getting Leo strapped in, I returned to the driver's seat, dripping sweat in the thick, still heat of the car. I looked over at him—still silent, with his jaw clenched and his hands folded uncharacteristically in his lap, as though he were a child at a desk. I blew into the interlock system to start the car and backed out of the lot. When I moved to turn the stereo on (the Lionel Richie cassette, still), Leo caught my hand mid-air. I thought he was going to bemoan my requiring a Breathalyzer to drive or scold me for having grown fond of "Three Times a Lady" but instead he said, "Not a word about this quackery to Claudia. I might need a second opinion."

"What, just because he didn't tell you what you want to hear?"

"He's wrong. He's making it into something bigger than it is. This was just a minor setback." He turned his head and looked out the window, repeating his common refrain: "I'm supposed to be out on that field with my men."

"You know, you say that, but I'm out on that field with your men and I've gotta tell you: you're hyping the experience too much." I half laughed. "They're *really* nothing to write home about."

He stared ahead out the windshield with a grimace. "Fuckin' MRI. Never gonna hear the end of it," he muttered, before sitting in silence for the rest of the drive.

● ● ●

AS WE DROVE, I considered how my need to prove myself to my father was an instinct so well ingrained in me, it was bundled with my earliest biological impulses. Eating, sleeping, hydrating, learning to swing a bat, seeking Leo's affections. Growing up, it was part of my personal hierarchy of needs.

It wasn't that Leo was emotionally withholding, exactly, as I knew a lot of fathers tended to be characterized. In fact, he heartily praised my tentpole successes as they came: graduating high school on the honor roll, getting into NYU, finding a job that paid well enough that I could afford to live in Manhattan and pay my own cell phone bill. Finding Ben. "Nabbing him." He was especially proud of me for that farce back when it looked like what we had might be the real deal.

But these were all things that had nothing to do with who I was at my core or what I was passionate about. I suspected his praise was more informed by his holding me against the yardstick of my sister's achievements than by my gaining autonomy. When it came to personal recognition for what I was really proud of, everything I accomplished was treated as something that was to be expected. The game-winning triple in the Little League World Series. The B'nai B'rith fundraiser I organized in high school for victims in Darfur. The first-of-its-kind speakeasy-style music festival I executed for my clients with only a week and a half's notice. Not to mention my encyclopedic knowledge of Yankees pitcher stats, Jackie Gleason bits, and Led Zeppelin songs.

"You hold Harp and me to different standards," I told him on a different drive years ago while "Bron-Y-Aur Stomp" streamed out of the tape deck. My sister would correctly identify

"Stairway to Heaven" six minutes into the song and my father would fawn and say how impressed he was. *Good ear, Harper!* Meanwhile, I could be in the back seat like, "Robert Plant penned this B-side track in a chartreuse-colored notebook on a rare sunny day in the Scottish Speyside, perched in front of a rented cottage's south-facing window while sipping orange pekoe tea," and Leo would be like, "Pfffff—everyone knows that!" He was enchanted by Harper and impossible to impress.

I'd already been dubious about my ability to return to Manhattan by summer, but the setback of my father's latest fall and now the possibility of what lurked within these scans made it seem like a far-fetched fantasy. The drive back to Glen Brook that day marked my indefinite return home. I felt caught between two sensations: panic and invigoration. Would I feel trapped, or would I spin this into opportunity? I'd left Glen Brook behind, in part, for the same reason large swaths of people leave their hometowns: To get out from under the weight of their parents' expectations. To craft a life without someone else looking over my shoulder and appraising every movement. But what would make it worth a return? The chance to step up in my father's moment of increasing crisis—the ancient prospect of demonstrating my worthiness—seemed too great to ignore.

Every Christmas Eve, our parents took Harper and me to see the Rockefeller Center tree, then to Smith and Wollensky to eat thick, salty steaks and wedge salads drenched in creamy

Roquefort dressing. On our way into the city, a countdown in the corner of the Panasonic billboard next to the Lincoln Tunnel would read 01: ONE SHOPPING DAY 'TIL CHRISTMAS. On our way home, it would be ablaze with double zeroes. We lived in the dreamy warmth of an anticipated moment, and it felt perfect. In the tunnel where the wall was marked NEW YORK | NEW JERSEY, my father always leaned across the dashboard with a long arm and left the rest of us in a different state, if only for the length of a laugh.

Now, in the tunnel en route from his appointment, he sat quiet with his crutches held together between his knees. Orange light illuminated his scowl in flashes. Still, despite the dour atmosphere, when we approached the state line, he lifted one crutch with his free arm and extended it across the dashboard. No words exchanged, because we didn't need them. I already knew what he was thinking: *I win again.*

The vantage point from the tunnel's exit ramp in Weehawken was my father's favorite view of the city. "That's your home," he whispered every time we drove it. "The capital of the world." I never knew if he was talking to me or reminding himself, nearly three decades after he traded in his Brooklyn roots for suburbia.

Still in silence, we eventually hit Route 9—the road that, growing up, always indicated when I was almost home. It's the same one Springsteen sings about in the first thirty seconds of "Born to Run."

● ● ●

AT HOME, I considered what Claudia or Harper would do in my shoes, then did my best impression of them. I took great care to fuss over Leo, finding a classic Yankees game rebroadcast on TV while he got as comfortable as he could in his spot on the couch. Baseball, in all its forms, was our family's go-to coping mechanism. "Jim Abbott's no-hitter! Nice!" I said to cheer him, but his face remained stony. I breezed into the kitchen and made him a perfect tuna melt on rye, then served it with iced coffee and his shower caddy of pills.

"Anything else I can get for you right now?" I asked, clapping my hands together, sounding like a cross between Claudia and a diner waitress. He shook his head, barely glanced up at me, and minded his tuna melt.

I walked out of the room, frustrated. *What more can I do?* I had put on my best caretaker act, channeling all the women my father preferred to me, and he seemed to hate it even more. I sat at the base of the staircase in the entryway, took out my phone, and scrolled to the photo I'd snapped of the doctor's note, tapping it to zoom in. It occurred to me then that sending this note to Claudia and Harper would only court more of what my dad didn't want. Their incessant lines of questioning, the fawning and the pity and the delicate treatment. When they acted this way, it made healing and returning to normalcy feel distant and unlikely to him, not something that he should be striving for.

Maybe what he really needed at that moment was someone like me: afraid to discuss illness or confront frailty, eager to talk about anything else but the obvious and life-altering circumstances hanging over both of our heads. He needed a distraction. I deleted the photo from my phone and walked back into the living room.

"We need to talk," I said, standing in front of the television, obscuring the Yankees' one-armed pitcher with my hands propped on my hips. Leo—shrunken at his post, his facial expression more sad than angry—tried to dismiss me, performing a shooing gesture with the remote in his hand. "It's important," I continued, reaching over to the TV's power panel and turning off the game. His shoulders deflated, and his head hung on his neck.

"Caroline, I don't want to—"

"It's about the lineup," I said, surprising him.

Leo's face lit up. He sat up and used his good arm to remove the stack of a week's worth of *New York Times*es occupying the sofa seat next to him. An invitation for me to sit down.

"Go on," he said.

"I think we need to switch things up," I announced, walking over, taking my seat. "You've got Pete Peretti leading off when Billy the Kid should be in that slot, and I should be batting cleanup."

He pulled a yellow legal pad and one of those clicking four-colored ink pens out from the pile of newspapers and looked at me over the tops of his glasses. "I'm aligned. What else?"

He was responding to me—not my imitation of anyone else, not who I assumed he'd wanted me to be. He looked animated for the first time all day. He was ready to strategize. I was ready to be his greatest distraction.

13

THAT NIGHT, I took Crispin up on his standing offer to drive me to the JAMS meeting. I stayed mum on the subject of my dad, but I'd never had a good poker face. Sensing I'd been quiet all night, on our way home he breezed past the exit to get to my house. "How about we drive east until we hit the beach?" he asked.

By then, we'd done this a few times. After the meetings, I relished the opportunity to sit in the passenger seat of his ancient Jeep Wagoneer, Route 33 going by the window in an eastbound smear. We listened to rock radio while I considered how my profile might appear to him from over on the driver's side. I liked being a fixture in his car. I wanted him to miss me when I wasn't there.

It was on these drives that I got to know Crispin through osmosis: all the late-night discourse exchanged at random over the center console of his car. By way of this banter, I collected all my favorite bits about him: the last thing he'd eat on death row (pork roll, egg, and cheese), the Crayola crayon he'd always wear down to a nub (Cerulean), the celebrity whose career he'd most like to have (Todd Rundgren).

When I balked at his celebrity response, Crispin flipped through playlists on his phone with a quick, intuitive thumb. The glow from his phone illuminated his front teeth, highlighting his smile in a way I suspected might end me. Three dramatic, descending beats and an angelic, feminine voice emerged through the speakers. The song was called "I Saw the Light," and some ancient part of me recalled hearing it on the radio in my youth. But knowing it was one of Crispin's favorites—watching the slow, slight roll of his shoulders and the roping muscles of his neck as he sang along, illuminated only in flashes by a sliding wedge of light—could make me a Todd disciple in an instant.

"He has a couple of his own bangers," he called out over the music, "but do you have any idea how much he's responsible for?" I laughed because I didn't have any idea and because it was thrilling to see this passion ignited in him. He could extol the virtues of Todd Rundgren forever, and because my affections picked up where I'd left them fifteen years ago, he held my rapt attention. "He's, like, a fucking wizard of a producer. Badfinger, New York Dolls, Grand Funk Railroad. Meat Loaf's *Bat Out of Hell* album? All him."

He pulled the album up on his phone, and the stampeding sax intro to "All Revved Up with No Place to Go" burst forth from the speakers. I felt like I'd been punted in the ribs, thinking about the dance at Saint Christopher's. Did he remember it, too?

"I know you like this album," he yelled over the song, giving me a wink. "Even if Meat Loaf aged into a card-carrying conservative."

"Please," I begged, clasping the arm that held the phone, "let's never discuss 'aged meatloaf' again."

It was just like this; I came to know him again through sounds and stories.

And in return, he knew me, too. He knew I'd request a full Russ & Daughters spread before getting sent to the chair, would love nothing more than to paint the sky Razzmatazz, and that my most potent fantasy wasn't sexual by nature—it was to be Courteney Cox portraying a young fan, plucked from a jangling crowd of New Jersey lunatics by our fearless leader, Bruce, in his "Dancing in the Dark" music video.

Perhaps it was because we were able to trade these more innocent tidbits with each other that when the more serious items came up—like why I'd been so quiet at the meeting—I found myself being more forthcoming with him than I'd been with anyone else that year. The subject of my father's failing health sat like a dead molar in the back of my mouth. But I could only chew around it for so long.

I recounted the forty-eight hours that preceded our drive: the fall into the pool, the MRI, the diagnostic theories. "I'm trying to be a worthy distraction for him, help take his mind off whatever is going on in his body. But I have no outlet. I can't talk to my sister or my stepmother about it without setting off a big alarm."

"What about Bobbi?" he asked. He'd grown close with my mother during their frequent *Dolls and Guys* rehearsals. I knew my mother, in turn, was fond of Crispin, too. She so appreciated his sensibility and relied on his musical direction that she recently referred to him as her "consigliere," which was mortifying enough to make me reflexively smack my palm against my face.

"She knows what's going on, but I feel like whenever I mention it to her, it leads to more complication than comfort," I told him. "I suspect that when we talk about her ex-husband's mortality, it makes her upset to think about her own, and . . ." I shook my head like I was saying *no* to the tears that threatened to spring to my eyes. "I guess my dad's just worse off than I suspected, and I wasn't prepared for how fragile that would make me feel."

"Hey, you're going above and beyond here," he told me,

attempting to make brief flashes of eye contact while still looking ahead at the road. "Think about everything you've done for him so far; how selfless you've been in all of this. Uprooting your life in the city like that to come back here and help him out? Not everyone would be so generous."

I looked at Crispin's profile in the night, his silhouette illuminated by the crest of the moon. *I'd love to start over with him*, I thought. *I'd love to come to him naked and clean, no blemished record, no broken heart.* But now, weeks after we recrossed paths, he gave me an opportunity to practice the same level of honesty he had been giving me.

"It's true that the reason my dad called me home was to help out after his fall," I said. "But I can't pretend that's the only reason I came back. I sort of had to come back. I'd left my job and blew through my savings and couldn't afford to live in the city anymore. And all of that went down because I went through an atrocious breakup a couple of months before I left."

Crispin raised his eyebrows but stared straight out at the road, hands at a careful ten and two. "I had no idea. I'm sorry, Caro," he said, with sincere sympathy. It wasn't the kind of performative pouting I'd have done for him had he opened up to me about a breakup. I'd react to that like a salivating wolf in an old-timey cartoon, waiting for my turn.

"Thanks," I whispered, like a question. I never knew how to respond to an obligatory condolence. I could recall sitting shiva for every grandparent and responding to many *I'm so sorry*s with *It's okay*—desperate even in grief to please everyone around me.

We hit the crust of the beach at Belmar, and he pulled into one of the handful of narrow parking spaces lining Ocean Avenue. Crispin unclicked his seat belt and put his seat back a little, leaned, and shifted to face me. He looked like a kid at a campfire, like I was about to tell him a story.

"Not to be the Australian girl at the lunch table," he laughed, "but tell me more. Come on! I wanna hear about the prick."

I laughed, too, biding my time. Crispin seemed so eager for a juicy story, and I didn't know if this one would elate or disappoint. "All this time," I said, "you've been a yenta and I didn't know."

"What, you think I'm above some gossip?" He grinned. "Don't make me go out to the boardwalk and scrounge for popcorn." He extended an arm over the console, gripped my knee, and gave it a playful shake. It was a move that might've floored me if we had still been driving and I wasn't being coaxed into stripping down to my most vulnerable layer.

We had a plan: Ben would transfer to the satellite Los Angeles office, where he could continue to produce branded content (a job he found demeaning, but which paid him an outrageous salary and gave him the passing satisfaction of saying he "worked in publishing"). I would live off my modest savings and lean on him for a few months while I worked my connections and interviewed in our new city.

I told Crispin how Ben met me at Minetta Tavern for hamburgers and champagne. How, when he walked in, I saw him the way I saw him the night we first met. Tall and substantial, charming and boyish. He had a commanding gait, a hairline to write home about, and a face that gave nothing away. But when he sat down, he told me that I wasn't going to LA anymore. He was still going through with the transfer, but I was no longer invited.

"Wait." Crispin stopped me, snapping my attention back to the interior of his car by the beach, far away from Ben. "He blindsided you with this? After you had already quit your job?"

"Yes," I said, satisfied to let the story stop there. Then I sighed. "Well . . . in the spirit of total honesty? There were some, uh, warning signs."

We took a trip out to LA shortly before the breakup to sign a lease on one of the El Cabrillo Spanish revival courtyard apartments, the ones built by Cecil B. DeMille. Afterward, we drove out to the desert to meet a few of his friends for a long weekend. They were a lot like Ben and every other New York City private school boy I'd ever met: aimless because they had family money to fall back on, always in pursuit of benzodiazepines, and still somehow talking about private school—or else categorizing others by which private school they had gone to.

The girlfriends who accompanied them went to Spence or Sacred Heart and also had a weird way of making this common root the undertow of every outing, asking me without fail every time I saw them where I went to high school. My reply was always an uncomfortable, hand-wringing *I went to public school in New Jersey.* They would flash me a tight, pitying smile as though I had confessed to being educated at a Cinnabon kiosk inside Newark Airport's oldest terminal. I felt myself loosen up a bit around only one of them, a Carolyn Bessette look-alike who went to St. Ann's.

We rented a small village of geodesic domes in the desert, one couple per dome. The plan was to spend a few nights out there—drinking and swimming and smoking a loosely rolled joint around a firepit—then go to this "secret" desert party. It looked like a scaled-down Burning Man but without the giant scarecrow. After tiptoeing around a stone plunge pool that looked like rich-kid soup for two days, I was ready to let loose and have a good time.

One of the guys—a Collegiate alum who went only by his last name, *Galloway*—produced a handful of capsules, one for each of us. Ben plucked the first one from his palm and tossed it into the gulf of his mouth, swallowing hard. I looked at him with mild disgust as everyone else's hands darted in for their dose. I pocketed mine, and we split off into our own huddle.

"What now, Caroline?" Ben demanded, tugging on his face.

"Nothing!" I reflexively shrieked. But it wasn't nothing.

"You don't want to, I don't know, *talk* before you launch into psychedelia for the next ten hours? You don't want to discuss who's taking care of whom or ask if I'm comfortable with it?"

"Do you hear yourself right now? We're at a rave in the desert. I don't need to check in with you every thirty seconds. Think you'll let me take a piss without permission, or no?"

"That's not fair, I just—"

"I don't need you to take care of me, Caroline. Galloway's brother is a chemist. I didn't just drop some bad acid. It's a new compound he's working on. It's like MDMA crossed with peyote."

"Oh, well, I didn't realize the esteemed chemist Dr. Nobody Galloway cooked it up! Then by all means! I hear he's the next Owsley fucking Stanley."

"I can handle my drugs, Caroline," he said evenly, an irritating tactic he deployed whenever I raised my voice in order to make himself seem like the moral one. "Everyone here can. If you can't, just take half and shut up about it."

Because I hated being told to shut up more than anything in the world, I popped the whole capsule into my mouth in an act of defiance. It was still crawling down my throat when Ben pulled me into his side, gripped my forehead with his big hand, and held a kiss there. *He only loves me when I shut up and do as I'm told*, I let myself think before shooing away the thought.

As we made our way past the blaring lights and thrumming crowd, I could tell Ben's dose had already kicked in. He was slick with sweat, and his eyes looked like an old Mickey Mouse cartoon. The rest of our crew felt it, too. Each couple looked closer knit than Ben and me—rubbing their hands on each other, walking in lockstep, heads nestled in crooks of shoulders. *Is everyone high but me?* I was the wallflower at the rave.

The moment Ben noticed tears running down my chin, he let go of my hand like he was tossing away a discarded wrapper and stormed off ahead of me. St. Ann's appeared at my side, took off my neon cowboy hat, and started stroking my hair (either for her benefit or for mine, I still don't know), and asked how she could help.

"I can't get high like everyone else is high," I cried in a blubbering staccato. "Why is everyone else feeling it and I'm not? There's something wrong. Oh, God, there's something wrong, isn't there?"

"There's nothing wrong," she cooed, walking in time with me, pulling my head into the side of her chest as she continued raking her thin fingers through my scalp. After a minute, she eased away and pulled a pair of red plastic heart-shaped sunglasses out of her fanny pack. "Here, wear the magic sunglasses. Don't focus on the other shit—just focus on your own sensations. These glasses are bullshit blockers."

The glasses worked. Or maybe I just needed to relax a little. After a few minutes of walking on my own path in the dust—alongside the greater group but separate, like a stroppy teen whale swimming at a distance from the pod—I felt the drug's effect lift something in me. Like the first firework on the Fourth of July: a single stream of light traveling up my sternum until it reached its highest possible point. *Showtime.*

I jogged to catch up with Ben at the front of the herd, running alongside him as he accepted me back into his good graces. With our inhibitions miles away, it was difficult to remember why we'd been arguing. He morphed into breezy West Coast Ben, shirt unbuttoned, serene smile plastered on his face. I held hands across eons with my inner child, goofily smiling as I did jagged little dances to the music in my head.

We marched onward, euphoric, toward the crowd—a humming, living mass that multiplied in front of our eyes like cells in the womb. "We're going in!" I announced to our crew. "We're going right into the heart of the organism!"

In the distance, an amateur band played the greatest song ever. "This is the greatest song ever," I kept saying. "Do you know this song?" I turned to the group, who ignored me, save one or two dead-eyed head shakes. *No.* I tried to remember the words so I could look it up later and listen to it forever, and I realized it was like trying to hold water in a fist. I couldn't make out the words. They'd all gone soupy. The air got thicker, and it was hard to hear the music, or anything really. I felt as though my head was being held underwater by an unseen force. I turned to Ben in a panic, then projectile vomited on his torso.

I got hauled off to one of those designer portable bathrooms. My companions were the girl from St. Ann's (by then exhausted at the prospect of babysitting me) and a brunette with the most expensive set of hair extensions available west of the 405. We were still ten feet away from the Porta-Potty when I puked again, indiscriminately in the direction of their dust-covered shoes.

"Well, this is one way to sober up," Chestnut Ringlets said to St. Ann's over the hump of my back as I retched.

"You think I'll be sober after this?" I looked up at her with hopeful, twinkling eyes and bile dribbling out the corner of my mouth.

"No, that shit is already in your bloodstream," St. Ann's snapped. "She means that taking care of you is sobering *us* up *real* quick."

I'm going to die, I thought. *I took a shady club drug in the desert and I'm going to die and bring shame to my family.* I attempted a quick prayer, asking that the private school girls wouldn't try to hide my body to clear themselves of any wrongdoing, but my mind had trouble gripping the thought.

Ben appeared in front of me, the lights from the carnival ensconcing him in a full-body halo. He came to relieve the girls of their burden, making no attempt at hiding the fact that his somber ass looked like he was about to receive a court sentence. He made an honest attempt at cleaning himself up as best he could, but the crotch of his pants was wet with sink water and his body hair was a matted tangle from his chest to his belly button.

I straightened up and tried to summon an apology, anything to make him soften his face from the form it had taken. "I'm sorry," I eked out before I was back to heaving bile in the dirt.

"Sorry for what, Caroline?" he asked with his arms folded across his chest, standing over me like a bad dad. "What part exactly are you sorry for?"

He looked down at me like I was more trouble than I was worth. And in that moment, I knew it was true. He hated me for not being an easygoing, low-maintenance girl like the rest of his friends had managed to find. I was not the girl he wanted. I was high-maintenance and sensitive to hallucinogens and I went to public school all my life.

"I'm sorry that I didn't go to Spence! You unbelievable piece of shit! Why don't you just go fuck her?" I yelled, pointing to the girl with the hair. "I know you want to! Go pull on her extensions and talk about sister schools and make her fake an orgasm. But don't be surprised when she just lays there!"

Without a word, he turned on his heel and walked back toward the organism. St. Ann's followed him, turning back once to shoot me a look of disgust as I remained down in the sand on my knees. Chestnut Curls got down with me for a moment to let me know she wasn't a New York City private school girl. She wasn't even from New York. I couldn't have been further from the truth. She grew up in Hancock Park and went to Harvard-Westlake.

Back at the beach, Crispin lit one cigarette off the last and tossed the butt out the driver's-side window, a safe distance from the car.

"Look," he said on an exhale. "I have cousins who went to New York City private school. Those kids are unbearable. Who could blame you?"

I was quiet in the passenger's seat. With nothing to fidget, I kept my hands cupped in my lap. "When he left, I had no backup plan and not enough savings to pay my rent much longer. My dad asking me to come home was a mutual solve to two desperate situations. So that's why I left New York," I said in a near-whisper, invoking that essay genre Winnie and I had long loathed. "*And* why I don't do drugs anymore."

"Hey," he said, reaching out to me, "look at me." He put three fingers under my chin, then gently lifted it so my eyes could find his. An indefinite stay in New Jersey wasn't such a harsh sentence if this was what it could feel like. "A lot of people leave for a lot less, and anyway, we're happy to have you here."

I flashed him a weak smile and pulled back. He was just

saying that because he took pity on me, and I knew it. But I was grateful for the fact of being in his car, being at the beach, his hand just momentarily brushing my face.

"And I'm not just saying that," he interjected, as though he were reading my mind. "I haven't driven around town aimlessly or gone down to the beach just for the fuck of it since I was a teenager. I feel like I'm in high school again."

When Crispin drove me home, he idled at the end of my father's driveway while I got out of the car. I couldn't see him past the headlights, but I knew he was watching me as I walked to the side of the house, punched the entrance code into the gummy buttons, and disappeared beneath the maw of the garage door with a wild wave. Only once I was safely inside, once the garage door had returned to its position, did I hear the shift of his engine and his tires peel away.

I didn't know what I'd be doing if I were in New York that night instead—and, for the first time since I'd come home, it didn't matter. Nothing held the thrill of even just sitting with him. I felt a species of longing stir beneath my ribs that I hadn't felt for so long with Ben, something I had assumed just quietly died. I thought briefly of how Ben tried to minimize me when we were in a crowd or even alone together. How he made me feel cheesy and lowbrow when I'd talk about the things I loved and he hated: Billy Joel. Musicals. Margaritas. Shopping malls. Yankees baseball. "I'd keep that under my hat, if I were you," he'd liked to say.

Being around Crispin threw everything into such sharp relief: he wanted to hear my stories, the weird things I was obsessed with. No snobbery, only curiosity. He met my excitement with his own. He wanted to match my energy.

My friendship with Crispin wasn't a reunion; it was an act of reanimation.

14

JERSEY IN JUNE held a predictable brand of magic. There was a last-day-of-school energy about it, despite school being long over for everyone I knew. Fireflies drifted upward through the heavy air. Honeysuckle breached the fence of the outfield, sweetening the chase of every old man's hit. Dusk stretched out deep into the night as the line for soft-serve ice cream wrapped around the familiar brick angles of the Jersey Freeze, serpentine and buzzing with longing.

The *Dolls and Guys* production was underway. My mother's enthusiastic approval of Crispin as musical director signaled a merging of my worlds. When it came time for cast auditions, I showed up and sat in the back of the cafetorium to watch the process. My mother, her assistant director, and

Crispin looked on as an Instagram-famous drag queen from Asbury Park revived "Adelaide's Lament" complete with a steamer trunk of campy props. A trio of girls in starchy Catholic school uniforms reinvented the rollicking majesty of "Sit Down, You're Rockin' the Boat." A slight and pale buttoned-up man I recognized as my mother's accountant announced that he had come out for the part of Sister Sarah before launching into the "I'll Know" duet, pitch-perfect on both sides. When I'd drop in on my mother's Monday-evening rehearsals, she would stop everything to rush over and hug me like I was out of prison on furlough. Crispin would spy this out of the corners of his eyes, and I'd recognize the same peripheral smile he'd give me whenever I was a passenger in his car.

Tuesdays were for JAMS. Our meetings were held at an old American Legion hall in Neptune. The local chapter had a dwindling member base and were therefore generous with how often they let us use the space, although we, too, had a retention problem. This was somehow only the third- or fourth-saddest thing about JAMS as an enterprise. JAMS was trying hard to be the fun optional little sister to the mandatory MAPS program I'd already completed. Its mission was to provide community and social recreation, balancing out the harshness of a court-ordered reprimand in hopes of helping DUI cases maintain long-term sobriety, or at least consider it. I admired what they were trying to do, but the execution was never quite right: dismal board game nights and half-hearted ice cream socials in a musty wood-paneled room surrounded by faded photos of forgotten soldiers. It was accurate to say my interest in JAMS—and my perfect attendance record—had nothing to do with the programming and everything to do with its proximity to a boy I'd once loved. It was a sobriety strategy tailored to me alone: I'd stopped drinking and attended meetings, grateful for how good it felt to approach my days with a clear head and free from hangovers, but also because it afforded me quality time with Crispin Davis.

"I've been thinking about what's next for you," Crispin said when he drove me home after a meeting one solstice-adjacent night.

My stomach clenched like a fist. Even *I* hadn't thought about what was next for me. In fact, *one day at a time* was the single most useful thing I'd gleaned from the sober community, if only because it applied so conveniently to my situation and all the big, scary thoughts I hoped to stave off.

"I thought you hated when people ask you 'what's next,'" I answered blithely.

He laughed. "Not like that. I mean, what's next for you in the program. I have a feeling if I haul you out to one more sober bingo night at the Legion hall, we're going to lose you."

Before I could tell him it was impossible to lose me, he launched into a soliloquy about service—how it was one of the core tenets of the program. How once he found his footing, he committed himself to speaking at MAPS meetings and in detox centers to fulfill his service duties. I started to sweat a little; I was in no position to act or speak as though I were coming from an aspirational place.

"Maybe putting your own spin on a JAMS meeting could be your act of service," he said while my own head was still spinning, my long-dormant creativity starting to percolate. "You know, take your professional event experience and try to turn one of these outings into something you'd actually want to go to?"

As soon as he dropped me off at my dad's house, I ran to the basement where I'd stored supplies from a birthday party I'd thrown for Leo a few years back. Giant gold-foil fringe curtains. Mirrored centerpieces. A modest but effective disco ball. Claudia had wanted an upscale Studio 54 theme but dismissed my offer to track down expired quaaludes as party favors. Looking at the pile of schlock I'd gathered around my feet, I decided JAMS was a worthy heir to all the dusty glitz of a bygone evening.

The following Tuesday, I had Crispin meet me at the American Legion an hour before the meeting was due to start to help me set up. By the time he arrived, I'd already wreathed the space with streamers and gold foil and Christmas lights. It looked fit for a Pinterest board, or at least an enviable Instagram post. He chuckled in disbelief, walking between the matrix of round tables adorned in sequined shrouds and mirrored trays and olive wood planks of sliced meats and cubed cheeses. I pointed at the disco ball on the floor, signaling where I still needed his assistance.

"Be honest, Caroline," he said as he hoisted himself, mirror ball in hand, onto a chair and flexed his toes to meet the drop ceiling's rafter. "Are you turning my JAMS meeting into a rich kid's bat mitzvah?"

I snorted and walked over to the front of the room. "I don't want to spend another summer night on a sad Rummikub and Kool-Aid situation," I called out to him. "Jersey June is too precious for that! JAMS should be a thing of beauty and utility." I climbed up on the long, solid block of wood covered in navy velveteen, a makeshift stage for the veterans and bingo callers. I stood at the podium and asked him in my best infomercial voice: "Do you ever feel like you're afraid to expand your social circle beyond other sober people? Are you worried about how to behave in spaces that aren't conducive to those of us who, uh, just want to drink seltzer?"

He folded one arm over his chest, propping up his other elbow as he bit his thumb and smiled. *Yes.* He nodded beneath the sequined light of the disco ball he'd successfully secured.

"Well then, Crispin Davis," I said, picking up a microphone

and stepping to the side of the podium so he could glimpse my gold lamé halter jumpsuit in its full pleated glory, "welcome to Sober Karaoke."

I walked him over to Claudia's ancient karaoke machine, which I'd rescued from storage—the one she used in her permed social starlet days back in Ronkonkoma—and explained how instead of infantilizing little games, I thought our cohort could benefit from practicing our social skills. "I want them to feel less anxious about being out in the world," I told him. "A lot of the people who come to these meetings, myself included, are afraid they can't do things they used to love now that they're sober. And I figured, what's more nerve-racking tequila-shot fodder than karaoke?"

Crispin looked at me like there was a light behind his eyes. Like his mind was a filmstrip moving too fast, his mouth unable to keep track or catch up—no string of words worthy of his thoughts. I recognized the look, just not coming from him. It was the look I had come to expect from Robbie Walker after I stretched a double into a triple during extra innings, or from Ben in the early days when we'd stay up all night and I'd toss out an intimate, quietly profound thought. Getting that look from Crispin sent a tiny electric zap across my scalp and down my spine. Before I had too long to soak it in, Serene Jackson kicked a Doc Marten boot through the beaded curtain I'd hung at the door, entering the space and pulling our attention away from each other with a clatter.

"You weren't kidding, buddy," she said, I assumed aimed at Crispin, though she wasn't looking at him. "Your girl went all out!" She pointed to the display of seltzer cans I'd procured at Whole Foods and arranged into a massive, structurally dubious pyramid and raised her eyebrows as if to say: *Nice.*

"Well"—he smiled—"look who finally showed up to a JAMS session."

It clicked for me then that when Crispin said he shared a community with Serene, he meant the recovery community. Fantasies of how the evening might go sprang to my mind: watching a singer whose every album I owned and cherished sing karaoke in this decrepit hall, spitting into my stepmother's ancient microphone. The thought thrilled me so much that I floated through our vague reintroduction: my weak *Hi,* her *Yeah, yeah, from the Pony, I remember.*

Regulars from our group started to file in, entranced by how the room had been transformed—fingering the streamers and smiling up at the lights and plucking cubes of cheese off the tables. Serene, Crispin, and I—sensing we'd have to be the ones to get the party started—walked over to the karaoke setup, chatting about what we wanted to sing. I'd envisioned myself vamping around to a Rolling Stones song, or maybe even cajoling Serene into singing "No Scrubs" with me the way Winnie and I used to do at our sleazy old karaoke haunt down on Avenue A. But when I picked up the leather CD carrier that accompanied the machine to peruse our options, I unzipped the sleeve in abject horror. It was empty, save for one disc: *TV Land Presents: Greatest Theme Songs KARAOKE EDITION!*

I felt a surge of tears bite the back of my throat, but Crispin and Serene both threw back their heads and laughed. Before I could apologize or curse Claudia's existence, Serene grabbed the CD, grabbed the microphone, and leapt onto the stage.

"Hello, my loves, and welcome to the solstice edition of JAMS!" The crowd, modest but mighty and still growing, cheered louder than anything that American Legion chapter likely had ever heard. "Tonight we're gonna do some sober karaoke thanks to our brilliant cruise director, Caroline. She's right over there—let's give her a big hand."

Applause spread through the dark, glittering room once more, and my face reddened as Crispin clasped me by the shoulders, cheering and lightly jostling me in excitement.

"You've all been working hard at staying the course, and I know it can be tough to get back out there and start to do the things you used to without using booze as a crutch. Speaking from experience, getting up on a stage and singing stone sober for the first time was harrowing. Which is *exactly* why we should take a little trip down that runway and see how we fly tonight, all right, folks?" she yelled, turning to the side and mouthing *track five* to Crispin as she held up a flat hand. She turned back to her audience.

"It's the shortest night of the year, so let's not let a single minute go to waste. I'm Serene, I'm an alcoholic, and this is the theme song from *Greatest American Hero*."

Perhaps because it was an exemplary TV theme song—or, more likely, because Serene somehow managed to breathe new life into the genre—the crowd was willing to suspend their stage fright and their skepticism (though I did hear a couple of muttered questions: *Are we* exclusively *singing eighties television songs?*) and lean into the exercise. A group of grizzled old-timers teamed up to howl the theme from *Happy Days*. A pair of moms did their best Laverne and Shirley impressions, calling out *schlemiel, schlimazel* before launching into an angelic duet on "Making Our Dreams Come True." Colleen, our MAPS coordinator, showed up and belted the theme from *Full House*. I was coaxed into singing "My Life"— a Billy Joel ditty that played on the opening credits of *Bosom Buddies*, the short-lived sitcom that launched Tom Hanks's career.

Crispin closed out the night by dedicating a song to me: the theme from *Welcome Back, Kotter*, a show I'd loved as a kid and a song I realized only then possessed an uncanny parallel to my return to suburbia. "Welcome back," he crooned through a smile he couldn't conceal, looking directly at me in a way that sent heat rippling up the backs of my legs, "to the same old place that you laughed about." I buried my grinning face in my hands in mock horror while Colleen shimmied beside me, hyping up the crowd to join in on the chorus.

A smaller faction stuck around after the night wound down, eager to keep the energy going with a group outing to a bonfire on the beach, or maybe pie at the diner. Serene helped clean up, nudging me and telling me how impressed she was with the setup. "If we were on tour this summer, this conversation would be a negotiation," she said, too casually to solicit my racing heartbeat. "Our longtime tour manager has been threatening to retire for years now. I don't know if you've ever considered working out on the road, but . . ." She trailed off, looking around at what remained of my shoestring-budget immersive experience. Then she looked back at me, awestruck in her light. "I have a gut feeling you'd change the game." My mouth had gone too dry to speak, so I nodded a wide-eyed affirmation—wondering when I'd be capable of allowing myself the indulgence of such a *what's next* fantasy.

After that, the early-summer days sped and bled into one another: a JAMS meeting followed by a diner trip, summer stage at the Stone Pony followed by a stroll along the boardwalk. Daytime sweat relented to nighttime balm. Steam lifted off our heated pool in the dark, the green lozenge of light glowing in the deep end. One night after a game ended in filthy, frenzied triumph, I drove home with the windows down, marched to the backyard, kicked off my cleats, and dove in still clothed.

I don't recall an explicit invitation, or any sort of overt expression that I wanted him to show, I just know that as June melted into July, Crispin could reliably be found in the same spot on the bleachers behind home plate. Every Wednesday night and every Sunday morning. He clapped those guitar-string-chapped hands together and cheered on my behalf.

15

SUNDAY MORNING IN the Kline household: the dryer
was on its last leg, so my yellow Bialys tee was still damp and
smelled like mildew when it was time to hit the road. I had
misplaced my cleats, and instead of looking for them I la-
mented my inability to call them from the house phone. "You
know," I said leaning over the breakfast nook through a
mouthful of brown sugar Pop-Tart, "like when you lose your
cell phone in the couch or something?" But my musings went
unappreciated. Claudia and Leo were in the middle of a tense
twenty-four-hour standoff following an ominous phone call
from the specialist in the city the afternoon before. A test had
yielded inconclusive results, further delaying an official diagnosis or proper next steps. Their mutual fear and frustration
manifested as contempt for each other.

"How is he gonna give me a call like this on the Sabbath?"

Leo had boomed, even though we were not exactly performing the part of good Jews: we hadn't lit the candles in months, and Claudia was testing out a new paella recipe she pulled from the internet. Trief.

"News? What news? It's just more of nothing! You're not asking the right questions, Leonard. We're never going to get any answers at this rate," she said with her back to him, hunched over the burners, threatening to season the mussels with her tears. "No answers and it's all your fault!"

Because I hadn't heard *it's all your fault* escape the mouth of someone older than seven in several years, I took it upon myself to drive myself to the game. Because I'd completed my MAPS commitment, the Breathalyzer had recently been removed from my car and my license had been restored, so driving alone had a new airiness about it. I left early to have a little time to myself to warm up. That morning's game was at the ballfield behind the municipal swim club, where I enjoyed catching small whiffs of chlorine and snack bar fumes as I rounded first base.

I'd forgotten we were facing the Dicks again that morning until I saw Kelly Quinn setting up her spread. She had one of those camping chairs that folded out into a recliner with a giant milky cold brew nestled into the cupholder. Her daughters had their own picnic blanket covered in a Lilly Pulitzer–esque print: paisleys puking on other paisleys. They were accompanied by a little dog, white and fluffy and yipping, perhaps from being handled too gruffly by small hands. Nearby was an L.L.Bean tote bag packed with coloring books and sensible snacks procured for an unreasonable price at Whole Foods.

I'd come early to avoid a tableau like this: Tommy Mills stretching on the diamond where I had wanted to get my stretches in. Little girls shrieking and chasing the soothing song of the morning birds away. The childhood-friend-turned-rival boasting a smug sense of domesticity and ease wherever her wedge sandals went. As I clipped my bag up on the fence in our dugout, she appeared over my shoulder.

"Heard you're quite the ace now, Caroline," she teased, smiling. "How's it playing in the boys' club? It's enough to make you miss our old girls' league, I'll bet."

I laughed a little. "There have definitely been times when I'd prefer our team's bratty heckling strategy over the way these guys talk to me," I said. "We could be vicious back then, but at least it was a viciousness I was used to." I felt a sense of tentative warmth. Kelly Quinn reminiscing over our shared girlhood glory.

Kelly laughed and looked off across the field. "Hey, remember after that World Series game when my dad took us all to the Rainforest Cafe in Paramus to celebrate?" she asked, turning back to me. "Danielle Cohen bet us that she could get the waiter to serve her beer, and it was, like, the wildest thing we could imagine someone doing! For a second there we really thought she could pull it off."

I flashed her a pinched smile and rooted around in my bag for my water bottle. Something about hearing her recount this incident throttled me back into an adolescent mindset again. I could so acutely feel what I felt then, the sting of being left out of Kelly's orbit.

"Actually, I wasn't on that team," I told Kelly, careful to keep my voice casual. "Your father didn't pick me up in the draft that year." I felt like I was talking to an ex who was trying to reminisce over a bygone magical night, and I had to remind them the mind-blowing sex they were describing was actually with someone else.

"Really?" she shrieked, aghast, flattening a manicured claw to her freckled, sunburned chest. "I don't remember that at all! I could swear you were there with us."

"Nope!" I chirped, animatedly zipping my bag shut. "Not on the team. No Rainforest Cafe hijinks for me!"

"Kel?" Tommy yelled from the field, cutting me off and asserting his presence for the first time since my arrival.

"Coming, baby," she called back to him in a slight drawl before turning back to face me. "I promised my husband I'd pitch to him for practice. Good to see you again, though!" She cuffed and pumped her hand around my arm, right above my elbow, in lieu of a hug. The conversation coupled with the intimate gesture flustered me. I couldn't tell if what I felt was an urge to kiss her or to shove her to the ground.

She jogged out to the mound in her sandals and her romper, removed a silk scrunchie from her tanned forearm, and pulled her bleached hair back into a low pony. A bucket of aging beige softballs, furry to the touch, sat to her right. When she picked one up, I felt like I was watching her go back in time. Tommy was already in his stance: knees bent slightly, big arms pulled back, his shoulders filled with power just lying in wait. She whipped one at him—the windmill of our youth, unleashed with the same war hawk look in her eyes—and he swung and missed.

Clasping her square-tipped manicure over her nose, she hid a smile and yelled a muffled "Sorry, baby!" Her hands remained clasped over her face for another few seconds, but I could hear her laugh anyway. I realized then I could live to be one hundred years old and still identify that laugh.

Tommy's bat only got a piece of the ball on the next two pitches, and the one after that sailed right past him. "Babe," he yelled to her. A warning. She shook out her limbs as if to signal, *Okay, okay, I'm going to get serious now.* A windmill pitch as perfect as I'd ever seen cruised right over the surface of his bat. *Now he's mad*, I thought.

"This is for me to take batting practice," he pleaded, softened even in his anger. "Not for you to be showing off." I looked over to her, but she didn't dare look back at me.

"You want me to lob you the ball so you can hit like every other half-dead man in this league?" she yelled back from the mound, hand to hip. "You're supposed to be extraordinary. You're supposed to be the best. That means batting practice at full speed, as if the best pitcher in the league was here with the sole intent of running you down." It took me a minute to identify who she sounded like—why that sort of harsh pep talk was so familiar to me—and then I realized she was parroting her father. Big Steve never lobbed us practice pitches or let us cut corners on running laps. He liked to hold practices in the high noon heat.

Tommy resumed his position bent over the plate. "Besides," Kelly said, smiling, flashing her eyes at me ever so briefly, "if I decide to start showing off, honey, you'll know it. You won't even be able to get a piece of it."

They went on like this—Kelly reinforcing her arm's legendary status, Tommy hitting a couple of moonshots, perhaps an act of foreplay between them—until the teams started to trickle in and they cleared the field for battle. From the bench, I could hear Leo and Claudia gently bickering. My mother—making one of her periodic game day appearances—sat a few yards away from them in her own reclining camp chair, looking at me and raising her paper cup of coffee in a toast as if to say, *Isn't it great I got out of* that *marriage?* Crispin made his way from the lot to the field. I couldn't tell yet what, if any, effect his presence had on my performance. Of the few games he had been to, there had been no discernible pattern. A couple of bad showings, one great game, one that was just fine. He clapped for me whenever I stepped up to the plate, and for the split second after he hollered my name through the tunnel of his hands, I didn't care whether we won or lost.

Tommy and Kelly took to installing the oldest woman I'd ever seen into a foldout rocker chair down the third base line. Her skin was translucent, bluish in places, and she was wrapped in two or three little white blankets despite the forecast saying it would reach eighty-three degrees by the third inning. Tommy called her Nana and kissed her cheek and clasped her twiggy little hands before jogging back to the dugout. Kelly planted a red cooler at her feet and made a big show out of highlighting the array of juices and snacks they'd packed for her. The girls danced around her chair like a maypole. Nana looked like a milk Popsicle, about to be vanquished by the sun.

"What are you doing, gawking at Jeanne Calment over there? You need to be singularly focused on strategizing," Leo snapped, appearing over my shoulder. "Now, we have a limited number of games before the playoffs. This is your shot to make the last few months worthwhile. No more 'you win you get a hot dog; you lose you get a hot dog.' We need to win. Consistently. Or we're not going to the show."

"Okay." I turned around and nodded, studious and soldier-like. "Got it. Games actually count for something. Win, don't lose. No more hot dogs. Don't fuck it up just because I'm in the mood to burn it all down."

"Don't get smart with me, Caroline. I know you want to do your best because I know you want to impress your boyfriend over there," he said, pointing to Crispin.

I grabbed his finger with urgency, as though it were a gun and I was stopping him from firing at a precious target. "I promise to hit a home run if you promise never to call him that again."

"Do me a favor and wait until the bases are somewhat loaded. I'm sick of this solo home run shit. Make a real dent, Caro."

The first two innings ran smoothly in our favor. Against any other team, I'd say it was a good indicator, but against the Dicks, it could be anyone's game until the last out. Our perennially injured first baseman was out with a jammed index finger—sitting pitifully on the bench holding up a Popsicle-stick splint to any passersby—so I covered for him. It was a big enough shift in vantage point that I felt energized, even through a slow inning. The shake-up made me buzz with excitement. It made me louder.

We racked up a five-run lead as we headed into the bottom of the third. The Dicks had home advantage, so we were on the field. Tommy Mills stood down the third base line with the scorebook in his hands, shouting little messages of encouragement as each of his men trotted up to the plate: *Let's go, buddy, let's get a piece of it. We're chippin' away now! C'mon, let's talk with those bats, boys.*

But there was something else: a little blond birdie on his shoulder, hovering over the short stretch of fence that followed the enormous protective backstop. Kelly Quinn leaned so far over the fence, her sandals were half a foot off the grass. As if no one was watching, she levitated there, muttering suggestions before Tommy gave signals to the batter and the runner. A couple of times she even gave them the signals herself.

Leo caught one of those—Kelly motioning for a runner on first to steal second just moments before he took off—stood up too quickly on his crutches, and started screaming at the umpire before fully regaining his balance. "What is this?" he said, tilting his chin toward the third base line. "We have civilians giving signals now? That woman is not a coach, blue."

Kelly released herself from the fence as the umpire pulled the cage off his face and took several steps toward her. "Ma'am, I'm afraid I have to ask you to stop what you're doing," he said gallantly.

She held up her hands as though trying to clear her name. "I was just barely making a suggestion, blue. Didn't realize Caroline Kline is the only woman allowed to speak within a hundred yards of a baseball diamond."

"Are you fucking kidding me?" escaped my mouth before the thought had enough time to properly filter through my brain.

"Kline," the umpire called, gruff and unyielding now, pointing a fat finger at my head. "Watch that mouth. You've had enough warnings this season. I won't hesitate to issue a citation if I hear another word out of you."

Kelly stood against the short part of the fence, the ancient lady directly behind her and the little girls with their little dog at her feet. Her arms were folded across her formidable chest, and she looked at me with a smug smile across her suntanned face, head cocked at a slight angle.

It was funny how in our youth, we did everything to hide the bad blood between us once it became apparent. We always insisted otherwise, tucking it away as though the shame of not being friends anymore was too uncomfortable or improper to admit out loud. "Don't take it personally," she told me when her father iced me from the softball team. "We just grew apart," I told my grandparents when I showed up to spend a week in Connecticut alone that summer instead of with a friend. Suddenly as adults, it was all out in the open. Contempt radiating off us like heat rising on a stretch of Parkway asphalt.

Fuck you, I mouthed at her while maintaining relentless eye contact and hoping the umpire had occupied himself. She flashed me a saccharine, close-eyed smile as she swept one hand from her throat to her chin to an open palm in front of her. A gesture colloquially known as *fuck you right back*.

Kelly sat down in her luxury camping chair, positioning it mere millimeters from the short fence, and took to cheering loud enough so her presence was known to every person on the field and off. I wondered how my saying the word *fuck* was somehow a bigger disruption to the game than her unrelenting stream of obnoxiousness. She periodically shut up to fix her attention on Nana: holding a straw out of a Yeti cup filled with ice water to Nana's puckered gray lips, slathering sunblock on the woman's forehead so she looked like a gleaming piece of dried fruit covered in Cool Whip.

When it was my turn at bat, Kelly shot out of her seat and called to the right fielder. "Bring it in," she yelled through cupped hands. "Ball's coming to you and you're *way* too far out."

The threat of a citation was the only thing that kept me in the batter's box and not at her throat. I refused to be rattled, knowing not only that Crispin was watching, but Gary Feingold—the chairman of the league's board and the one who granted me official permission to play—had also decided to show up and take in the game on this idyllic summer Sunday morning.

I wouldn't let her play to my insecurities. I had fought my way from league pariah to one of the bona fide best bats on the team. A notable switch-hitter with a reputation for clutch moves, I'd recently ranked eighth in the league in RBIs. It said so on the municipal website. Robbie Walker managed the standings and had beamed with affectionate pride when he pulled up this accomplishment on his phone to show me the week before. I thought: *Fuck this provincial bitch, with her bad taste and her yappy dog. All I have to do is talk with my bat.*

In my periphery, I saw their right fielder take five big steps forward on the grass. I hit a squibbler toward first, which the pitcher scooped and softly tossed to the first baseman before I could run it out. I kicked up a nuclear cloud of dirt in frustration on my way back to the bench. Kelly sat down in her chair, satisfied.

Our lead slipped over the next two innings as the Dicks tied then eclipsed us by two runs. A valiant offensive effort was made by Ryan Buckley and Billy the Kid, both of whom were used to being labeled the bad boys of the league but were starting to look like Cub Scouts next to my antics. They knocked a couple of line drives into left-center, but no one was able to step up and bring them home. There was a lot of trudging on our part as we took the field in the bottom of the later innings. The sun got hotter, and our morale waned.

We got to a boiling point: Dicks at bat, loaded bases, but two outs. Ryan Buckley threw a tricky pitch and their guy couldn't quite get the meat of his bat on it. It was a hit, to be sure, but not a moonshot. It went just past third base, where my temporary replacement—Timmy the Tortoise—had to summon all his strength not to let that little blip turn into an RBI. The batter charged toward me full force. Timmy put his full weight into the throw. It looked like it was going to fall short, but I extended every tendon of my limbs to keep my toes on the bag and watched the ball sail into the basket of my glove.

"*Yes*," I moaned down in the dirt, knowing that this out held them.

"Safe!" cried the umpire.

"What!?" I shrieked loud enough to tear the blue sky in two.

The bench emptied behind me, paws of the league's men and the onlookers laced into the links of the fence, a lot of jeering. *What are you looking at, blue?*

Ryan, still planted on the mound and no stranger to chaos, was hell-bent on continuing the game without confrontation. He knew if things went left, his rough-and-tumble brother would jump in and both of them would face discipline. "Kline," Ryan yelled, tugging on his bun in frustration, trying to get my attention. But I was focused on the crowd yelling in defense of the Bialys at the umpire, who lumbered over to silence the protests.

"Her foot came off the bag when he crossed it," the umpire explained to the crowd, pointing at the toe of my cleats, as though there was still some evidence to look down at. Ryan kept calling to me, and I continued to ignore him.

Leo furrowed his brows and hoisted himself up against the links with the help of a crutch. "Now that's a bush league call, blue, and you know it."

Crispin stood behind him, just as riled up after feeding off all the stray energy. "Yeah, man, totally bush league," he echoed, not entirely sure what that meant but knowing it was derogatory.

"Caroline!" Ryan yelled again. "I need the ball back! Now!"

So I turned my back to the congregation and whipped the ball at him sidearm. I only knew it was too hard and erratic a throw after it left my hand. It happened in both the blink of an eye and in soupy slow motion. Ryan dove to block the ball from going anywhere, lest the loaded bases continue to empty toward home plate. But he missed it, landed in the dirt, and left the ball to sail on a horrific trajectory: easily clearing the low panel of the left field fence as it went straight for the ancient woman in the chair.

She made a noise like a toy with a drained battery.

"Nana!" Tommy Mills cried, abandoning his post at second base and leaping over the low fence with ease, like an Olympian over a hurdle. The crowd swarmed around the old lady, whom, it was important to note, had *not* been hit by the ball, but was a victim of a close call by a matter of millimeters. Nevertheless, the incident scared her enough to render her unconscious and slumped over in her chair.

"You almost killed Nana!" Kelly screamed several times in my direction, as Tommy worked to revive her with ice water. Once they were able to rouse her, they received a round of applause and the attention quickly turned back to me.

Ryan stepped to the umpire to negotiate with him. "Ron,"

he said, holding a flat hand out as an apologetic barrier between them. I'd never heard Ryan Buckley or anyone else use an umpire's first name before, so I knew it was bad.

"Throw her out!" Kelly called from the sidelines, fanning Nana with a mass market paperback. "She almost killed Nana!"

As chairman of the board, Gary was one of the few who felt comfortable shutting Kelly up. "With all due respect, Mrs. Mills," he said genially as he walked past her, "that's quite enough. You have no jurisdiction here, and we're going to handle this accordingly."

Gary stepped onto the field, arms crossed and head bowed, walking swiftly toward the pitcher's mound, where Leo balanced on his crutches beside me, Ryan Buckley, and the umpire—known in some circles as *Ron*. Ryan continued peacemaking, no doubt deploying tools he and Billy the Kid learned during some sort of court-ordered training. "Look, Ron, no one was hurt. There was no malintent; it was just a wild ball. She really didn't mean it."

But Ron turned to address me, sausage fingers in my face and all. "Listen, young lady," he said—like he was my father, in front of my father. "That woman could have been seriously hurt. And the fact that she's Corporal Mills's grandmother—"

"Great-grandmother," Timmy Moriarty cut in, suddenly part of the scrum. He replaced his fist over his mouth in quiet observation.

"Whatever she is," Gary said, picking up where Ron left off, "the league and this town owe a debt of gratitude to the Mills family. Aside from the official rules, I'm letting you know right now, Caroline: screwing with them is just bad optics."

That angered Leo. "Oh, get out of here with that, Gary," he said, waving his hand like he was swatting away a cluster of gnats. "There's no special treatment in this league. You're just arguing in bad faith now."

Ron cleared his throat, determined to regain control. "I'm going to let you finish out the game, but I'm warning you right now: you better keep those emotions in check. Another outburst like that and someone could get seriously hurt."

Gary gave a solemn nod, and I could practically hear his thoughts. All the deliberation that led to letting me join the league. How I was already on thin ice just by virtue of existing. That I should keep my mouth shut and just be grateful to play.

Everyone resumed their positions. I stood guard at first base, thinking about earlier in the season when Billy the Kid shoved an opposing third baseman off the bag with two hands because he didn't like a look he'd flashed in Billy's direction. I thought about how when his team didn't make the playoffs last year, Pete Peretti cried after the last out. I thought about how, after ghoulish Tony Scolari got thrown out of a game in May, he knocked down every bat leaning against the dugout fence in an atomic clatter, swept every Gatorade bottle off the bench into the dirt, and ripped the game's page out of the scorebook and into confetti.

I wondered if any of them, or any other man in this league, had ever been reprimanded for being too emotional.

We lost to the Moby Dicks, 10–7. I strode back to my car without looking in Kelly's direction.

16

BANGERS ON BANGS had serviced Asbury Park musicians since Crispin's grandfather opened it in the early 1960s. It attracted the shore's young rock talent looking to break in: Bobby Bandiera, Billy Rush, Vini Lopez. Steven Van Zandt and Southside Johnny became patrons by the store's first birthday, with Bruce and Clarence and the rest of the scene becoming regulars by the time the Stone Pony opened in 1973. Crispin's mom worked the cash register then and took Polaroids of every musician who bought an instrument there, saying she wanted something to remember them by when they became rock stars. Every photo got tacked to the wall. A mélange of nobodies and somebodies, pinned together in the biggest band for all eternity.

Even after retailers on the main drag shuttered or moved,

the shop managed to stay open for the next few decades—selling hard-to-find instruments, catering to a loyal handful of Monmouth County's most famous musicians. By the time the economic stimulus came to Asbury in the mid-aughts, Crispin's grandfather was ready to call it quits. But the rest of the family wouldn't hear of it, including and especially his Berklee-bound musician grandson, who was something of a prodigy, albeit a lazy one.

The Polaroids still hung above the register, matted and framed now, so customers would feel confident about the lineage they were buying into. A small curated collection of vinyl records occupied a corner of the shop. Crispin was a one-man show: handling inventory, sales, and teaching music lessons to the locals.

This was where I found him when I surprised him one Thursday on my way to spend the evening with my mother. I tried to make a casual entrance, but who could be casual with a bell tied to the door? Crispin was perched on a reclaimed wooden barstool in the back, leaning over and rearranging fingers on a fretboard. The fingers belonged to Sarita O'Brien, hiding behind a long curtain of dark hair, unbuttoned denim shorts cut up so high she almost looked naked.

Sarita went to a different high school, but I knew of her when we were teenagers. We shared some mutual friends back when Winnie and I made it our priority to run around and get in trouble. It was unlikely she'd remember me, but she was hard to forget—practically Freehold township royalty. She had a Mexican mother who was allegedly a minor pop star before she came to the States and an Irish father who was a retired lieutenant. A bona fide wild child when we were teenagers, but famously sober since twenty after she was arrested for stealing her father's police cruiser and taking it for a joyride. They found her driving on the wrong side of a ramp on Route 18, drunk and high on dextromethorphan. Now she was a semi-renowned tattoo artist down the shore and the host of *Dry Goods*, a sobriety podcast with a moderate local following.

It was difficult to imagine she was the same girl on the stool in the back of Bangers, singing George Harrison's "My Sweet Lord" in an angelic tone, close enough to Crispin that they could smell each other's breath. I'd been in the store a full two minutes and he hadn't looked up from what he was doing. Maybe he was just an attentive teacher, I thought, but it seemed more likely he was drawn into the force field of her magnetism. Her voice, the agility of her hands, the chaotic collage of tattoos running up and down her arms. That glossy black hair and those sapphire eyes.

Sarita was hard to take your eyes off of, and I'd bet, watching him move her hand, she was hard to keep your hands off of, too. She was one of those girls who was curvy in all the right places: her ass, her breasts, the apples of her cheeks. I knew from social media that she dressed like an Instagram It girl with a closet full of nineties vintage and an outsize collection of beauty products. I watched at a distance as she sat propped on that stool, singing about God, flashing a small smile whenever Crispin's fingers pressed down on hers.

By the time they finished, I'd been in the store nearly ten minutes and had convinced myself Crispin Davis was in love with Sarita O'Brien, and that she definitely loved him back. "Hey, girl," he called coolly when he saw me, giving a wide wave. He stood up and replaced the guitar Sarita had been playing back on a rack before walking up to meet me. She followed, standing and looking suddenly like she'd been caught in an intimate act, running her fingers through the crown of her hair, gently dabbing her lipstick, buttoning her denim shorts over the pouch of her stomach. The buttoned shorts looked too tight to breathe in, much less sit comfortably in for an hour.

"Sorry about that," he said to me in a near-whisper. "We're just wrapping up." He wore a faded yellow Serene Jackson tee from a tour she did a few years back. It looked like an old-school fan club advertisement, an illustrated postcard that read: *Tell Serene: I WANNA BE A HOT ROLLER! Write to us: PO Box 314, Asbury Park, NJ 07712.*

"Thanks again, Crissy," Sarita said, sauntering up the sheet music aisle toward him at full force. She pushed her inked arms into the counter, hoisted herself up on it, and said in a lower voice, "I'm gonna be living in the material world any day now." She turned to me, winked as she smiled, and gave me a quick appraisal. I was right: she didn't remember me.

He let out a quick, single burst of laughter even though what she said wasn't funny and didn't entirely make sense. "All right, Sarita," he said, and I could tell he was trying to shoo her out, even though she seemed to want to stay and shoot the shit. "This time next Thursday, yeah?"

She jumped down off the counter, and her flip-flops landed on the tile with a smack. "Yeah, sure, but I'll see you before that, though, no? You'll be at Monday's meeting? I'm going to harass Serene to bring a bunch of her tour shirts to the church for me," she said, reaching over and pinching his T-shirt away from his body for a second. "I'm jealous of yours."

He told her he would be there and would see her later, firm enough so she knew it was really time to go.

"I've gotta get back to the shop," she said, pulling a tattered pink lanyard with a fist of keys out of a Louis Vuitton tote. She performatively directed it at me, as if I didn't just watch Crispin practically ask her to leave. "These men's asses aren't gonna tattoo themselves." Again, despite not saying anything particularly funny, she laughed as she pushed her way out of the store and onto Bangs Avenue, bell dinging a goodbye.

Crispin gave me a quick, tight hug to properly greet me,

then busied himself with all the counting and tedium that came with working the register. A summer storm brewed outside; cracks of lightning illuminated the row of storefronts across the street and the thunder rolled.

"Hey, can I ask you something?" he said, stopping to lean over the countertop. I looked at his tanned arms folded over each other, the light grip of his hands on his alternate biceps. I'd waited half a lifetime to be in those arms. I was preoccupied thinking he was about to finish his thought by asking: *Do you think Sarita O'Brien would prefer an emerald-cut diamond in her engagement ring, or a round cut?* But instead, he said, "So, I can't come to your game next Wednesday, but I was wondering if you'd meet me down here in Asbury after."

Wednesday's game was scheduled against Century 21 Realty. A bunch of bums. I felt confident I'd walk away from that one victorious. "Of course," I said. "I mean, I'll be filthy, but sure. What's the occasion? Are you running previews for the musical already?"

He smiled. "I can't tell you all the details yet, but I'm going to be part of this after-hours thing at the Stone Pony, and it would mean a lot to me for you to come. I think you'll be really stoked when you see what it is."

I couldn't help smiling back, matching him. It was hard to think about him depressed and struggling for so many years. His joy was contagious.

"I'll text you all the details," he insisted. "It's not *Dolls and Guys* related, and I'm not setting you up for a secret dinner society or a silent rave or anything, I swear." I'd be lying if I said I wasn't moved that he remembered some of my biggest experiential-marketing pet peeves.

Suddenly, the sky opened and rain poured down so thick and dramatic, we couldn't see the other buildings on the street. I looked out the storefront window in mild horror and confessed I'd parked far away and hadn't brought an umbrella. I shifted my eyes to him, hopeful. "I know I seem like I have my shit together," he laughed. "But not so much that I carry an umbrella. I have one in my apartment, though. I can give it to you to take to your mom's."

He locked up and we made a run for it, foolish enough to think some scaffolding and commercial awnings would ease the blow for us. The water moved like rapids through the street, decimating our shoes and splashing all the way up our legs. I was cackling, hopeless, by the time he pulled out his formidable Jim Morrison impression—*rain in the streets is up to my ankles, rain in the streets is up to my knees*—for the last block of our sprint.

The lobby of his building tried its best to pay homage to its art deco exterior: gold inlay work and plush emerald benches and a couple of ornate lamps, illuminating artwork that was trying too hard. We looked like stray dogs, soaking the small stretch of carpet that welcomed us in. He couldn't look at me without doubling over in laughter, which only sent me into a torrent of my own.

"You cannot walk into your mother's house like this," he said with authority, leading me up the stairs to the door of his duplex. I texted her to let her know I was running behind, though how far behind remained yet to be seen.

The prospect of seeing all of Crispin's personal effects and ephemera made me light-headed. The anticipation made the tips of my fingers buzz. Crispin took a few steps into his apartment and reached to hit the light switch in the kitchen, but nothing happened. He looked over at the clock on the stove. Blank.

"Shit, the power's out," he muttered, turning to me. "Wait right here." He took off his soggy shoes and quickly jogged up the stairs, his wet jeans making a horrendous swooshing noise. When he returned his arms were full of dry, soft clothes and a folded towel. "They're clean," he said, handing them over and reaching to hit the light switch in the bathroom, forgetting it was impotent. "Why do I keep doing that?"

I showered by candlelight, impressed enough he had a candle somewhere ("I learned my lesson after Hurricane Sandy," he said, shaking his head like he was trying to rid himself of a bad memory) that I was willing to overlook his rather utilitarian approach to shower accoutrements. A 2-in-1 Head & Shoulders and a minty Dr. Bronner's soap the size of a water tower. I said a prayer that my hair wouldn't turn to straw and let the soap cascade over my skin until my limbs tingled. *This is where Crispin Davis showers every morning*, the fourteen-year-old living inside my head thought. *This is Crispin Davis's soap. The mint on your skin is the mint on his skin.*

I wrapped the towel around my head and pulled on the long flannel pajama bottoms and big sweatshirt. My bra and underwear were still soaking in a tangle on the edge of his tub, so I had nothing on underneath.

I had a flash of an old memory, or maybe it was several bundled into one: the week of graduation parties after the last day of eighth grade. Every day, a different house with a different pool and the same catered fare. At a couple of them, the ones where the parents knew us well, a bunch of us stayed after most people went home. Communal sweatshirts and sweatpants were distributed so we could change out of our wet bathing suits and get warm. Huddled together in an air-conditioned basement, crowded around a big-screen television, not enough seats on the couch so we were all splayed too close, legs across legs, shoulder under the crook of an unexpected arm. This was intimacy as we had never experienced it, and perhaps wouldn't experience again for a few years: skin wet and soft under someone else's clothing, the ease of the environment coaxing us into relaxing atop the bodies of our peers. The forgiving glow of a beloved movie in the dark, bathing its audience, making us beautiful.

When I emerged from the bathroom, Crispin was swathed in similar attire and planted on his couch, scrolling through his phone. He was humming a song I knew intrinsically but still took me a minute to place: Led Zeppelin's "Fool in the Rain." One of my favorites.

The path toward him was illuminated by pillar candles featuring the faces of patron saints, the same kind you can buy at ShopRite in the aisle with the bags of dry beans and cans of coconut milk. I took in what surrounded me: The eclectic mix of furniture, likely inherited or thrifted, with some supplements from IKEA. The guitars mounted on the wall, four in a row, like hunting trophies. The narrow ladder bookcase filled with rock and roll biographies and a couple of meditation guides. A psychedelic framed portrait on the wall: Homer Simpson on a sheet of acid blotters.

"Second chances!" he called out, pointing at me as he scooted down the couch to give me ample space. I looked down at the sweatshirt he gave me, and that was what it said in white lettering across my chest. *SECOND CHANCES*.

I asked what it meant, and he said it was the sober house he'd lived in for a few months before he moved here, gesturing around our cathedral-ceilinged surroundings. I felt happy for him and envied him in that moment for what he had: a beautiful apartment, for one. A job adjacent to his passions. Undeniable talent. A community. Sobriety and accountability and a commitment to the pursuit of rigorous honesty. I looked at him, nestled into the soft arm of the couch in his hooded sweatshirt, and thought about how he had done more introspective work on himself in the last year than most people would do in their entire lifetimes.

"I'm impressed by the commitment to Catholicism," I noted, leaning in to examine one of the candles. Saint Jude. Even I knew that one. Patron saint of lost causes. My man.

"I have a confession to make," he said, putting his phone down on the coffee table, screen side up. I sucked in my breath, bracing for him to tell me about a blooming romance with Sarita. He smiled. "I've tried to turn on a light switch no fewer than five times since you got in the shower. I might've even reached for the TV remote."

I laughed, more out of relief than amusement. I couldn't recall a recent power outage, a real one. The kind that lasted hours and forced you to develop your own temporary culture of darkness with your house. I'd even missed out at the height of Sandy; my apartment in the city was somehow spared.

"My favorite thing my parents used to do when we were kids and the power went out," I told Crispin, "was let us camp out in their room at the foot of their bed in our floral-patterned sleeping bags. And we had this emergency kit in there—everything worked by winding a crank. Crank radio. Crank flashlight. And my sister and I would always want to put on a skit or something, and my parents would say, 'How about we play charades instead?' Probably to save themselves the migraine. They shined the crank light on us like a spotlight at Carnegie Hall and we just went for it."

Crispin laughed, and I realized in the last couple of years that the most pristine, happy memories I returned to were the moments that had seemed completely ordinary at the time. The time we stayed up and played charades deep into the summer night could very well be one of the best nights in my life. It made me crave my parents, even though they were still right there, my mother literally just blocks away. I missed them already. Versions of them I couldn't get back.

We sat in silence, perched on opposite ends of the couch, looking out the enormous window behind us. A front-row seat to the storm. Ropes of lightning ripped through the sky followed by rocky, unnerving bursts of thunder. When a loud strike startled me into a little jump, Crispin slid down the couch and gripped my knee. I looked down at his hand, studying the veins and valleys I could see in the shadows. I didn't realize I was holding my breath until he gave my knee a friendly shake, as if to say *it's okay*, before removing his hand altogether.

Closer now, I could hear the soft rhythm of his breath; take in his clean laundry scent. I stared at his face in profile, the sharp angle of his jaw, lit by flashes in the sky. He turned to face me, and I felt a warmth roll through me. My body was angled by intuition. My mind went blank. I leaned in.

Instead of meeting me, he eased himself back toward the far end of the couch. It was a miscalculation.

A few seconds took an eternity to tick by before he whispered: "I'm just trying to do the right thing here, Caroline."

I sat there, cheeks burning pink in the dark, trying to recover my heart rate without breathing too loud. I looked over at him, but he was back to watching the window. Rather than let silence ferry us away from the moment, I punctured it with the question I had to ask.

"Are you dating Sarita O'Brien?"

A short, staccato laugh. An incredulous twist of his eyebrow. "No," he said plainly. "What makes you think that?"

I shrugged. "She was all over you back at the shop. Pretty territorial once I got there. She didn't want to leave." I wanted to say, *She was also dressed like an Instagram model in unbuttoned Barbie doll–size clothes, and you just rebuffed a kiss from me*, but I kept that to myself.

He chuckled and looked down at his hands. "That's an interesting take," he said. "I didn't read it that way. Sarita's a great girl, but I'm pretty sure I'm not her type."

Great, I thought, *now I'm giving him ideas. Boosting his confidence and letting him know I think he has a real chance with her.*

"Look, I'm not really supposed to *think* the word *dating*, let alone actually throw my hat into the ring until I get my year in September."

"Is that one of the rules?" I asked.

He tossed his head back and forth. "AA doesn't have hard-and-fast rules, it's more just common sense, honestly. No big changes in the first year. Like, don't quit your job. Don't move across the country, don't end a relationship, don't start a new one. Stuff like that. I'm surprised that never came up in any of your MAPS meetings."

"So, it's not forbidden, but it's one of those aspects of recovery you, personally, are strict about?"

He laughed a little and shrugged. "*Half measures availed us nothing.*" A quote from the big book.

I wanted an outright repudiation of my original accusation. Something like, *I'd never date Sarita O'Brien, with her annoying laugh and perfect ass!* Instead of what I got, which I interpreted as: *I'm not allowed to date Sarita O'Brien until September.* I realized then that I wasn't going to get that assurance from him. He was keeping me at a distance on purpose. Whether it was because he wanted to be with someone else or because he was holding on so tight to the mores of his program, I couldn't be sure. But I felt it in the moment: maybe this was as close as he was ever going to let me get to him.

The heat of tension spread between my shoulders. I spent all my time away from Crispin craving this kind of physical nearness, and now all my impulses were telling me to bolt from the building. That I'd embarrassed myself and he didn't want me.

Crispin, perhaps sensing my panic, stood up from the couch, walked to the other side of the coffee table, and turned to face me. Solemn as a fence post. He flashed me a peace sign.

My eyes widened, almost against my volition. "Two words," I said tentatively, wondering if I had it in me to stick around and put the unrequited lean-in behind us.

He pantomimed a crank next to his eyes, like an old-timey film camera.

"Movie," I said, elbows pressed to knees, hands interlocked, fingers laced at a point against my lips in a gesture of sincere contemplation. I relaxed into his game.

The shadows of the saint candles danced across his torso, his cheek. I knew that soon I'd be sleeping on my mother's pullout couch in a Victorian house just on the other side of Wesley Lake. I'd be thinking about the shadows of this evening, the sheer proximity of it all making it difficult to fall asleep. But in Crispin's living room, in the soft darkness, I let the moment bloom uninhibited.

He held up one finger in the dark.

"First word," I said through a smirk.

17

I WENT TO the city the following Wednesday for a half-hearted interview with Film Forum's director of programming—the result of my still, somewhat hopelessly, dashing off sporadic job applications—then a late lunch with Winnie. We ate matching vegan taco salads with cashew cream perched at the counter at Fern Bar, one of our old haunts. She conquered a candy-hued Aperol spritz while I nursed a seltzer and watched the clock. I had to catch a train within the hour to make it to the night game on time.

"Dare I ask how things have been going with local teen idol Crispin Davis?" she asked, cocking an eyebrow. I pressed my forehead against the bar and groaned.

"Did you know that people in AA aren't allowed to date for a year?" I asked, picking my head up.

"Yeah," she said casually while forking seitan chorizo into her mouth. "There's a whole episode of *Sex and the City* about it."

I groaned again. I didn't want to tell Winnie how it was going. I didn't want to admit to misreading a cue and leaning in for a non-kiss. I didn't want to say Sarita O'Brien's name aloud. I deflected and asked Winnie what she was up to for the rest of the day.

She regretted telling me the truth, as she pulled up the digital invitation with a sheepish look on her face: CHARLES-TON KING IS TURNING THE BIG THREE-OH!

I could argue we knew Charlie because he was engaged to Poppy Sadler, a fixture in our NYU friend group who was now something of a local celebrity. She owned Poppy's Sundries— a sustainably sourced shop on the Lower East Side—and every brand looking to tout environmentally sound practices courted her as an influencer partner. Earlier in the year, Winnie and I ran into her at some organic skincare launch, and afterward the three of us went downtown and stayed out all night in our dressy attire, barhopping and drinking gin and tonics and singing pop songs.

"Fame doesn't seem to have really gone to Poppy's head, right?" I asked Winnie as we crawled into her apartment the night we re-created our college life vibes. Poppy didn't seem too different as a public figure. Just super committed to not making any garbage. Her dress was vintage, and when we stopped for a dollar slice, she asked for no plate and took a cloth napkin out of her purse to dab her mouth with.

"Yeah, but she got her corgi from a breeder," Winnie countered. "Doesn't that seem, I don't know, morally misaligned?"

Regardless of her opinion on Poppy's ethical practices, Winnie kept in touch with her and had even been seeing her a bunch since I'd left town. When I'd gently tease her about it, she would act like I left her no choice but to replace me with a mega influencer who we just so happened to once see vomit a perfectly intact maraschino cherry in the common room of our freshman dorm. "I'm not even bringing that up to shame her," I insisted, laughing myself into a bind when Winnie responded with a disapproving look. "I was sincerely impressed by that! I still am!"

But here was the thing: we didn't just know Charleston King through osmosis. Before he was Poppy Sadler's fiancé, or even her boyfriend, he was one of Ben's closest friends from high school. I knew all about Charlie. Diplomat parents with fuck-you money. He grew up in a penthouse on the Upper West Side with Picassos on the wall. "It's small, but it's definitely a Picasso," I remember murmuring to Ben at a party once out the side of my mouth before taking a big slurp of single malt whiskey. "Caroline," he said back through gritted, smiling teeth, "don't be gauche." Charlie had graduated from

Yale and moved back to the city a few years ago. His return made Ben a benefactor of runoff luxury: suites at playoff games, Cohibas on the rooftop, access to a glass house in East Hampton, and, just once, a helicopter ride over there.

"The Odeon," I said, pursing my lips and scanning the details on the screen of Winnie's phone. "Digital invite. Not premium, but hey, no waste. Good for Poppy."

"Caroline, come on," she said, reaching to get her phone back.

"I just want to know why you felt the need to shield me from this!" I said louder than I intended, trying to laugh and indicate I was being a good sport—exactly the sort of thing a bad sport would do.

"You're not really drinking or partying right now," Winnie tried. "I wanted to be sensitive to that?"

I let out one incredulous, breathy laugh. "You know, I might've actually believed that if we weren't eating lunch right now in a literal bar that you picked out." I hated being made to feel like I had to be handled with kid gloves. I wanted to still be the sort of person my friends felt like they could take anywhere. Not the sort of friend who might behave erratically or get triggered by certain places or substances or the appearance of ex-boyfriends.

"Is this about Ben?" I asked her.

She closed her eyes and threw her head back in despondent

exasperation—a gesture that was shorthand for *I'm not answering this question right now* but also an answer in the affirmative.

"You got this email weeks ago and probably RSVP'd immediately. What do you know that I don't?"

"Don't make assumptions," she said, picking her head up but not looking at me.

"Don't quote *The Four Agreements* to me," I shot back. "That's the fifth agreement, actually. Haven't you heard that one? *Stop fucking quoting this book.*"

"I didn't want to speculate before I saw it for myself," she conceded. "My plan was to go tonight, see if Ben shows, and report back to you in painstaking detail. Swear to Joni Mitchell." She held up her hand like she was taking an oath.

Winnie went on to explain that she heard a rumor that Ben was going to stick around the city longer. She'd also heard, more devastatingly, that he'd been spotted out with a friend of his younger sister's. But his sister wouldn't do me like that, would she? I needed to believe she was as devastated as I was that I'd been given the boot. Ben was all but confirmed to be there tonight.

When Winnie stepped away to use the bathroom, I called out to the bartender. "Can you refill this glass I'm drinking out of, but with a gin and tonic instead? A double?" I slugged it as soon as it was set down in front of me.

I thought about how I was supposed to be settled and

comfortable in Los Angeles by now. How I'd never have gone home had it not been for Ben thwarting my plans and scuttling my future. How all my problems could have been avoided. I'd have been three thousand miles away when Claudia called to tell me that my father had fallen down, and then what? No homecoming. No DUI. No playing softball in a league of brutes or running into Kelly Quinn or wondering who Crispin Davis had a crush on and why it wasn't me. When Winnie returned, I was scowling and flushed and crunching ice from my empty glass between my molars.

"It's getting late for you, no?" Winnie said. "Which train are you trying to catch?"

I ignored her. The pull of knowing the right thing to do but the compulsion to do the wrong thing anyway had, I feared, always been particularly strong in me. My whole life. Buying into the Columbia Record Club as a kid. Trying at-home wax strips as a teenager. In adulthood, I'd had this same feeling of *what the fuck did I just get myself into* every time I showed up uninvited to one of Mitch McConnell's improv shows or whenever the tip of Jackie Meyerson's tongue made contact with my clit. I knew in every instance where I was going was no good, but I had a hard time stopping myself from doing it anyway. Sitting there in silence, I powered down my phone—holding the button so long it felt as though I was strangling it—and let it sink to the bottom of my purse.

I watched as the clock behind the bar eclipsed the

departure time for the last possible train I could catch and still make the game. Winnie offered to close the tab, but I refused and ordered another cocktail, this time out in the open. We were going to be at Fern Bar until we left for the Odeon together and Winnie knew it.

"Don't you have a game tonight? What about that thing at the Pony with Crispin?" Winnie finally asked. She was getting explicit, which led to my telling an explicit lie.

"Game got called," I said without looking at her, fishing around for my credit card. "Ground is still soggy from that storm. And Crispin's thing at the Pony doesn't start 'til late, I have time to kill." Maybe Winnie had enough drinks in her or maybe she knew better than to argue with someone wading into an active spiral. She just nodded in concession, ignoring the fact that it had been sunny all week and a soggy field was unlikely.

I gathered my things and examined my reflection in the antique mirror next to our station at the bar. I was grateful to be, at least, dressed up enough to go on an interview. My dress was fitted and black and exposed just enough to keep things interesting. Leather-heeled mules could be better, but worked. Hair was a little flat, but fine. Lipstick was a matte shade of brick red. *Dynamite.*

Winnie was quiet. That was how I knew I really might be in for it. She wasn't looking forward to showing up to the party with me. It was the first time in a long time I watched her walk through the streets with a slight curve to her posture, her arms folded in front of her like she had a chill. She was dressed in what she called her Jody Watley outfit: skintight and shoulder-less mauve velvet dress that wrapped around her biceps, black sheer tights, shit-kicker boots, topped with a ridiculous mini top hat and hoop earrings she could fit her arm through. It was the sort of outfit one wore to a party one was attending alone. A conversation piece. An icebreaker. Now that she was bringing an interloper, she wished she'd dressed in a way that made it easy for her to disappear.

I'd been to birthday dinners at the Odeon before, but this was different. The interior was completely rearranged: not to accommodate a dinner, but for a true party, where everyone could cluster and gather or move freely and slink off to find a quiet corner if they needed one. It should have felt odd, walk-ing into a restaurant we had frequented so much over the years to find all the seating tucked away, the cacophony of conver-sation and inorganic laughter greater than on even the busiest night. But it wasn't off-putting. There was a magical quality to it. Beneath the suspended globe lights, against the wood-paneled walls, everyone looked like the epitome of youth and glamour. Clutching the stems of their martini glasses. Pinch-ing each other's elbows in greeting or dismissal. The scene looked like exactly what I'd been missing.

Winnie handed me a lowball glass with a wedge of lime floating in it and surprised me when she commanded, "Drink that as fast as you can." I cocked an eyebrow and knocked it back. It was water. I hated when she mothered me like this.

Poppy released herself from a group of older folks—no doubt members of the King family, the ones footing the bill for the evening's festivities—and made her way over to us. When she approached Winnie, she bent her elbows and fanned her hands out beside her face to express that performative brand of surprise—*you're here!*—that hosts feign at parties. When she turned to me, it was a closed-mouth smile with eyebrows arched up to her hairline, hands jutted out with palms toward the sky in unmistakable confusion. *YOU'RE here?* But she didn't pluck at the thread. Poppy was adept at a lot of things I wasn't: P&L projections, shopping secondhand, and good old-fashioned manners.

"Ladies, ladies, ladies." She clicked her tongue, leading us through the crowd. "Let's get you a proper drink and a bite." She turned to us, and upon closer examination of my eyes, she said, "Or maybe the other way around. You're just going to die when you see the menu, Lynn curated it herself."

I scanned the crowd for the owner who famously won the restaurant in her divorce settlement. For a split second, I forgot that I was not there to schmooze, but rather to catch a glimpse of the man who broke my heart and dismantled my future. At least, I forgot about that until I spotted him in the crowd: tall enough that his head poked out among the gaggle of five-foot-nine Jewish men, and he could see me with ease. We made expressionless eye contact. I had forgotten that Ben was tall, depending on the context.

By rote, my face still slack, I lifted my pointer finger and bent it in his direction, like I was itching the air. A small, dumb gesture of ours. Waving to each other with a finger. Reaching for each other like God to Adam, or E.T. to Elliott. Shorthand for whenever one of us needed attention. Winnie caught me doing this and grabbed my finger in her fist like she was going to break it off. She closed her eyes and exhaled, long and audible, in quiet exasperation. Poppy handed me a small plate of tiny purple carrots and a baby ramekin of dip.

"I really am so thrilled to see you, Caroline," she said, eyebrows crimped a bit, trying to cover her own tracks. She was embarrassed she hadn't invited me, but she shouldn't have been. Not inviting me was the right thing to do. She should have been pissed I had the audacity to show up anyway. I was a land mine in a Spode shop. She knew better. Why didn't I?

When I didn't answer immediately, she tried a different approach. "Winnie tells me you're living back at home right now? How is the commute treating you?"

"Oh, I don't commute," I said, not even attempting to hide the path of my eyes behind her, scanning the crowd where Ben had been standing. "I quit my job to move to Los Angeles and then was abruptly informed that I wouldn't be going to Los

Angeles. So, I'm not with my agency anymore. But it's okay. I'm the ringer on a small-town men's softball team."

"Excuse us," Winnie said, taking me by the elbow to a private enclave where she could have a word with me, the way a parent would escort a child throwing a tantrum out of a shopping mall.

But before she could scold me, I heard my name called out a few yards away, the tone laced with pleasant surprise. I turned and saw Lacey Drew, barely five feet tall, natural blond hair pulled into a high ponytail that swung as she trotted toward me. Ben trailed her, looking like Lurch behind her boxy little frame.

Lacey Drew was a close friend of Ben's family. Her father was a prominent sports doctor, who was Ben's dad's roommate at Columbia. Lacey was a gymnast who was supposed to go to the Olympics last cycle but got sidelined when an old injury acted up. I'd spent a considerable amount of time with her—the Drews came on vacation with us twice, once to Aspen and once to Oahu—but stopped short of feeling any affection for her. She never had much to say, and we had little in common. To me, she was a provincial shiksa—nine years our junior and better suited to follow Ben's younger sister around, anyway.

Lacey greeted me with pursed lips and a quick, hard knock of her jaw against mine—a clumsy attempt at sophistication.

Ben greeted Winnie before me, bending down to plant a quick kiss on her cheek as he said, "Hey, Win," in the same soft, sympathetic tone one would use when saying hello at a funeral. When he got to me, I barely whispered *hi*. It occurred to me I was nursing a bone-dry gin martini and I wasn't entirely sure how it got into my hands.

As if he had managed to hit a panic button like a subtle bank teller, Ben was suddenly flanked by his crew of private school boys, forming a half-moon around him. Each of them was toasted and, therefore, happy to see me. "Caro!" They waved their paws through the air and pulled me in for a hug. I supposed any familiar face was a treat when that much Moët had been consumed. Their last real memory of me, the fiasco back at Joshua Tree, was apparently vomit under the bridge.

After a solid seven minutes of small talk, Winnie and I extracted ourselves, saying we needed another drink. Instead, we headed for the doors, desperate for fresh air and a long cigarette.

"Well, that's a relief," I said, coughing on my first pull. I'd been smoking scented vapor for so long I'd forgotten how harsh and perfect a real cigarette was. In an instant, I tasted like a cowboy.

Winnie looked at me like I was insane. "What do you mean, *that's a relief*? What part of that was a relief to you, exactly?"

"I mean, I *know* he's not fucking Lacey Drew. It's a relief that he didn't even bring a date to this thing. He's just here hanging out with a family friend. It's embarrassing. Like inviting your cousin to prom or something."

"Just because she's a family friend means they're not fucking?"

"Win, she's practically a child," I retorted. "We've been on vacation with her. Attached at the hip to her parents. She got *her hair braided* in Hawaii! And besides, she's not his type. Physically. He's very particular."

There was more I wouldn't say. I asked Ben on that Hawaii trip, just once, what he thought of Lacey Drew's body after she sauntered her flat ass past our poolside lounge chairs in her high-cut little rust-colored bikini one too many times for my liking. She would have been eighteen or nineteen then.

"Not for me," he said simply, confidently. We were in bed, the cool white sheets and too many pillows surrounding us like a nest. He traced a finger from my bottom lip, down my throat, past the expanse of rib cage where my splayed breasts had pulled the skin taut. "I only want what you have," he said when he got to my belly button. "A body like a statue of Aphrodite."

Winnie was silent, one arm folded over her chest, propping up the elbow that was keeping her cigarette close to her lips. She smoked it to the filter, lit another, and stomped the first one out before she spoke again.

"I think you're wrong, Caroline. I think they're together."

The cigarette activated the soup of liquor sloshing around inside me. Before I could argue with her, a torrent of nausea sent me back inside, beelining for the restroom. I would *not* let myself get sick in front of that group of people again. I believed I could get it to pass—I just needed to sit and calm myself away from all that chaotic energy.

I picked a clean-looking stall in the far corner and vowed to camp out there as long as it took for me to feel better. I dug around in my purse to find my phone and turn it back on, thinking I might as well check my email or play a word game while I rode out the storm. But it wouldn't turn on. I tossed it back into my bag. Out to sea. No communication.

Other women came and went, clicking and drunkenly chatting, occasionally stopping for a quick key bump. It was my mission to remain silent and still. One jerky motion and it was Joshua Tree the sequel.

When two loud girls burst in, it made me jump. I saw an unfortunate pair of red-heeled strappy sandals beneath the door of my stall. *Lacey.*

"I'm just dying to get back out there," her companion said. "You know, I'm from there originally."

"Oh no way!" Lacey chirped, drunk and insincere. "I had no idea."

"Yeah, my whole family is from Pasadena, actually. They were all out here for a long time—I went to Dalton—but now they're back there again. What I wouldn't give to have Will consider moving there. I'm so over winters in New York; it bums me out every fucking year."

"Well, you'll just have to come visit us. Our apartment is amazing, and we have plenty of space. Two big bedrooms."

I looked out the bottom of the stall to double-check. Tall red sandals. Definitely Lacey. *Our apartment. Come visit us.*

"It has this, like, Spanish-style design. The apartments all belonged to this famous director back in the day. I forget his name. They're landmarks or something."

It was Cecil B. DeMille—*she doesn't even know Cecil B. DeMille?*—and that was *my* apartment. The one I picked out and went to painstaking lengths to obtain. I could feel my heart freeze then start to samba as the realizations washed over me, the severity deepening with each passing word. Lacey and Ben *were* together. They were moving to Los Angeles together. They were moving into the apartment—into the future—that I had picked out.

"I'll bet it'll be tough to leave where you're at now, though," the Pasadena-born compatriot said. I heard a gentle riffling; someone digging around for lipstick or drugs. Then the soft jangle of keys. Drugs.

"I mean, how could I not miss the Upper West Side?" Lacey laughed between sniffs. "And that apartment, with those built-ins and that walk-in closet? Don't get me wrong, I could stay forever. But Ben's already lived there for so long. I owe it to him to let him get a fresh start."

"You both deserve it," the friend said, followed by a snort.

After three years of tap-dancing around us moving in together, all that pushing and prolonging and an eventual breakup, Ben asked a girl he couldn't have been dating for more than a few months to move in with him. This blond shiksa gymnast who was barely of legal drinking age was living in the jewel box apartment he inherited from his grandparents. When I thought of her red suede hooves clonking against the hardwood floor in the foyer, it made my stomach turn again.

I tamped down the nausea. I knew the name of the game that night in that bathroom was to remain invisible, but I'd gotten more insight than I had come in search of. It became apparent in light of this new information that, with the exception of Winnie, I would never see these people again. That I should have heeded my best friend's apprehension and never shown up. I rose from my crouched position, dusted myself off, and burst out of the stall to the surprise of the Dalton alum and the horror of Lacey Drew. She opened her mouth to speak, but I pushed my way out of bathroom doors, back into the undulating masses, and over to the front, where I slipped out unnoticed.

Without a phone to summon a car on demand, I hailed a taxicab the old-fashioned way and slid in across the stiff, familiar seat. "Penn Station, please." I didn't know what time it was or how long I had to make it to Asbury Park in time to see

Crispin. I only knew that it had gotten dark while I'd been at the Odeon.

The landmarks of my recent past went by in a smear out the window. The restaurant where Winnie and I would split cacio e pepe and mascarpone gelato and orange wine. The movie theater where I would get high off a vape pen and take in old black-and-white films. The corner past the park where Ben and I kissed for the first time. I didn't even feel it anymore. I loved it, and then I longed for it, and seeing it all just felt like pressing down on a fading bruise. I made it all the way to Twenty-Ninth Street before vomiting into my own lap.

"Did you just throw up in my cab?" the driver asked me in a thick accent.

"No," I said like I resented being asked the question, even though I was obviously lying. The ghost of Andy Gibb was on the radio, singing about how love was higher than a mountain and thicker than water.

"Miss," he called again, "if you dirty my cab, you have to pay. I'm warning you now."

"Sir?" I yelled back, leaning into the partition, "could you please stop talking over Andy Gibb? I really love this song and I'd like to hear it. The man is dead, have some respect."

He glared at me in the rearview mirror. Then he shrugged and, to my surprise, turned up the volume.

In my stupor and without my phone, I had an outline of a plan. Get to Penn Station, buy a train ticket to Asbury Park, buy a giant bottled water, and attempt to sober up on the ride out, then walk to the Stone Pony upon disembarking. I felt badly about showing up late and possibly drunk, but I had to push past my guilt and focus on just getting there. I worried about Leo and Claudia finding out I'd been drinking and the impending fallout from missing the game, but I wouldn't let my mind linger on those anxieties at that moment.

As we got closer to the pit of midtown, I willed myself to release the shame I felt over every decision I'd made since two o'clock that afternoon. In the home stretch, my mouth started to water again. I tried to swallow, and my throat locked.

We were a block from the station when I relented with a gag I couldn't stifle anymore. It was just a little one, but it was audible. The driver threw the cab into park, got out of the car, and ripped open my door to witness perhaps one of the more pathetic tableaus he had seen in his entire medallion career. I saw how I must have looked in his eyes for a moment: curled into myself, dress and hair dripping in partially digested hors d'oeuvres, snot and tears and vomit mingling on me. A real trifecta.

"Fine!" I cried, pulling all the cash I had out of my wallet and handing it over as I heaved myself out of the back seat. "I threw up in your cab! But it barely touched your cab! It was mostly on me!"

I ran toward the open mouth of Penn Station and trotted down the steps into the catacomb of the New Jersey Transit.

• • •

WHEN I ARRIVED in Asbury Park, it was quiet enough that I could hear actual crickets. Signs the end of summer was imminent: a calm street at the Jersey Shore and a chorus of crickets chirping their back-to-school song. Typically, my heart raced at the prospect of meandering around in the dark alone, but that night was different. I was an active repellent. Nobody tried to mess with a crying girl caked in her own vomit.

Conscious of how late it was—but not yet sure if I was too late to make it to the Stone Pony—I took off running down Cookman Avenue toward the water. The main drag was cozy and cool at that hour of the night. The flowers in the public garden were bathed in glistening, restorative moonlight. The marquee of the movie theater had gone dark. The cats who lived in the cat café were curled into a single sleeping pile, a soft breathing mass.

Farther down the block, where there was a row of bars, I caught the sounds of a dissipating crowd. I saw some random stragglers make their way toward me. A couple. He was drunk and doing a funny little shuffle and she was amused, laughing like she'd never seen him like that before. A gaggle of girls dressed to look younger than they really were, lips augmented past their natural borders with filler. They were all wearing yellow wristbands and dresses that were cut so short you could see the crescents of their ass cheeks.

As I reached the next block, I encountered another group on the same side of the well-lit street as me. I felt deep shame at the prospect of even a bunch of drunk strangers seeing me in this state: running like I was desperate, sweat and alcohol rising off my skin like heat on a long stretch of road. The four of them slowed down, then stopped in front of me, blocking my path. It was two dudes dressed in head-to-toe black, thick biceps straining the cuffs of their sleeves, flanking Sarita O'Brien, whose hair was done in two long black braids that hung down to her rib cage. She was in a stretchy cropped tube top and another microscopic pair of shorts. Crispin Davis stood two feet in front of her, a hard gig case in his hand, his knuckles bone white around where he grabbed the handle.

Too late. I had missed it.

This was the moment that cemented what I'd suspected all along: I was unworthy of him, in no uncertain terms. I looked at someone who had worked on himself to such a degree that he had gone from near-dead to living in a state of honesty and gratitude within a year. He had a good life and an undeniable talent. He had friends who didn't forsake their promises and turn off their phones just to watch their own lives circle the drain.

"Crispin," I said, not knowing what would follow, but the sentiment oxidized and died as soon as it hit the air. I was everything he needed to get away from. I was a walking MAPS violation: my blood more gin than anything else, hair filthy and matted, makeup eroded. How could I ever be a match for someone who was striving for authenticity? I was all veneer.

We were standing in front of his building. He stepped toward the doorway and punched his code into the number pad. He had no intention of confronting me; he just wanted me to know that he saw me. Sarita gave me a long look up and down before trotting up the stairs after him, calling *Crissy*, but I didn't see him turn to face her before they rounded the corner up the second flight of stairs and disappeared from view. Tears sat hot on the corners of my eyes, overflowing like a hastily served cup of tea, spilling down my cheeks. I bolted for the boardwalk so I could walk to my mother's house in Ocean Grove and crash there for the night. I fished her spare key out of a flowerpot and let myself up.

Once I was on her pullout couch, I plugged my phone into the wall next to my head. It perked up, glowing too bright in the dark. *Fuck you*, I hissed. I could see the silhouette of a bitten apple behind my eyelids when I blinked.

After a moment, the cascade of every communication I'd missed since that afternoon appeared. A flurry of unread text messages: concerned ones from Robbie Walker, threatening ones from Ryan Buckley. One from my mother: **Hi snoopy, the team is trying to get in touch with you—how late will you be to this game?** Voicemails from Leo and Claudia I couldn't bring myself to listen to just yet.

Texts from Winnie she must have sent while I was hiding in the bathroom, then when she realized I'd left:

> Collective noun for a group of girls from
> Spence: A Gwyneth.

> Collective noun for a group of boys from
> Collegiate: A depression.

> Alright, you must be really sick to ignore
> my brilliant jokes. Can I bring you water
> or something?

> Ok, just let me know you didn't hit your
> head or some shit. I know you think it
> would be New York as fuck to die here,
> but please don't ruin the Odeon for me.

> Girl, wherever you are, you need to call
> me when that phone battery's back. I'm
> not playing around with you. I don't
> appreciate being scared like this.

And then, the spate of texts from Crispin:

> Hey, are you close?

I have to put my phone away now, but I left your name at the door! Just let them know at will call that you're with me.

Where were you?

Where was I? I didn't have an answer for that. It had only just happened and I already could not fathom what force pulled me so dutifully toward that birthday party, and for what? To prove to Winnie that I could handle my liquor? That I could still attend social functions? To see Ben? To confirm what, deep down, I already knew? He had moved on, quickly and with someone easygoing enough to be palatable, because I wasn't worth the trouble.

I gulped down cool tap water from the Mayor McCheese souvenir glass I pulled from my mother's cabinet. I settled back into my spot on the couch and tried to piece together the evening through social media. Crispin had zero presence, but Sarita O'Brien was an influencer by Monmouth County standards. Hundreds of other peoples' photos and videos from that night had been uploaded under the Stone Pony's geotag.

I watched the animated tiles dance across my phone, telling the story I should never have missed. Serene Jackson welcomed Crispin to the stage to sub for her bass player. They opened with a cover, a Pretenders song I love, Serene doing a perfect spin on Chrissie Hynde warning she might come and go like fashion. Clips from her classic *Shark River Blues* songs, peppered with loud whoops from the crowd. Riffs off the latest album with voices from the audience rising to meet the lyrics.

That was enough to fill me with regret on its own, but it wasn't the end of the show. A stranger's video captured a grainy upshot scene: Serene at the edge of the stage, dripping with sweat after a long set, laughing and taking in the energy of the audience. "You guys wanna hear a little something from my parents?" she growled to the crowd. Then, in the living epitome of a Jersey June romance, Bruce Springsteen and Patti Scialfa stepped up and launched right into "Tunnel of Love" with the Hot Rollers on backup. A live chemistry experiment onstage in the church they had consecrated.

I saw Crispin's face, euphoric, bobbing in and out of the frame as his bass made up the backbone of the song. The crowd was so loud it made the music near impossible to hear. Bruce was known to show up at the Pony every once in a while, but you had to be in the know to catch him. Crispin had tried to bring me into the fold, and I'd ghosted. I watched a couple of more clips where he was featured beaming in the background. Sarita O'Brien posted a video of Serene returning to the mic to join Bruce on "Jersey Girl" to close out the night, Crispin at the front of the tableau, a heart-eyed emoji in her captions. For all I knew, she fancied herself the Patti to his Bruce and he felt it right back.

Only when I'd exhausted the tag, watching the lo-fi video of every last stranger who bore witness to what I'd missed, did I decide to call it a night. I deleted every fitful text draft I typed out to Crispin in the dark, *sorry* being too weak a word wherever I tried to deploy it.

18

THE FIRST THING my father said to me when I arrived home after my shameful escapade was: "Caroline, we're about a cunt hair away from not making the playoffs." The second thing he said was: "We need to talk." He instructed me to go sit in his office and wait for him. A holdover disciplinary tactic from my youth meant, I suspected, to build anticipation and dread.

When I hadn't showed up to Wednesday's game, the Bialys had been forced to forfeit. One teammate was on vacation, another was sidelined with a sprained wrist, and Billy the Kid was on suspension for his last outburst. But Leo had anticipated these absences and factored them into the lineup. It was my unanticipated no-show that put the team close to elimination. A win the coming Sunday would secure our spot in the playoffs, but a loss would send us over the edge. I braced to be reprimanded for abandoning everyone, as though the unanswered texts I finally sent to Crispin in the light of a new day weren't a painful enough reminder of my mistake.

I went to my father's office and sat in his massive leather desk chair, knowing I'd be shooed from it the moment his shadow darkened the doorway. He had barely spent any time in here since leaving his post as in-house counsel for a big financial institution near Wall Street. He had retired officially the year before—Claudia threw him a big party in Jersey City at a restaurant on the water, and a live band played the Beatles' "When I'm Sixty-Four." His desk wasn't cluttered with its usual effects, just some photographs of Harper and me as kids and straggler artifacts from the brief era he'd had between retirement and his fall down the stairs. Paint swatches. Israeli travel brochures. Tucked beneath a picture frame was a handwritten list of things he wanted to accomplish in his first year of retirement.

Build a sports court in the backyard. Start writing my memoirs. Take a family trip to Aruba. Go to 18 Yankees games. Take a wine tasting class. Win the World Series.

"Out of my chair." I heard Leo before I saw him, stashing his list back behind the photo in a flash of mild panic. Much to his chagrin, he had begun using a walker to get around the house, but he still refused to use it in public. "Unnecessary fodder for my enemies," he called it last time I'd rolled my eyes about it.

"I have some disappointing news," he said finally, after his long shuffle and slow process of sitting down was complete.

My thoughts, still soggy from the night prior, buzzed with grim possibility. *The Bialys are not only out of the playoffs, we've been ousted from the league. Crispin Davis was featured in the paper for his performance last night and quoted saying, "Thank God that bitch Caroline Kline didn't show up and ruin everything!" Claudia booked a family cruise and was expecting us to actually go.*

"You're going to have to finish out the rest of the season for me," my father continued, solemn as a brick, as if that wasn't very obviously already the plan.

"Yeah, Dad," I replied, picking at the corner of a Post-it Note pad. "I know."

"No, you don't know," he said, reaching out to yank the pad away from my fidgeting fingers. "That 'conclusive report' I've been waiting on from the doctor? Well, he called yesterday with the results." He paused, hesitant to deliver the actual bad news. "It appears the diagnosis they're going with is primary-progressive MS."

Anxious heat settled between my shoulders. *Multiple sclerosis.* A question answered and a sentence served in one go. Leo's days of attempting to feign normalcy, despite appearances, was over.

"Pop, I—" I heard myself start to squeak, tears stinging the corners of my eyes.

He cut me off with a halting grunt and held up his hand, palm flat facing me. Leo's universal sign for *no waterworks*. "I'm looking into a second opinion. But that's not my point. My point is, I misled you. Told you this would be a temporary solve for a couple of months. But my chances of getting back out there are dwindling." He looked over to the framed Mickey Mantle portrait he'd hung on the wall for emphasis, then looked back at me. "I mean my chances this year, to be clear."

I nodded. I knew what he meant, but I also knew there was a good chance this year's circumstances would affect all his years left to come. He knew it, too, but wouldn't dare say it.

"So, no more fucking around, Caroline. You hear me? No more missed games or general sloppiness this close to the World Series."

My wary laughter dislodged a tear; I couldn't help it. I caught it with the tip of my tongue as it dripped down my face. "Only you could get a diagnosis like this and still be preoccupied with the World Series."

"Caroline," he said, reaching his hand over the desk and placing it on top of mine. "I still believe we can win it all." He gave me a steady, reassuring look. I wanted what he had, in that moment. His recalcitrant refusal to give up hope.

●　●　●

HARPER SHOWED UP on our front door on Friday morning, fresh off the red-eye. "Where's Sil and the kids? Didn't want to come out for this festive family reunion?" I jabbed as she stepped into the foyer.

"I murdered them and I'm on the lam," she deadpanned, lowering her sunglasses. She hugged me, retreated to the living room, and planted herself next to our father on the couch before passing out cold for six hours.

It felt unjust that time hadn't stopped for my father's diagnosis. I wanted more time to sit in the reality of it, to let the gravity of it wash over me. But a softball game to end the week was as assured and undeniable as the sunrise. "No sulking," Leo snapped when I took three minutes longer than usual to arrive downstairs for departure. "Remember: the best cure for a big scrape is rubbing a little baseball-diamond dirt in the wound." That Sunday brought us full circle: a game against the Door Crusaders, the first team I had faced in the league.

"Tony Scolari is the worst of the worst," I told Harper on the car ride over to the Twin Pines complex, while we were stuffed in the back seat of Claudia and Leo's car like a pair of overgrown children. "Nastier than all the Moby Dicks combined."

"First of all, don't talk to me like I don't know who Tony Scolari is," Harper retorted. "*I'm* the one who told *you* to watch out for that walking pile of dick cheese. Need I remind you that vampire pulled out his uncircumcised schlong in front of my friends and me all those years ago, before he realized we were only seventeen?"

Who could forget that? A big barbecue at the McMansion

of the league's then commissioner, whose poor daughter—Harper's best friend, a beauty and a prude—had ended up face-to-face with that puckered little anteater muzzle. Scolari was toasted and somehow thought exposing himself on the diving board was a worthy joke. The girls in the pool screamed. Harper's friend had never seen such a thing in her life. It traumatized her.

"Second of all, the Moby Dicks aren't actually dicks, they're just *good*," Harper pointed out. "Annoyingly good. You're making enemies with Glen Brook's sweethearts. No one's gonna see it your way. Except for me, of course."

"Why can't you just be here all the time?" I said, laying my head down onto her shoulder like when we used to trade naps on long car rides as kids. She tucked her chin on top of my temple.

Our mother was waiting on the bleachers when we arrived, pawing at the air as soon as Harper stepped into view. "My baby," she said, clasping my sister around the neck. "I can't believe you flew all the way out here for my *Dolls and Guys* premiere." Harper and I exchanged incredulous smiles.

"Look who decided to show up today," Ryan Buckley said when he spotted me. He went to clip his bag up onto the fence but missed because he was too focused on trying to roast me. Joke was on him, though: I'd reached a new level of feeling dead inside. There was nothing left to roast.

"Welcome back, *principessa*," Pete Peretti spat, snapping

on his batting glove. "Pray tell, what was so fuckin' important that you just *had* to leave us high and dry the other night?"

Billy the Kid, loath to miss a chance to pile on, burst in with a sharp, cruel laugh: "Let me guess: Got caught up at that margarita joint and stranded without a ride?" The rest of the bench took turns snickering at the comment or pretending they didn't hear it.

"I don't see anyone getting up your ass for missing the game," I snapped back, pink faced and roiling. "But you can't go four pitches without a suspension, lunatic!"

Billy threw down his glove, and Ryan dove in front of him, buffering the two of us. "Hey!" Ryan screamed at me. "He's fucking working on it!" He turned back to Billy, and the two of them mirrored each other's deep breaths.

"You good?" Robbie Walker appeared behind me, affixing a gentle palm to my shoulder. He was the only one whose worry outweighed resentment.

I flashed a quick, close-lipped smile at him. "I'm fine, Robbie, really. Just a bad case of food poisoning. I'm sorry I didn't get back to you sooner. My phone died; I was completely out of it."

"Food poisoning?" Scolari said, disgusted, passing by our dugout. A perfect intersection of two things he was known for: arriving late to the game and sticking his nose in other people's business. "This is why my theory holds up: women should only ever be allowed to eat a fistful of food a day," he continued, holding his hand up in a ball over his head as he joined his team.

Robbie looked incensed and my father went wild-eyed, but before either of them could say anything, Harper yelled over from the bleachers: "Hey, Anthony! I know exactly where you can put that." Scolari looked up at his fist, then back at her, then me, and murmured: "Oh great, there's two of them now."

Before the first pitch, Leo requested the Bialys suspend their collective disdain for me and refocus on what was really important: our mutual hatred of Tony Scolari and the desire to vanquish his team from the playoffs. We started strong: I batted cleanup and drove in two RBIs in the first inning alone. Everyone was a hitter, rounding the bases like that Bugs Bunny cartoon. Meanwhile, the Door Crusaders let the August heat get to them, struggling to get even one man on base at the top of each inning.

By the bottom of the fifth, we were poised to invoke the mercy rule on them. I was already fantasizing about the game ending early: driving down the shore with Harper, parking by the beach and walking through Ocean Grove, admiring the pastel-hued gingerbread houses as we meandered up and down each long street. With two outs, I knocked what could have been a pop out into left center, but the shortstop dropped it.

I got loud on first base, cheering on Timmy the Tortoise as

he stepped up to the plate, yelling for him to bring me home. "God, shut the fuck up already," Scolari muttered, loud enough for only me to hear. He stood guard as first baseman, getting increasingly agitated as the innings peeled by. He had always been a bona fide schmuck, but this season really brought it out in him. He was frustrated being stuck on a bum team. I bet he wished more than anything he was a Bialy. I could imagine how it must have felt for him to see me—*some bitch*—running away with the victory.

I ignored his request and whooped even louder, clapping and raising hell. Harper caught my drift and stomped her feet onto the bottom rung of bleachers, drumming up even more fury-inducing support. Timmy racked up a full count, then took a step outside the batter's box to compose himself, adjust his gloves, and buy himself a quick moment of respite.

We relaxed in our posts for a split second, and Scolari turned his back to the umpire to hiss at me: "I wonder what's going to take longer, him dragging his old ass to first or you hauling your fat ass over to second."

"You'd better stop thinking of my fat ass in motion," I said without making eye contact. "I have it on good word you don't wear a cup."

Timmy threw all his weight into his last swing, hitting a low lob right to Scolari for the third out. Scolari stepped on the bag and rolled the ball to the mound. As I trotted back to the other Bialys, he came up behind me, grabbed his crotch, and hissed: "One day I'm gonna make you choke on this dick, you stupid bitch."

Without a beat, I stopped and dug the heel of my cleat into the dirt, aligning it at a harsh, perfect angle to send him tripping over it and into the dirt. The distance he got was cartoonish, and he landed on his face so quickly, so sincerely, his reflexes didn't have enough time to send his arms out in front of him. His front teeth were left to break the fall against the hard ground.

Both teams and both sides of the bleachers buzzed with noise and horror. Above the din, I heard Harper's voice, soft and sober: "Oh shit." When Tony picked his head up, blood spilled from his mouth. His two front teeth were chipped to such a degree there was barely anything left of them. The middle part where they met was gone, chiseled in a sort of inverse fang situation. A tiny black pyramid shape occupied where a shit-eating grin once lived. It was, frankly, terrifying and hilarious.

"*I'll kill you, you bitch!*" he growled through blood-drenched lips, turning over and propping himself up on his elbow. Ryan Buckley and Billy the Kid were already flanking me, making sure Scolari didn't make good on his word. Still down on the ground, he made a weak attempt to grab for my ankles while the umpire ambled over, but Billy dug a quick cleat into his wrist to deter him. Ryan was silent but livid—he knew there would be a reckoning in the coming days, perhaps one like never before. Billy was silent but giddy, if not jealous, that he didn't get the opportunity to knock the teeth from the mouth of his greatest rival himself.

The umpire, Leo, and Gary Feingold—who had a knack for showing up just in time for my worst behavior—all joined us on the infield.

"What are we going to do with you, Caroline Kline?" Gary Feingold said softly, shaking his head at the pool of Scolari's blood, scarlet against the tan bed of dirt. Leo kept his eyes trained on the blood, not looking at me.

"What are you going to do with *her*? How about what you're going to do with that animal?" Leo cawed, pointing to Scolari as two lackeys assisted him in walking to the dugout. They'd procured ice wrapped in a washcloth and Advil from a nearby mom.

"Quick question," I asked, a finger planted to my lips. "Does he threaten everyone in the league with sodomy while they're on base, or is that an exclusive offering for ballplayers with tits?"

"Whatever he said"—the umpire raised a meaty hand in objection—"doesn't warrant that sort of violence. This is a family complex, ma'am. This is a league built on a solid foundation of respect."

"You would say that, wouldn't you?" I practically spit,

looking him up and down. "Let me ask you this, blue: What do you do for work when it's not a Sunday? Are you a cop in real life?"

Leo, too exhausted to scold, led me by the arm toward the parking lot as the umpire swept his finger through the air to indicate in a dramatic boom that I had, indeed, been thrown out of the game. The Bialys mercied the Door Crusaders half an inning later, ending the latter team's season. In the parking lot, Gary told Leo and me he had to speak to the rest of the board, but that I should expect a disciplinary hearing sometime that week.

Harper whisked me down to Ocean Grove like I'd dreamed about, but there was no glory in it. We walked down the main thoroughfare—a long stretch of grass surrounded by four-story Victorian homes and a giant cross-bearing auditorium—and ate rum raisin ice cream.

I'd barely talked since the game. The shame of scuttling my chances to shine in the playoffs felt too great. This, on top of the weight of our father's diagnosis and Crispin's palpable absence in the bleachers. I thought I might cry if I opened my mouth to speak.

Harper seemed not to notice as she prattled on about the joy of being back by the Atlantic Ocean, buoyed and energetic without her own kids flanking her.

"Alright, clearly my distraction methods aren't doing much for you," she said finally. "Care to comment on your performance today, Ms. Kline?" She held her ice cream cone out in front of my face like a reporter's microphone.

The thought of disappointing my dad after trying so hard to prove to him—to both of us—that I could pull off this men's league folly made my entire life feel small. "This stupid game, this stupid team," I sputtered to Harper, pushing her ice cream cone away. "It was the only thing I hadn't fucked up yet. The only measly part of my life that wasn't moving backward. A chance to win."

I stopped in my tracks, feeling winded and dizzy. She slung an arm around my shoulder. "Not to mention," I continued, "after a lifetime of Dad fawning over your every move, I felt like he was finally starting to come around on me. And now I'm pissing away my chance at that, too."

"Are you fucking kidding me?" she yelped, retracting her arm. "Every single time he calls me, all he does is drone on and on about what a godsend you are."

I narrowed my eyes at her in doubt, then softened. "Dad said that?"

"He's said the phrase 'best natural hitter in the family' ten too many times and repeatedly marvels at how everything I had to train *so* hard at just comes *so* easily to you," she recounted, rolling her eyes. "Like a duck in water, I swear. Plus, whenever I get on his case about his health, he mutters about how *Caroline never interrogates him like this*."

I considered my father's appraisal of me as we walked a

block in silence. "Here's the silver lining to the whole Tony Scolari situation," Harper interjected. "I'll bet that greasy fuck ball spends a lot of time at a lot of clubs with black lights."

I wasn't following. "Okay, so?"

"Well, you know how when you're at a party with black light, your teeth and your tennis shoes and anything white glows purple?"

"It's been a while since I've gone anywhere like that, but yeah, sure. Like a glow-stick effect. I remember."

"Well, Scolari's going to have to get veneers, and those don't glow like bone does. Any girl Tony tries to hit on at a club, he's gonna smile and it's gonna look like he's missing two front teeth. For the rest of his life. And just think: *you* made that happen!"

I mustered a smile as Harper amused herself with Tony's grim dating future, but when I looked up at the auditorium in the distance, where the outline of the cross met the pristine sky, I wondered if I'd ever feel compelled to repent for all the things that I'd done.

19

I CALLED CRISPIN to see if he'd be willing to meet. I wanted to apologize in person. I tucked myself into different corners and tried him at all hours of the day: in the morning from the Wawa parking lot, in the afternoon on a sanity walk, and in the evening sitting poolside. I left a quiet, pleading voicemail while I dipped my toes into the chilly water and vaped out of my father's eyeline. But he never answered the phone. He eventually responded via text message, twenty-four hours after my last attempt: All good, Caroline.

I had a fantasy of showing up for *Dolls and Guys* on opening night—to show Crispin I was capable of course correction, that I *could* show up—and telling him everything. Really, everything. Rigorous honesty. I'd tell him I wanted to drive east until we hit the beach every night. I would tell him I wore his cologne in ninth grade so I could keep a piece of him close and how the worst, most dramatic breakups in my adult life somehow seemed like nothing next to the night he walked away from me at the Saint Christopher's dance. How I'd loved him half a lifetime ago and that I was certainly in love with him now. How even though my life looked nothing like how I imagined it would, when I was with him, I felt the possibilities of what it could become.

I wanted to sweep in and tell him all of it, standing with confidence on the scuffed linoleum of the cafetorium while an amateur actress cawed about how if she were a bell, she'd be ringing. But I was double-booked for opening night—the league scheduled my disciplinary hearing at the same time.

It was silly of me to assume the board meeting would be held in any sort of official setting. There was no pomp and circumstance; no municipal building or big, faintly bleach-smelling boardroom with portraits of dead Glen Brook assemblymen lining the walls. The meeting was, instead, held in the basement of the home of Gary Feingold. I was corrected each time I referred to it as a meeting. It was a *hearing*. At least, that was what they called the part that pertained to me.

Like many Glen Brook houses I'd grown up hanging around, the Feingolds' home was an eighties art deco style, adorned with laminate furniture, glass accent tables, and clamshell lamps. The basement was a neutral respite: blond wood and nubby, mismatched sofas worn past their prime. I'd been in this basement a few times growing up. Gary's son was my age and would have people over for small parties. I remembered gathering there once while home from college on winter break: too young to hit the bars but curious to see if anyone's semester away from home had aged them into someone I found worth making out with.

We sat in folding chairs typically reserved for crowded Passover seders, rearranged artfully over beige carpet. The men on the board took their seats facing Claudia and me at a makeshift dais, a long plastic table topped with faux wood. They bore stern faces, my father included—knowing he would have to recuse himself from the decision and being "angry as hell" about it, as he'd incanted the entire drive over. It was hard to take him, or anyone, seriously in this atmosphere, though: the low popcorn ceilings, the wine-stained carpet, and the accoutrements from Jeremy Feingold's Wayne Gretzky–themed bar mitzvah strewn across the walls.

My outfit was wasted on that crowd; a dry-clean-only camel number that looked like something Faye Dunaway might've worn in her *Bonnie and Clyde* heyday. I wore my hair blown straight because I'd read in a magazine a dozen years prior that men subconsciously considered wavy hair to be chaotic and unruly in a corporate setting.

Across town, there was a man in a red skirt who answered to "Sister Sarah" and sang on behalf of the Save a Soul Mission. I wanted to be where he was: Glen Brook Middle School, surrounded by the cast and crew of *Dolls and Guys*.

Is he there? I texted Harper while we waited for the attending members of the league to take their seats. It brought me relief to know that at least Harper was at the cafetorium and therefore her ass was planted on an old beige folding chair identical to mine and Claudia's as we sat in Gary's basement.

Actually, he skipped town, left a note, and now the teenybopper who plays Benny Southstreet is conducting the band with an eyeliner pencil, she wrote back immediately.

Of course Crispin is here, what kind of question is that? she wrote again after a beat. **He's the musical director! It's opening night!**

"I call this hearing to order," Gary Feingold said, banging a literal gavel he'd had custom made for an occasion such as this. It had a little gold plate with his name engraved on it and everything. As the tinny bangs of the gavel rang out, I knew I wouldn't get to confess my undying love to Crispin Davis. There wouldn't be any grand sweeping gesture. Not as long as I was being held hostage by the men of the Glen Brook softball league.

"First order of business is the disciplinary hearing of Caroline Kline of Ringer's Bialys, who has received two warnings and a citation since her debut in the league this spring," he continued. Claudia grabbed my hand.

"You'll remember we voted on Miss Kline's eligibility before she formally joined in April. Following an argument that the precedent for a woman replacing an immediate family member in the event of injury or illness was set with the Ruby Winnick case in 1977, a four-to-three vote passed in her favor. This vote includes Leo Kline recusing himself due to conflict of interest and Mo Levine abstaining from voting."

I flashed a quick, narrow-eyed look at Mo Levine, bowed at the dais with his hands folded in front of him, fluorescent light reflecting off the shiny top of his bald head. According to Leo, Mo acted like he couldn't be bothered at these meetings. He was one of the oldest board members and had originated the league's sponsorship model. For decades, a team played under his shop's name, Mo's Mercantile, until he shuttered the business. His lack of passion was a key differentiator between him and every other man on the board and in the league, all of whom practically foamed at the mouth with enthusiasm. No one had any idea why he still showed up.

"'The indiscretions at the beginning of the season were mild infractions,'" Gary read off a printout. "'Foul language, nothing out of the ordinary or foreign for anyone in this league, but certainly something to be cognizant of. It seems there have been issues sparked by facing certain teams, or specific members on certain teams, where a preexisting relationship dynamic affects Miss Kline's ability to comply with the league's behavioral code of conduct.'"

Gary lowered his glasses and spoke off the cuff. "Caroline, I voted in your favor last time around. Because your father is not only a fellow board member and an asset to this league, but I consider him a close friend. I argued so vehemently on your behalf in April that the board has requested I recuse myself from this vote."

Claudia seized my hand in a tight squeeze. Neither of us expected Gary to recuse himself. We knew my spot on the roster wouldn't survive without him. The rest of these men could decimate the last few months of my life in a single power trip.

"Mr. Chairman," Claudia said, standing, smoothing out the skirt suit she wore, looking ready to defend some disenfranchised soul in a Grisham adaptation. "A word, if I may."

He gestured to let her know to proceed, and she did. "I'm addressing the board not only as Caroline Kline's stepmother, but also as her attorney. I feel qualified to defend her character to this organization while also pointing out that the insidious harassment she has faced throughout her tenure in this league is wholly unacceptable."

It was funny, perhaps, that I had never thought about my relationship with my teammates and rivals in those terms before. I'd regularly name *harassment* as it happened to me at work—albeit, never to the institution and mostly just to Winnie over a bottle of Pét-Nat—but the same consideration never crossed my mind with the league. The word seemed too formal for what I'd endured as the lone woman infiltrating a boys' club, but it was accurate.

"Her infractions, though minor, as you mentioned, not only pale in comparison to the behavior of other league members—

some who have seen court-ordered therapies before they've seen a hearing like this one—but are also a natural defensive reaction to discriminatory aggression."

She recited all this with ease and agility, no notes in front of her. I looked over to my dad to indicate that I was impressed, but he was fixated on his wife.

"Caroline's father—your beloved Leo, my beloved Leo—is ill. It is an uncertain time for the league and a trying time for our family. She has brought levity and talent and visibility to the team, but at the end of the day it's not even about that. It's about stepping up for her father. Caroline's presence in this league is a mitzvah. Don't let whatever legal action that kochlefl Scolari has threatened blind you to her contributions."

Two Yiddish words in one argument. My father met my gaze after that with his subtle smile and arched eyebrows, as though to say: *Get a load of this shiksa.*

"Mrs. Amaro-Kline, you've done a tremendous job bringing your courtroom acumen to several board meetings this year. I thank you for bringing a layer of legitimacy to this operation," Gary said, followed by a collective chuckle from the other board members. "But with all due respect, I think the board is most interested in hearing what Miss Kline has to say in her own defense."

I wanted to defend myself against how I'd been spoken to by the other players and how I'd been singled out by the umpires. But it was more than that. I wanted to defend how I'd turned this opportunity on the ballfield into something bigger than I could have imagined. How I won over my obnoxious teammates and how I helped poise our team for the playoffs. What I didn't want to lose, it turned out, was everything I'd gotten from being here. The chance to be a part of something bigger than me. The time I got to spend with my father. I couldn't bear the thought of returning to whatever came before this. I wanted to be here. I wanted to stay and fight.

I stood to speak but didn't know exactly what would come out. "I'll start by saying that at first, I wanted nothing to do with this league or any of you," I said, eliciting gasps from the crowd. "And I don't need to tell you all the resistance I've been met with in this league. But hitting my stride with the team, I've helped win games, draw crowds, and make top rankings." I laughed then. "Though, now that I think about it, maybe that's why I'm being held accountable like this. It doesn't matter how much you love my father. You all still see me as a threat instead of an asset."

I looked down the dais, where each board member either watched me with rheumy-eyed intensity or made notes on the yellow legal pad they each had in front of them. Mo Levine, sitting all the way at the end, did neither. He fixated on his own hands, picking a finicky cuticle.

"Reluctant as you may have been to let me take Leo's place while he recovers, I was just as reluctant to leave behind my life to come and play. Before this, it had been a decade since

I'd spent more than a night in Glen Brook. This was not something I was willing or excited to do. But now, even though it's nothing like how I imagined it would look, I'm dedicated to what I'm building here."

I looked over to Leo, then to Claudia, both looking back at me in anticipation and awe.

"My duty to this league and what we've accomplished together is an essential piece of my life now. One I'm not willing to relinquish quietly. If given the chance, I intend to serve as a better example to the people who watch us play and to the people we play with."

I looked around, taking in the energy of the eyes that were on me. I wasn't sure what to do next, although I felt oddly compelled to curtsy. I cleared my throat and said softly, "I yield my time," before taking my seat.

"Thank you for that, Miss Kline," Gary said studiously, pushing his readers up the bridge of his nose. "And let me be the first to say that no matter the direction the board votes this evening, we appreciate your contributions to the league. I've known you since you were a little girl running around the bases between innings with your sister. Having you play among us was something we couldn't have anticipated, and I'm moved by how you've stepped up for your father in his hour of need."

A shuffling of papers; Gary rose from the dais and helped my father do the same as Leo announced: "As Gary and I have recused ourselves from this vote due to conflict of interest, it is up to the remainder of the board to decide if Caroline Kline shall have a place on the Ringer's Bialys roster as we head into playoff season, or if she shall be suspended for disciplinary violations."

"All in favor of removing Miss Kline from the league, say aye," Gary said by rote. "All opposed, nay."

He went down the line of hunched men, soliciting votes aloud, so I could watch my fate unfold in real time. Without Gary's vote, I was in obvious danger of falling short.

Nathan Golan (whose team lost the World Series in an upset to Leo's right after we moved to Glen Brook, a fact he's never forgotten) was an aye. Antonio Malmo (so old-school Italian, you could just *tell* he'd never performed an act of cunnilingus in his life) was an aye. W. P. Kahn (a league founder as old as Methuselah himself) was a nay. Barry Babitz (one of the league's original players who was only ever described as *a real mensch*) voted nay. Mark Gould (never once described as a mensch but once described by Leo as "possessing more wily charm than an entire brothel") voted aye. Robin Walker Sr. (veteran of the league and father of Robbie) voted nay.

Mo Levine, the last in line, looked agitated when the vote arrived at him, like someone had just roused him from a long nap. If he abstained again, we were left in a tie and the vote could be put to the league as a whole—something I knew was very bad for my prospects.

With a heaving sigh, he rubbed his brow with an arthritis-gnarled hand and squinted out at me in the crowd. When our eyes met, his face softened, and his eyebrows turned up in an expression of almost childlike surprise. A brief flicker of a smile accompanied a single nod: "Aye."

Fuck.

Gary looked down the row and saw Mo beaming like he'd given me a second chance even though he just voted me out of the league. Gary clarified, "Mr. Levine, *aye* is the affirmative in removing Miss Kline from the roster, I'd like to make you aware."

Mo's face rearranged itself. "Oh, no, no, no. Aye to her. Affirmative to her." He pointed at me with a tan finger, curved by the mercilessness of age.

"So, nay? Nay is what you're saying? Nay to her removal?" Gary suggested, frustrated.

"Nay," he confirmed, with another definitive nod.

"The motion passes four to three with two abstaining," Gary boomed as he banged his little gavel, "in favor of Caroline Kline remaining on the Ringer's Bialys roster for the remainder of the season, barring any additional infractions." A small smile snuck its way onto his face.

My breath hitched and my armpits dampened. Claudia hugged me in my metal folding chair, and Leo clenched both his jaw and a quick fist in quiet victory, his hand under the table but still visible. Robbie Walker, sitting two rows behind us for moral support, clapped loudly twice then stopped when no one else clapped along with him. My affection for him perhaps never quite grew into what he was hoping for, but it also never waned.

"On to the next issue," Gary continued, refusing to linger on the drama of my existence for even a moment. He proceeded to talk about food vendor budgets for the championship game.

No longer needed, I began to gather my things and checked my watch, trying to estimate how quickly I could fly down the back roads that would get me from the Feingold house to Glen Brook Middle School.

I'm assuming we're in the second act? I texted Harper.

> Second act? A sixty-five-year-old woman
> just finished belting "Luck Be a Lady."
> There's, like, two songs left in the whole
> show.

The eyes in the basement followed me as I tiptoed over to the carpeted stairs to make my getaway.

• • •

MY MOTHER HAD a hard-on for eleven-o'clock numbers. It started when she played Rose in her high school's production of *Gypsy*. Just as an addict recalled that first high, Bobbi looked back at belting, "How do you like them eggrolls, Mr.

Goldstone?" and claimed it as her origin story. She taught Harper and me the words to "Memory" from *Cats* before she potty trained us. When she wrote *Hannie*, she was praised for young Agatha's showstopper, "I'll Try It on for Size," about leaving the Midwest behind for good in favor of a new life in New York City. A local theatre blogger said she showed "shades of Jule Styne," invoking the Jewish master composer of the Great White Way.

This was why, agnostic of the situation with Crispin, I was glad I made it to the middle school in time for "Sit Down, You're Rockin' the Boat," even if I had to ignore the speed limit to get there. It was one of the most iconic eleven-o'clock numbers in the history of musicals, and I knew my mother wouldn't let it go to waste. She solicited her dental hygienist, Dawn—who Mom knew had a great voice because she would sing while she scraped to calm the nerves of her patients—for the part of Nicely-Nicely Johnson. Zany as she was, my mother had an eye for this shit. Dawn came out onto the stage in a linen checkered suit and tap shoes and tossed the bowler hat that covered her long box braids into the audience. The energy shift in the room was palpable.

A single beam of dusty light hit Dawn, and she began to sing about bringing her dice along on a boat ride to heaven. Then I saw Crispin in the shadow of the stage, leading the orchestra with a slender wand.

Harper and I had always fought for my father's affections

by honing our swings and developing strong opinions about the American League East division. We sought our mother's appreciation by learning the choreography to half of *Liza with a Z* by adolescence and identifying every Hollywood starlet who had to have Marni Nixon's singing voice dubbed over theirs on film soundtracks. We picked out the eleven-o'clock numbers from every show she took us to see and ranked our favorites in a marbled notebook.

"Remember, girls," she chirped once from the front seat as we sped home from a matinee through the Lincoln Tunnel, "it's not just the fact that it's the penultimate song that defines the eleven-o'clock number." She had a list of criteria: it should be a solo, it should be a showstopper, and it should demonstrate a change of heart.

My mother had really punched up the act: all the girls huddled in the mission were clad in dapper suits, tap-dancing across the stage even though the song was typically performed with little-to-no choreography. It made me wish I'd gotten there earlier to catch the rendition of "A Bushel and a Peck," performed by the group of old men she collected at the VFW.

It made sense, my mother's fondness for the epiphany moment. I could imagine how she saw her own life in those terms. I understood what Harper and I refused to try to comprehend all those years, how the life she lived with Leo was inauthentic to whom she had become. I couldn't see her from my vantage point at the back of the room, but I imagined what she looked like waiting in the wings: Her hair pulled back into a tight, slick bun. Dramatic eye paired with a tasteful raisin lip. Proud but focused—nodding in time with the sharp beats of Dawn's tap shoes against the ancient, scuffed floorboards of the stage.

What had to change to provoke a change of heart? If you had asked me back in March under what circumstances I'd consider leaving Manhattan, I'd have said *kicking and screaming*. The reality wasn't a far cry from that. The night I'd fucked up and missed Crispin's show, I'd needed to cauterize my longing and nostalgia and recognize how much I didn't need what I'd left behind. Ben, the job, the city. It hadn't been taken from me, or lost, or even missed. But coming around on what was possible now—who I might become in an environment I'd once so adamantly resisted—felt pretty showstopping.

Dawn sang about being dragged by the devil and having too heavy a soul to float as she kicked a high leg over the heads of the congregation. They slid toward her, arms splayed to the side, chiming in for a final *Sit down, you're rocking the boat!*

The conclusion rolled along, mirroring an outcome closer to the MGM film adaptation than the original book for the stage. A double wedding in Times Square, but no duet on "Marry the Man Today" ("I am not pushing *that* agenda," from my mom). The house lights went up, and the ensemble crossed over the front of the stage to the rhythm of syncopated clapping. I craned my neck, looking past them for the man attached to the baton.

The principals were next: a twenty-four-year-old exotic dancer as Nathan Detroit. A bona fide Asbury Park drag queen as Miss Adelaide. My mother's accountant as Sister Sarah. Her once-timid friend Sue as Sky Masterson. They took their bows, then extended their arms out to the orchestra and, finally, to Crispin, who bowed twice in quick succession.

My mother sashayed onto the stage, arms outstretched to the cast and then to the audience until someone gave her a microphone. "Frank Loesser never approved of the way they cast the 1955 adaptation of this musical," she said, using her press octave so she sounded like a cross between Barbra and Lady Gaga. "He never forgave them. I'd like to think he's looking down on us tonight and rolling over in his grave." Her comments were met with raucous laughter as Crispin materialized at her side with a dozen peach roses before retreating back behind the curtain.

Harper appeared next to me clutching a corsage she'd ordered from our mother's favorite florist. "Bobbi's having a cast and crew shindig at that diner on Route 33 that serves cocktails," she said with the hushed tone of an informant. "If you want to catch him, go out to the parking lot now and wait. They've been coming out the side entrance that the janitors use. Mom keeps calling it the stage door. I think she wants me to get people to crowd around it and demand her autograph, but that ain't happening." I barely hugged her before I took off running.

There was something perverse about being in a school setting this time of year: the still, heavy heat of the night mingled with the dismal whine of crickets in the distance. I used to count their cries, simultaneous with mine, imagining that they, too, did not want to return to school. They'd make their first appearance in early August; a warning. By Labor Day, they'd be out in full force, overlapping in a treetop cacophony. If we had our way, the crickets and I, the summer would never end.

I supposed there was also something perverse about hanging around a middle school parking lot at twenty-nine years old, furiously sucking on a mango-flavored robot cigarette, which was how Crispin found me when he emerged from the janitor's door like an outlaw. His eyes darted in my direction, but he either didn't see me or he didn't think I was waiting for him. I called out to him and asked him to wait up. He stopped in front of his car.

"That was amazing," I said, breathless after jogging over. "*You* were amazing."

His smile was weak, and he wanted to shrug it off. "Thanks," he said dimly. "Yeah, that band is really something. And your mom, too. She's really cut out for this."

"All she does is sing your praises," I told him. After a beat of painful silence, I asked, "So, has my mom tried to rope you into collaborating on her fall production?" She had plans to adapt *Bye Bye Birdie* into an homage to Gen Z fandom culture and the Boomers who bemoan it.

I wondered, *Is this it?* So much for my grand gesture. Did I come so far to have it fizzle in a parking lot all over again? The truth worked its way up my spine, but my limbs were numb in waiting, unsure of what to do.

He rubbed the back of his neck and squinted into the moonlight. "I'm actually going on tour with Serene soon. Her bassist is out of commission longer than expected, so I'm gonna be a Hot Roller for a little while." He reached into his pocket for a cigarette and pulled out a tiny matching vape instead. Took a drag. Mint. "I'm trying to quit, eventually everything," he said sheepishly, holding it up.

I felt small then, talking about a regional theatre gig when he was about to traverse a continent. Serene's fall tour was not a minor one. A weeklong residency at the Stone Pony to kick off at the end of September, then all of the US and some of Canada. They wouldn't be back until the holidays. Even though I hadn't seen him since the night I messed it all up about a month prior, the thought of him being that far away for that long made the muscles in my chest seize.

"I need you to know how sorry I am about missing that show," I told him, trying not to cry, trying to tuck my heart back into my chest. "Before you pull out some empty *It's all good, no worries, whatever*—I need you to really listen to me and think about it. How deeply I regret not showing up for you. How dire things were to make me miss it."

"I can't do this with you, Caroline," he said, unlocking his car. "I should never have assigned such importance to you being there. I have no control over whether or not you show up. That wasn't right." He tossed a bag in the back seat, straightened his spine, and turned to face me. "I don't want to be angry about this anymore."

I felt my eyes get wide and wild. "*Angry about this?*" I huffed. "I'm still waiting to see this alleged anger! All I've gotten so far is disappointed looks and silence. If you're mad at me, then get mad! Why won't you yell at me about it?"

"Because I'm—" he started, but I cut him off.

"I did a fucked-up thing. I stepped out and totally blew you off. You should be pissed! But I never get any of that from you. You're just so laid-back all the time. So chill. *So zen.* I'm shocked to hear you even have another mode. I'm dying to see it."

His cheeks reddened, and his eyebrows got sharp. His face was fixed in a serious way I'd yet to see. "I do everything in my power," he shot back, the volume of his voice finally rising, "to keep the angry part of me in check. Okay?" His eyes bore into mine. Tension locked between his shoulders, making him look angular and hulking. "All of my energy this year has gone to trying to control those emotions, not to mention every other impulse I have."

I nodded, somewhat satisfied I'd at least roused a new reaction from him.

"But instead of getting mad," he said, his voice easing and posture softening, "I need to manage my disappointments better. Examine why I had you being there that night built up to such a degree in my head."

Good, I wanted to say, *examine that!* But I couldn't. My breath was caught in my chest, sharp and unmoving.

He opened the driver's-side door and tucked himself into the seat. I grabbed his forearm as the rest of his body maneuvered behind the wheel. "Crispin," I said, my voice laced with more urgency than I'd ever let him hear, "if you want me there, I will be at every show you play until you're older than Springsteen. I will be Courteney fucking Cox in the crowd every night for you. You need to know that." The truth, or close to it. I couldn't think of somewhere I'd rather be or anything I'd said out loud in the last year more rigorously honest than that statement.

But he turned the key in the ignition anyway. "I've gotta go, Caroline." The headlights beamed a path in front of him, the one he would follow home.

20

THE PLAYOFFS RESTORED a natural, nearly ancestral energy to the Kline family home. Some of my most potent memories from growing up under my father's roof took place during postseason, both in the MLB and in the Glen Brook Men's Softball League. When his team made it to the highest ranks, my father sank into this regimen of random activities he called "conditioning." During the playoffs, he woke up every morning at six to swim laps and eat Product 19 cereal served with sliced bananas and strawberries. After dinner, he'd watch a classic Yankees victory on VHS so he could go to sleep with a vision of success in his head, prepping his brain to lace glory into all his dreams. He'd spend an hour at the batting cages and an hour in the gym. Last season, he had pinned a bouquet of eucalyptus behind his showerhead to help him breathe better.

"I don't think that thing really works," Claudia said then, unimpressed with the soggy leaves crowding her headspace.

"My ability to breathe deeply will allow me to vanquish my rivals," he replied, eyes closed, calm as a monk.

Whenever the Yankees made the playoffs, it was a different level of insanity. The whole family had to get involved. I remember coming home late from a friend's house one October evening as a kid and walking into the living room like I was walking into a war zone. Harper sat in the corner of the sectional, rigid spine, head held high, diligently chewing on a plastic blue-striped drinking straw. Bobbi sat primly in the leather armchair, wearing her oversize Tino Martinez T-shirt, legs tucked beneath her. Leo barreled across the hardwood in his underpants, wielding a Louisville Slugger he got on Bat Day at Yankee Stadium in 1976. Graig Nettles's name was engraved across the barrel.

It was 2003; game seven of the ALCS against our greatest rivals, the Red Sox. An altar rested on the mantel above our fireplace: seven tealight candles, a baseball signed by the entire 1961 Yankees roster, a framed postage stamp of Lou Gehrig, and the beaten-up old cap my father was wearing on the night of the Pine Tar Game—the night he met my mother. In front of the television, a small malachite urn holding the ashes of our family dog. We always groaned in horror when our father brought her out. "She's been with us five World Series rings," he would argue, placing the remains on the hardwood floor. "Two of them she was even alive for."

"Caroline!" Leo boomed that night all those years ago, the moment I made myself known in the doorway, "get to your post, we need all the help we can get." He pointed to the far side of the sectional between my mother and my sister. I took the opposite end—the one with the recliner attached—and he quickly shooed me away, telling me I was threatening the juju.

"Let's hold it to a vote," Harper muttered from behind her straw. "All in favor of abandoning these superstitious poses, say—"

"This is not a democratic household," Leo cut her off, facing the TV, bat raised in the air like an Olympic torch, "and I am not a rational man. This is *THE PLAYOFFS*." I looked over at my sister, pitifully, knowing she must have been drinking iced tea and had that straw in her mouth when something good happened. She wasn't going to be allowed to stop chewing on it until it was all over. We had already gone into extra innings.

When Aaron Boone stepped up to the plate in the eleventh, my father sprung over to my mother's chair and cried, "Rub this bat! I have a feeling this schmuck is about to do something!" Bobbi blinked away an eye roll, laid a lithe hand onto the base of the bat, and gave it a little pet.

When the ball sailed over the wall, the fat base of the bat

popped and crunched seven jagged holes into the ceiling as my father pumped his elbows while running around the room. When Mariano ran out to collapse and cry on the mound, we were allowed to move freely once more. We all leapt from our posts, screaming and dancing, covered in plaster until we were christened with champagne. My father later had recessed lighting installed to cover up the holes, but their crooked, arbitrary path was undeniable. "Did your contractor have a seizure when he was installing these?" Claudia asked shortly after moving in.

To this day, my father will deny he has any obsessive-compulsive tendencies. But during any postseason broadcast, he goes about rearranging the remotes, the seating, the lighting—just about any detail he can exert control over—as though keeping the game aloft with ritual.

"Don't make me sound like a lunatic," he'd tell Harper and me whenever we got into one of our *remember when crazy ol' Dad did this* jags. All we had to do was look at each other, wide-eyed and incredulous, recalling the horrific sight of Harper's straw, decimated by bite marks, presented to her in a Ziploc baggie before the first pitch of the World Series. My father's expectant face, not considering for a moment that she would refuse to chew on that straw for what would become six more games.

"I still can't believe you saved that thing," Harper would say as an adult with a palm to her forehead.

"I still can't believe you refused to chew!" Leo would shoot back, indignant. "Need I remind you how the 2003 World Series ended? All because you turned your little nose up at the straw that could've saved us."

Postseason was a special time for the Klines. We operated with a proprietary blend of strategy, magic, and deft precision. It was with that heritage running through my veins that I channeled all my strength and focus into achieving what I came to Glen Brook to do: to go to the show, as my father never stopped saying. With Leo officially out of commission—his level of physical weakness varying day to day, the stair-cases at Gary's basement hearing forcing him to reconsider using a motorized scooter to get around—I picked up the mantle of his routine. I, too, began hitting the batting cages and watching *Yankeeography* before bed for inspiration.

I jimmied the Lionel Richie ballads out of the Saab's tape deck with a butter knife and got a new cassette stuck in there, expressly for postseason. It was called *Yankees Greatest Hits, Volume 2: The Dream Season*, and it featured amped-up sports anthems interspersed with John Sterling and Michael Kay calling key moments from the 1998 championship season. I listened en route to my first playoff game: a recording of David Wells's perfect game segued perfectly into Steppenwolf's "Born to Be Wild." Sunday at dusk on Labor Day weekend. The night was a trial that would shape the remainder of the season. Monday was the bonus day that followed, though we

weren't sure yet what sort of day it would be: one of trium-
phant celebration or one of sober reflection.

I was light on a cheering section. Harper had gone back to
the West Coast but promised to consider returning if we made
it to the World Series. ("*When*," Leo corrected her sternly.
"*When* we make it to the World Series. How many times do I
have to remind the two of you about the laws of attraction?")
My mother was still knee-deep in *Dolls and Guys*, which was
running through the end of the long weekend by popular demand. Crispin was, of course, a notable absence on the bleachers, likely never to return. Just as I strode up toward the field
from the parking lot, consoling myself by remembering Dad
and Claudia were still loud enough to make me feel like a star
in an empty stadium, I spotted her from a distance—sitting
on the top rung of the bleachers and wrapped in a little shawl.

"Are you really here?" I asked, standing directly beneath
her, chin tilted up like an inquisitive child.

She was startled. "Oh shit, there you are. Look, don't tell
anybody I'm here," Winnie said, removing an enormous pair
of acrylic tortoiseshell sunglasses from her face. She had a
silk scarf wrapped around her hair and tied underneath her
chin, like an incognito starlet driving a convertible. "It's bad
enough my parents know. They *cried* when I showed up to the
house. Do you believe that shit? The Jewish guilt is *strong* in
those two."

Feeling like I might cry, I laughed instead. "I mean, you *are* the prodigal daughter of this town. And you haven't been home in, what, nine years?" I said, exaggerating. "This is big. This is Harry Bailey returning from war."

She put the glasses back on and cocked an eyebrow. "Does that make you Jimmy Stewart?"

She looked me up and down like she didn't know what to make of me. Tan and muscled, hair pulled back into a neat ponytail, tied in a yellow ribbon to match my Bialys tee. Back straight, head high, eyes clear, brain sharp. I told her I hadn't had a drink since the Odeon. I considered it postseason conditioning, but, if I was being honest with myself, I felt better the longer I went. Crispin hadn't been to any JAMS meetings lately owing to his busy theatre and band schedule, but Colleen welcomed me with open arms.

Winnie softened and quit her movie star act then. She removed the shawl to reveal a matching sweatsuit composed of her own ancient bat mitzvah favors. The top read *I SURVIVED WINNIE'S TITANIC BAT MITZVAH* across the chest, with a graphic of a capsizing ship. She did the absolute most with that theme—wore a Heart of the Ocean replica necklace and everything. She moved to the bottom of the bleachers to be eye level with Claudia, who explained the likelihood of going to the show, loud enough to be embarrassing. Winnie sat, rapt, absorbing every word of it.

Because it was a crowded and competitive field of candidates that year, the frequency and stakes were both higher. The playoff schedule was one day on, one day off, making for as many as four games in a week. So many contenders had passed the threshold of wins this year, and a larger-than-usual number of teams were in knockout situations. A few one-game playoffs were slated to thin the herd a bit. Next would be eight teams competing in the quarterfinals (what Leo called the division series), then four in the semifinals (the championship series), and of course two in the final (the World Series, known around these parts as "the show").

The Sunday game itself was technically considered a pennant playoff. Our opponents, Royal Dental Spa, hoped to intimidate us but wore teal T-shirts that featured an anthropomorphic tooth in a crooked crown.

Ryan Buckley and Billy the Kid had taken to their annual ritual of growing out playoff beards, which went against every fiber of my clean-cut, Steinbrenner-honed tastes. The other men on the team tried to follow suit, showing up with varying degrees of scruff and stubble—looking unkempt at best and like budding cult leaders in a few instances. Robbie Walker had a weird mustache coming in that didn't appear to be growing in tandem with the hair sprouting across his jawline. He smoothed it over with an index finger, looking at a fuzzy Timmy Moriarty as though his face were a mirror. "I don't think I can do this facial hair thing," he said pitifully, patting the bald patches where his mustache should have met his burgeoning beard. "I'm missing my connectors."

Hideous as they were, the beards seemed to give these men the confidence they needed for Ringer's Bialys to easily win the run off and move on to the next round. Ryan pitched all nine innings without breaking a sweat, Robbie hit a three-run home run in the seventh, and with the bases loaded, Timmy the Tortoise got hit by a pitch and sauntered over to first with pride. I hit a rocket into deep center in the second batting lefty and another one in the fifth batting righty against each of their two best pitchers. I had four RBIs, including the game-winning double. By the bottom of the ninth, Winnie had practically frayed her vocal cords screaming for me.

"She's back!" Billy the Kid yelled to the crowd as I slid into second. "Caro-line drive, back in action!"

"What do you mean 'she's back'?" yelled Claudia. "She never left!"

After shaking hands with our opponents, their shoulders rounded with the knowledge they'd be going home until spring, the Bialys barely waited until we were back in our dugout before giving me the MVP treatment. I'd been privy to it before as a participant, but never as the recipient. While they chanted "MVP" (interspersed with Leo's hopeful cries of *We're going to the show!*), they doused me in whatever liquid they had on hand: neon Gatorade in squirt bottles, wide-mouthed jugs of water, Pete Peretti's lukewarm sugar-free Red Bull.

Timmy pulled out his Squeeze Breeze from two decades ago—a combination spray bottle and foam fan to keep him from overheating—and misted me with it.

I was a laughing pillar of sugar in the night, courting the mosquitos and gnats that hovered over the field in buzzing clouds. Ryan Buckley cried out, "Victory lap at Locals!" as he slung his bag over his shoulder. A couple of claps and a couple of groans. I was with the groans. "Fifteen minutes. No exceptions."

I walked back to Winnie then, knowing her response to this celebration forum would be a staunch *abso-fucking-lutely not*. She surprised me when she relented without argument and said she'd meet me in the parking lot.

21

LOCATED IN ONE of Glen Brook's oldest strip malls, Locals Bar occupied what was once an old-timey pharmacy before the CVS/Walgreens wars rolled out across every suburb. It took a true visionary to see the space and think "bar," but the Murphy siblings (local elder millennials, two brothers and a sister) who leased the building were onto something. Despite the abject cringiness of the place—including a sans serif LED sign out front, announcing LOCALS BAR in an obnoxious shade of blue—it was always packed.

Inside, the dark wooden walls trapped a mingling scent of sweat, fried pickles, and tonic water shot from a rarely cleaned soda gun. The team gathered in a giant booth in the back, which was rather generously referred to as "the lounge." The "locals," whose patronage was the sole objective of the Murphy family's mission, had already begun to pour in.

It was a mix of people my parents' age and some old class-mates I recognized. Lots of the Facebook moms from my high school crowd and their slick-haired husbands. Sarita O'Brien, poster child of the local Alcoholics Anonymous chapter, was inexplicably holding court at a round table of gravel-voiced men, drawing tattoo sketches for them on cocktail napkins, holding them up against their biceps, which were tan and losing tone. Winnie and I sat at a two-top off to the side. She drained a vodka soda while I nursed a seltzer with lime in a lowball glass.

"So, what's the plan here?" Winnie asked bluntly, nearing the bottom of her glass. "Like, what will you do next?"

I looked over wistfully at the small circus in the big booth. Billy the Kid and Pete Peretti pounded the table, trying to get the old-timers to down cheap shots of cinnamon-flavored whiskey. Everyone was in a great mood, egging them on. Even Robbie got in on the chant.

"Probably just let Robbie Walker impregnate me already," I said with my head still turned to them. After a few seconds, I looked back at Winnie. "I don't know—start interviewing for a new job in earnest once the season ends? Get back on the dating apps, I guess?" It felt a little sad, laying it out like that.

"But are you coming back to the city?" she asked, an undertow of urgency in her voice.

"I'll be back eventually, Winnie," I said, exasperated, like a teenager trying to convince her parents she's turning over a new leaf. She looked away from me. She wore a tense expression that only made an appearance when she was on the defense. Her eyebrows were pulled back, jaw tight. Her ears even appeared half an inch higher than normal.

She was silent for a moment before she said, "Look, there's no easy way to say this," and I was hit with a pang of an old, familiar feeling, like I was being broken up with. "My old editor sold her pilot to one of the big streaming services. They ordered a full run, and she wants me to help her build the writers' room from the ground up."

"Winnie," I said, eyes wide as the moon. "This is incredible, holy shit. So, you're leaving *The New Yorker* to take it?"

"Actually," she said back, "I'm leaving New York to take it. The job's in Santa Monica, so I'm moving to Los Angeles."

My mind was a hurricane, thoughts speeding by at a record pace. I thought about how Winnie had generally regarded Hollywood as a concept and any of our friends who went west. All that bravado. All those years of calling newly minted Angelenos "soulless." "That's why the California workday ends at two in the afternoon," she once said after returning home from a reportage trip there. "It's all people who couldn't crack the New York work ethic. An army of the weak willed."

I'd never lived more than a short train ride away from Winnie in my entire life. I grew up counting paces between our houses, skipping over fences of shared backyards. Even living at home the past few months hadn't been devoid of her presence. When she left, I knew it would be the death of something. The end of a spontaneous book reading in Dumbo or an exhibit at the Whitney or a basement show on the Bowery. No more trays of afternoon oysters just because we felt like it.

I remembered her reaction when I'd told her I was moving to LA with stunning clarity, though I'd tried to tamp it down. She told me I was making a mistake. She told me I'd be back, that this dynamic with Ben was untenable and I was letting myself drift away on a raft of fantasy. She had turned out to be right, but she was cruel in her delivery. I thought about what I wished she'd said instead, and then I grabbed her hand across the table and said it:

"This is going to be fucking amazing."

· · ·

AFTER I WALKED Winnie out, I lingered in front of the strip mall, bathed in the unnatural blue glow of Locals. I took several hits off my nicotine pen, making myself dizzy as I dialed Harper. Her phone sent me to voicemail. *Fuck California.*

Sarita slid out of the bar, clutching a dwindling bottle of water and a pack of cigarettes in one claw. She stood at a distance, but after she lit a cigarette, she looked at me and asked if I wanted one. "The real thing," she said, pulling one out of the pack and nodding at the smooth piece of metal in my hands. "You gotta get tired of that shit sometimes." Hers were the kind with little balls of menthol hidden in the filters. I thanked her and took it.

I wanted to ask, but wouldn't, what forces drew Sarita to that bar. Or any bar. She was, I supposed, the sort of sober person who wanted to have free rein and go where the action was. Crispin had mentioned he knew some people in the program who were like that: wanting to go anywhere like anyone else, refusing to feel confined by sobriety. But for the most part, he avoided it. He laughed back when he told me. "At one of my first meetings, one of the old-timers said, 'If you hang out at the barbershop long enough, you're gonna get a haircut.' And I just never forgot that."

"You seeing the Hot Rollers at the Pony in a couple weeks?" Sarita asked, still standing several paces away, one arm crossed under her rib cage, propping up the other, which was holding the cigarette. She flicked her tongue when she exhaled a plume of smoke, just to give it something to do. "Serene hasn't shut up about your stage design at that JAMS meeting. And you know it's Crispin's official debut with the band."

"Crispin must be exhausted," I said, dodging the question and looking down at my cleats. "He's been doing the musical direction on my mom's show, and now the Pony residency . . ."

"Wow, yeah," she replied, eyes widening as she thought longer about it. "And tour's coming up. And he just got his one year! We had the celebration meeting last night. Got his coin and made a speech and everything." I could imagine the warm sensation of pride spreading through his limbs as the coin was placed into his hand. The crinkles around his eyes he got only when he was sincerely, inconsolably happy.

"A year of sobriety," I said in a voice so small it sounded like it didn't belong to me. It had been weeks since my last drink, and I felt like I deserved a Presidential Medal of Freedom. "That's an amazing accomplishment."

I realized that since I'd found out about the AA dating rule, I hadn't thought about what the one-year milestone might mean for him. I was so focused on what it might mean for me. No more excuses—either he could start dating Sarita, or he would have to turn me down in earnest. I'd also let myself fantasize, briefly, about a different possibility. That maybe he'd felt the same and he was just playing by the rules and waiting for the year to pass. It all seemed so foolish in retrospect. What did I think was going to happen? A year would be up, and we would run to each other across the distance of twin municipal fields like lovers in a meadow montage? Of course it was never going to happen for us. I couldn't even get him to talk to me unless I chased him down in a parking lot.

"So, I can tell them you'll be there?" Sarita said, closer now, head cocked with a smile. "You'll come to the Pony opening night?" She smelled like spun sugar and cigarettes. *This is who I'm up against*, I thought. I couldn't blame Crispin if he wanted to run to her now that his year was complete.

"Sarita," I said, swallowing audibly, "I can't go. I-I let him down so badly last time, he won't even speak to me now."

She tossed her head lightly from side to side as though weighing the evidence. "Yeah, he was pretty in his feelings about that whole thing," she conceded. Then she laughed. "But my thing is like, how is he gonna stay mad?"

I looked at her then, surprise betraying my stoic face. "You and I have both known him a long time," she said, "and he doesn't really hold on to things like this. It's actually kind of annoying how reasonable he is. Never holds a grudge. If he's feeling it intensely, he just sort of stops in that moment, breathes, says *nothing is fucked here*, and moves on."

I laughed then, too, at her pitch-perfect analysis—thinking about a couple of times in the last few months when I'd gotten flustered on the road or in a crowd and Crispin took me by the shoulders and said exactly that. *Nothing is fucked here!* I thought about my Pavlovian response, the calm that settled between my bones when he spoke.

"I mean, think about it," she continued. "He has to really, *really* give a fuck to stay mad like this, you know what I'm saying? He's so diligent about the program and everything else because he hates feeling like he's out of control of a situation. And I think you tapped into some feelings he maybe wasn't ready to face."

I tossed my cigarette to the ground, twisted the toe of my

plastic cleat onto the ember, and made no attempt to mask the slow, tight smile spread across my face. It hadn't occurred to me that she might be on my side. I wanted to hug Sarita O'Brien but decided against it. Then she dropped her cigarette and hugged me, that long, cool curtain of hair blanketing my shoulders as she hooked her chin into my neck.

"I'll let them know you're coming," she said with a wink when she pulled back. She disappeared back into Locals while I took a few more minutes to stand stunned on the sidewalk. I had been so sure Sarita was my rival, selfishly ticking off days on the calendar, lying in wait for Crispin to hit his mark so she could make her move. And yet that five-minute conversation yielded more hope than every minute of the two weeks prior combined. I'd had more adversarial cigarette breaks with my best friend.

Back inside Locals, the Bialys cawed for me to join them in the oversize banquette. They wanted me right in the middle, in the action. Refusing to file out properly to let me in, or perhaps too drunk to coordinate, they had me walk over the table to sit down among them, cheering as my cleats knocked into plates and cups. They'd ordered "bottle service," which was just Hannah Murphy—one of the proprietors—coming back and forth from the kitchen with bottles of Jack Daniel's atop metal buckets of ice. They had appraised her body in increasingly explicit terms with each passing round, but they knew to pipe down about her hips, her lips, after I sat at the table.

WELCOME HOME, CAROLINE KLINE

I survived forty minutes in the sweaty crooks of my wild compatriots, but with my seltzer long gone, I decided to emancipate myself, crawling under the table to get out and return to the bar for more. Then it occurred to me I could just track down Hannah Murphy and see if she was willing to throw an extra bottle of club soda into the mix just for me to nurse.

When I spotted her, it was down the long, dark corridor that led from the kitchen to the back alley. Hannah was up against the wall, her long copper hair sweaty and ruffled, hands gripped across the back of her enthusiastic make-out partner. Pressed against her was Sarita, whose hands clasped Hannah's face as they devoured each other. Their bodies were soldered together, courting rapture in a dark, quiet moment of respite before the table of lunatics had enough time to notice how long their server had been gone.

22

WAS IT ARROGANCE or clairvoyance that assured me we would make it to the World Series? After sweeping the Throckmorton Salt Lords in the division series, we vanquished the Monmouth QuikLubes in the championship series to win the pennant. Our dynamic was tighter than ever. During our pregame ritual on the night we won the pennant, the team presented me with an entire case of blue B_{12} gummy vitamins. "To make up for the times you got skipped," Ryan said, smiling. I worried, just for a moment, as they all looked at me, that I would cry. Instead, I slung myself over the box, laughed, and said: "Here's all that juice I've been asking for!"

The league's newsletter recaps were littered with Bialy achievements. Ryan Buckley showed off his iron pitching arm. Billy the Kid and Pete Peretti at last let only their bats do the talking. Robbie led the league in stolen bases. Pop flies went to die in our gloves. The old-timers playing deep in the outfield didn't let a single moonshot go over the fence. Timmy the Tortoise's on-base percentage was out of control. I didn't hurt things by keeping up my local reputation as Caro-line Drive, switch hitting my way into history. My father's draft selection for the team seemed like a carefully prepared gelatin dish that had simply taken this long to finally set. At any rate, Leo was right from the beginning: Ringer's Bialys were going to the show.

I felt both buoyed and dizzy at the prospect of rising to the occasion. We were about to play the World Series against our greatest adversaries, the Moby Dicks. I not only wanted to defeat them, I wanted to lead my team in the charge. Months ago, no one suspected a woman would ever be allowed to play, or that the question of it would ever come up. My presence thus far was unprecedented, but I wanted to be indelible. I wanted to take it all and remember, years from now, that something had made this brief hometown stint worthwhile.

I drove alone down Route 18 to the World Series that Sunday. It was a crisp late-September morning in New Jersey and I had the windows down, arms chilled by the sweet air. I parked the Saab butt-end facing the field to avoid taking a ball to the windshield. I squinted into the distance as I popped my trunk, spotting a couple of players occupying benches on both our home side and their away side. I slung my bag over my shoulder and walked toward the bleachers with conviction, where I knew my support system was building camp.

On the bleachers: Harper and Sil nursed coffees the size of their heads to regain consciousness after catching the red-eye. My niece and nephew, Nina and Tolon, were hanging all over my mother, who was dressed like Elton John in her spangled Dodgers zip-up jacket and enormous round white sunglasses. Claudia sat beside her, long acrylic nails clutching a pearl-pink tumbler filled with coffee-flavored water from her instant pod machine. Leo was nearby, tucked away in the dugout, reviewing his handwritten lineup for the umpteenth time.

To my surprise and delight, Winnie was perched behind my mother and stepmother, wrapped in dramatic autumnal layers, despite the forecast indicating the temperature would likely creep to the high seventies before the game was over. She came prepared with a peppy DIY sign cut from a shipping box and covered in thick marker scrawl. *Better bitch than mouse*, it read. I felt like I had to tuck my heart back into my chest. In a few weeks' time, Winnie would live on the other side of the country. My sister would go back to the life she had built separate from us. Crispin would be away on tour. I didn't know where I would be beyond this game, what would happen when it ended.

But the moment of sinking into my feelings was interrupted

when I noticed who appeared alongside them on the bleach-ers. Sitting on the far side of the bottom-most rung was Tommy Mills, dressed in civilian clothes and wearing a sling over his arm. Before I had a chance to properly register what was in front of me or the impulse to ask a question, I looked over to the Dicks' dugout.

Amid the players clipping their bags to the fence and stretching their hip flexors, Kelly Quinn had her right cleat-clad foot propped up on the visitors' bench. Her long blond ponytail was pulled through the back of her blue cap, cascad-ing over her shoulder as she reached down to lace up her cleats. She righted it when she straightened up, looked over at me, and smiled.

● ● ●

"GET GARY ON the horn," Leo muttered, careful to remain expressionless beneath his Wayfarers and cap pulled low. "Caro, get over here and look at me, only at me. If we show any emotional response, they'll think they're capable of rat-tling us." Claudia followed, punching numbers into her phone and handing it to Leo as he maneuvered his electric scooter over the curb and into the parking lot with a rickety thud.

"What kind of stunt are you trying to pull here, Feingold?" he hissed. He hung up after less than a minute, turned back to me, and said Gary was two blocks away from the field.

"We're going to sort this all out," he assured me, but it sounded hollow.

Gary pulled up, and a motorcade followed. It wasn't just the Dicks and the Bialys and our families who came to watch; it was players from across the league who had been knocked out in earlier rounds. They'd come to root for whoever beat them in the pennant race to make them feel like they hadn't lost in vain. Or root for the opposing team out of spite. Or maybe they just came for the drama.

"I demand to know what the fuck is going on," Leo said, scooting over to Gary and rolling over his toe with an audible crunch. He backed up, the scooter beeping as he went, then hoisted himself up on the vehicle's platform so he had a couple of menacing inches over Gary.

But instead of acquiescing, Gary jabbed a finger into the niche of Leo's chest. "I'll tell you what the fuck is going on," he growled. "This league is a fucking free-for-all now because of her," he said, voice full of venom, pointing at who else but me.

Claudia positioned herself behind my father, sunglasses pushing her hair back off her face, exposed and ready to jump into the pride. "Point at her or touch my husband again, Gary, and I'll break your hand off at the wrist." The scene we were hoping to avoid making was now gathering mass and speed, like a hurricane off the shore.

"I got a call last night at ten o'clock," Gary said, ignoring Claudia but taking two steps back. "Tommy Mills. Our league's most valuable player. On the eve of the World Series. He can't make the game, he says. Reactivated an old war wound doing yard work. Allegedly."

I looked back at the bleachers, where Tommy had his head turned to listen to the unfurling ruckus, but otherwise stayed put. I wondered what was really going on under that sling. Kelly pulled their catcher onto the diamond and started whipping practice pitches at him, ignoring what her presence had incited.

"'But it's okay,' he tells me," Gary continued. "'I have a replacement and we're going to be just fine. Better, maybe.' His wife, she's a star pitcher from back in the day. A real powerhouse. And he's chuckling and I'm getting an ulcer, thinking about these kids showing up today for a chance to see Captain America play."

"Stop talking about this guy like he's Derek fucking Jeter, for Christ's sake," Leo yelled, disgusted. "He's small-town, just like everyone else out there who busted their ass to get to the World Series."

Gary put up his hand. "But he's not like everyone else, Leo, and you know it. You know he changed the face of this league when he showed up to play. Think about the fundraising. Think about the T-shirt vendor over there who made

Tommy Mills apparel to sell today. Elvis's signature Captain America sundae he's gonna be slinging. Win or lose, this guy's the draw. His presence courts major funding for all of us."

"Nine times outta ten," Claudia said, looking down at the asphalt, "it all comes down to the almighty dollar."

"I'm sick of you acting like this league lives and dies by one player. It doesn't, and it never will." Leo paused to look back at the growing crowd. He was seated atop the scooter again, tired from standing. "If anything," he said, "half those people are here to see Caroline. Don't underestimate her pull in all this."

"Regardless, I had to let him sub her in on the roster for the same reason we had to let Caroline play. This Ruby Winnick precedent from '77. The loophole no one thought to go through until *someone* dug too deeply into the files."

Claudia cocked an eyebrow and crossed her arms in front of her chest, regretting nothing.

"Gary," Leo said, attempting but not quite achieving calm, "I need you to understand the context here. There's sour grapes between this girl and Caroline. They're pulling a big act because they know there's a very good chance they're going to lose and they don't want to go down without trying to take her down, too."

It was then that Kelly and Tommy ambled over with someone in tow behind them, walking with authority. It took me a minute to focus my eyes and realize it was Big Steve—Kelly's father and my old softball coach—gone completely gray, but mustache still intact and shoulders as broad as ever.

"This is the big show," Leo told Gary before they got within earshot. "Every single person on that field worked hard all season to get here. And now she's gonna waltz on for some intimidation campaign against my daughter?"

"Everything alright, Gary?" Kelly asked as she stepped into the scrum, voice innocent as honey. She addressed Gary but looked around at all of us, checking our eyes for fear or resistance.

"No, everything's not alright," Leo answered, turning to face her. "You've got a lot of nerve, missy, trying to start some shit right before the World Series. Despite what you may think, this town loves this game, not the drama. They take it seriously. They're going to remember this."

Tommy opened his mouth, prepared to launch into a rebuttal, but instead Kelly arranged her shoulders to make herself taller and got there first. "So, are you saying exceptions should be made only for you? For your daughter? The league's rules shouldn't be upheld by the board equally across all teams?"

I felt the gravity of the situation as much as I could appreciate the absurdity: the ultimate matchup between the two best teams in a single town that lives and dies by baseball. A war hero drawing out a crowd and bringing in essential funding. One woman, now two women, threatening the ecosystem of delicate egos and calcified assuredness of the way things had always been. The tension and the stakes were apparent; each team refusing to consider themselves a possible loser. But on the other hand, a bunch of grown men arguing about the infiltration of their adult softball league—one with a sixteen-inch ball and underhand pitching—was nothing short of hilarious.

"What are you saying, Mr. Kline?" Tommy said, finally getting his chance to speak in that earnest, soft voice of his. "You think this is a farce? You don't think I'm really hurt?"

"Can't say I do," Claudia said, looking him up and down with her mouth fixed in an arch. Big Steve, who until that point had been quiet, saw this as an opportunity to take Claudia— a stranger to him—down a peg.

"Are you calling into question the integrity of this *veteran*?" he demanded to know, stepping close enough to Claudia that Leo hobbled over to provide a physical barrier between them.

I crouched down and chuckled into my own collarbone. When the rest of the group noticed the peals of laughter coming from underfoot, they stopped yelling over one another and looked down at me.

"What the fuck's so funny down there?" Leo wanted to know, failing to adjust his combat voice to address me. Or maybe he was actually mad.

"If you have to ask why this is funny," I said, rising back

up so quickly I sparked a tiny head rush, "then you'll never know. I can't help you there."

I turned to Glen Brook's all-American couple. "Tommy, I hope you feel better soon. Kelly, I'll see you out there." I extended my hand—an act to demonstrate I could be above all this, that maybe women were above all this—and she shook it.

•   •   •

BACK IN THE dugout, Leo shared the lineup and the men were solemn, clapping one another on the back in anxious solidarity. A couple of them whispered about Kelly Quinn taking the mound, and a couple of others hissed not to mention it right now.

The typical pomp and circumstance: when we were announced, we took the field in V formation like geese while the national anthem played, hats over our hearts, and the crowd mirrored us. A pair of local radio stars took their posts at a makeshift booth to announce each team's lineup and proceed to call the game. "Subbing in for pitcher Corporal Tommy Mills," one DJ said, "is Kelly Quinn-Mills, in her Glen Brook Men's Softball League debut."

She waved as she jogged out onto the field, turning a tiny pirouette as she inserted herself into the queue.

Sil volunteered to manage the scoreboard, which seemed magnanimous, but I knew he really just wanted to leave the kid corralling to my sister. Elvis parked directly behind the bleachers, selling festive breakfast sandwiches for the occasion: pork roll, egg, and cheese or toasted peanut butter and banana. A stringy-looking kid (likely an intern at the radio station) perched behind a card table with a laptop and a PA system, ready to deploy each player's chosen walk-up music. A sign taped to the front of the table read: NO "ENTER SANDMAN"! The umpire reset his hand clicker, pulled the cage down over his face, and cried *batter up* into the crystal clear morning.

The catcher—a paunchy stoner who went to my high school—led off for the Moby Dicks. He hit the first pitch Ryan gave him right to me and was out at first. An inaugural out I took as a good omen. I waggled a single finger in the air. *One dead.*

Their first baseman followed with a base hit when a grounder eluded our first baseman's glove. He stole second before their left fielder struck out, but barely anyone was paying attention to him making a run for it. The crowd was focused on Kelly Quinn taking practice swings in the on-deck circle—making it clear that the Dicks would indeed let Tommy's wife sub for him in his traditional spot, batting cleanup, rather than opting to move her down the lineup.

I shouldn't have been surprised when Kelly sauntered to the plate to the tune of "Sweet Caroline"—the walk-up music she'd chosen for herself—but the oblique taunt made my breath hitch when it came on the PA system. I heard chatter and giggling disbelief radiating off the bleachers. I punched my glove, maneuvered it against the front of my thigh so that it opened wide like a mouth. *So that's how it's going to be.*

When she swung, it was with all the ferocity she had when we were kids. She swung like she was playing for keeps.

• • •

KELLY WAS ACCUSTOMED to fast-pitch greatness. It took all her energy to dial it back and relinquish the ball before going into a full windmill, but after a couple of innings she got the hang of it. By the bottom of the third, we were in an okay spot despite Kelly's competency and a couple of bogus calls. The score was 3–2 Dicks. We were down with one out, but batting at the top of our order.

Billy the Kid batted leadoff all series, and it worked for him: two swings later, he was resting comfortably on first base. Pete Peretti popped up to right field for the second out. Kelly walked Robbie, putting him on first by the time I stepped into the batter's box to the tune of "Psycho Killer" by Talking Heads. My walk-up music was a personal homage to Nana Mills, who showed up to the World Series straight-faced and wearing Tommy's combat helmet, much to the amusement of everyone around her.

Power surged through my biceps after striking out my first

time up, and I drove the ball down the line, reaching the left fielder chest-high on one hop. Billy the Kid put his head down and chugged for home, bent elbows pumping like he was running for his life. He dropped down and slid even though it was clear he'd beat out the throw even if he stopped to dance across the bag.

Billy picked his head up from the dust cloud he'd created just in time for the ump to yell, *OUT*. I knew enough to know that an entire season of mostly exemplary (for him, at least) behavior was about to come undone with that call. It was the third questionable one this umpire had made in as many innings. We all saw Billy beat the tag. By the time he got to his feet, he was purple in the face. He unleashed a string of expletives and fury upon the umpire, so close to his face that flecks of spit were flying through the cage of his mask.

That umpire was known to have one of the shorter fuses in the league. He wouldn't hesitate to pull the plug and keep it moving. Stout, shiny faced, and eager to wield the strange sliver of power Glen Brook had bestowed upon him, he was quick to make an example out of the league's best-known bad boy. When he gestured for the ejection, he put a little jump into his step to add some heft to it.

Kelly and I may have served as a temporary distraction to the league's antics of yore, but getting tossed out of the World Series reanimated Billy's reputation as a perpetual problem child. This was an atrocity the Buckley brothers wouldn't take lying down, and Billy was going to remind every onlooker that he was the real liability on the team. Ryan called time and ran out onto the field screaming, tempting the ump to consider back-to-back ejections, while Billy ran around the infield, ripping the bases off the ground from beneath our feet.

"We made it this far, they're not playing without me," he screamed into the dust, despite being neither a captain nor a manager and therefore having no right to forfeit the game on the team's behalf. "If I'm out, the team's out." He was visibly weeping. Hot tears and snot dripped off his face, stippling the dirt underfoot.

Baseless, I trudged over to the side of the fence, where Winnie flashed me a wide-eyed look of secondhand embarrassment while Harper—who had a better arm than half the men out there—sidled up to the fence and got in my ear. "This is why they shouldn't let men play," she said with a sigh, pushing her sunglasses up the narrow slope of her nose. "They're too emotional."

The Dicks took a knee at their posts. Some of them were accustomed to seeing Ryan and Billy ensnared in mayhem. Kelly, though certainly aware of their reputation, kneeled on the pitcher's mound with her cap pulled low and her fist to her mouth, looking genuinely rattled. On the sidelines, the crowd had a *Justice for Buck!* chant going as my father and my stepmother, attorneys-at-law, made their way onto the field with two legs and four wheels. Claudia went in to put some distance between Ryan and the umpire, and Leo summoned his patience and peacemaking prowess as he stepped in to negotiate.

"Look, you're dealing with irrational people," he said, parking his scooter next to the umpire. The cacophony of the Buckley brothers' dissent carried on in the background. "I need a rational moment with you." He agreed the men on this team could be a bit of a nightmare but pointed out there had been no time given after the warning to let Billy compose himself. "You called him out and then you threw him out. Let us have a little time to calm down. Let the game be decided on the field and not through an ejection."

An earnest plea, and then a deal was struck: the run didn't count, Billy was still out at home, but he wasn't out of the game. He returned to the field with the bases bundled in his arms and quietly redistributed them to line up where each ghostly box lay in the dirt. Each team retired to their respective dugouts, the Bialys retrieving what we needed to get back out in the field. When I remembered we were the home team, I realized we'd be the last to bat. No matter what, we still had a bona fide chance at winning this thing.

"We get last licks," I murmured to no one in particular. My hands were close to my face, pressed together in a pose of prayer.

• • •

THERE WAS NO trouncing in the cards. Instead, each team crept up on the other, eking out a run or two throughout each long inning, cutting the tension only with a rogue walk-up song here and there. We were tied going into the bottom of the seventh, when Pete Peretti came back around and took his place at the plate.

By then, the crowd had grown restless, wringing their hands with anticipation. Some of the league's loudest characters—and our greatest adversaries—had shown up to hang on the fence and make predictions no one asked for. Tavoularis sat in a camp chair off to the side by himself, smoking a cigar and wearing a visor with one hairy, bony leg folded over the other.

Tony Scolari was surrounded by a semicircle of young bucks who let him do most of the talking. When he arrived, he took one look at Kelly on the mound and cackled. "Oh, you gotta be fucking kidding me," he yelled. "One wasn't bad enough, they got *two* of them out there? Jesus Christ. Good luck out there, boys." He glanced over at Tommy Mills and shot him a quick, insincere salute. "How's it going there, Captain?"

Nana had been transported to a transparent bubble tent with a portable outdoor air conditioner of questionable capacity. The tiny Mills girls caused a stir right behind home plate, attempting to scale the side of the bubble while Tommy tried to deter them with his one free arm. The struggle ended with both of them in his lap, screaming like they had just seen a puppy get pinned beneath a set of tires.

Distracted by the cries of her children, Kelly threw a wild pitch. Pete Peretti chuckled to himself at the plate. He'd have liked to get a hit, but he'd take whatever she gave him if it meant getting on base. The next one was perfect, and he just looked at it. "Eye on the ball, Pete," Leo barked, not about to let anyone get lazy as we army crawled toward the finish line. Kelly threw one a little low and a little outside, but he swung at it anyway for a foul tip. He committed to getting the meat of the bat on the next one, but just before he followed through on the swing, the younger of the two Mills girls unleashed a screech that could rip an eardrum. He struck out swinging.

He turned to the umpire, who was already fed up with us. "No crowd interference, blue? You're just gonna let these kids scream like banshees? You don't want to ask them to pipe down or try to preserve the integrity of the World Series?"

The umpire stood facing Pete, arms folded, imposing his presence as though willing him back toward the bench. But instead of accepting the strikeout with grace, Pete pointed a finger at Kelly halfway back to the dugout. "How about you get off that mound and tend to your kids? Go be their mother. Tommy could still whip all our asses with *both* arms tied behind his back. We don't need you here, sweetheart."

He spit, and before his saliva hit the dirt, a rosin bag beaned him in the left eye, jolting him and shocking the onlookers. Everyone looked over to Kelly, whose rosin remained at her feet. It was Ryan Buckley's rosin that hit Pete, and I was the one who threw it at him.

"Yo, Pete," I screamed, white lightning in my veins, "you're out. Now how about you shut the fuck up and sit the fuck down?"

He was so stunned he actually listened to me, wordlessly moving back toward the bench with a batting-gloved hand cupping his brow. Tony Scolari and his band of degenerates were up against the fence behind us, fingers laced through the openings, rattling it in the loose spots. "Ah, better luck next time, buddy. See? All these bitches only out here for themselves. That's the real team right there. Them against all-a-you."

I looked over at Kelly, expecting to see her face mirroring my rage, but she hung her head and shook out her hands. Just like she did when she got rattled on the mound as a kid. She took a deep breath then pitched the ball to Robbie.

The entire time I'd been home, I hadn't heard anyone refer to her as just Kelly. It was always "Mrs. Mills" or "Corporal Mills's wife." It'd been years since anyone—including and especially me—had publicly acknowledged her in terms outside of being a military wife or a Facebook mom. I didn't know what circumstances brought her out there that day. Maybe Tommy really was hurt, or maybe she just needed a moment of starshine and he wanted to give her a shot at regaining something she'd lost. Whatever the case, she was more than holding her own. She was a better athlete than a vast majority of the guys out here. Scolari knew it. They all knew it.

For a second then, I let myself consider: maybe it was a little bit like she and I were on a team against all of them. There were plenty of men out there who had a ton to prove, but no one worked harder to do it than the two of us. Out on that field, right at that moment. I dipped my toe into the pool of a fleeting fantasy: the two of us saying *screw it* and running off together like Velma Kelly and Roxie Hart starring in their own merry murderess revue.

When it was my turn to step out of the on-deck circle, I kept my bat hoisted over my shoulder, turned to Scolari, and said, "If it were you in this game, she'd get you so good you'd cry in the car on your drive home. But you'll never have to know, because I kicked your ass and sent you home first."

I didn't wait for a response. I got pulled to the plate by the vocal stylings of David Byrne singing all the French I've ever known. I lined the thick of my bat up against the far corner of home base. I looked up at Kelly. I saw a flash of our old familiarity flicker across her face. For just a moment, it felt like we were eleven years old again. The two of us on the same team. That girlhood camaraderie that couldn't be explained or imitated. I stared at her face and knew she was feeling some of the same. The tension in her brow dissipated. I felt my lips relax into a soft smile before we moved into adversarial territory again.

My hit went deep into left center. I made it to second without having to slide, and it kicked off a rally. We broke the tie and added three runs before the end of the inning.

• • •

LEO LET HIMSELF get excited, scooting over to squeeze my shoulders every now and then. "We're doing it, Caro," he muttered. "This is it. The big show!" His certainty that we would win—that we were destined to win all along—made me certain, too. It seemed like a foregone conclusion: everything else in the last few months may have gone wrong, but Ringer's Bialys *will* win the World Series.

Ryan Buckley didn't let the Dicks score any runs in the eighth, but just barely. Before getting the last out, he loaded the bases with a hit from their second baseman, a walk to their shortstop, and a weak little squibbler from their rookie. No runs scored, but then we didn't score any in the bottom of the inning either. We were left with the top of their batting order— their best hitters—in the top of the ninth.

If we had a suitable replacement, we would have subbed Ryan out after the first two were on base. But anyone else's best relief pitching efforts were far below his abilities—even in his state of exhaustion. Still, no matter how pragmatic our approach, we dreaded losing our grip. The tying run was at bat. Ryan wouldn't make it through extra innings. The sloppiness became impossible to ignore when he nicked the Dicks' first baseman and loaded the bases for the second time in as many innings.

Kelly stepped up to the song that bore my name, and it felt like I was watching a ghost play ball. She was every inch the girl I grew up with. The way her feet were planted at a calculated distance from the base. The measured stance she perfected at all those weekend softball clinics. The sturdy jaw she kept clenched when she focused on the ball's trajectory.

It would have been enough to be the woman who showed up to the World Series at a moment's notice. That was what small-town lore was made of. It would have been enough had she just replaced her superstar husband, struck out a few men, gotten a good hit—maybe even found a way to stretch a single into a double. But that wasn't enough of a story for Kelly Quinn-Mills. She had to take it a step further.

A home run wasn't elusive in the men's softball league. The scale of the field, for one, worked in our favor. It was much smaller than the major league field dimensions, therefore making it very possible to send one over the fence and into the greenery. But a home run wasn't easy to come by either. It still took power to send the ball that far, even without MLB-length fences. Few were ever hit in the league's World

Series, when impenetrable pitching lineups were deployed and the pressure was on. But every once in a while, it was known to happen. What was unheard of was hitting a grand slam in the World Series.

When we were kids, Kelly's father scolded her every time she swung at the first pitch, which was often despite his coaching. "Use the first one to gauge the pitcher," he'd told us, explaining that if it was a ball instead of a strike, the pitch count would load faster and we'd have a better chance of getting on base. She couldn't help herself. It was a habit no amount of yelling could curb. As I watched her hit—the result of a swing at a first pitch—sail over the center fielder's head, back beyond the fence, I knew we were watching a moment the whole town would talk about for the next decade.

Almost instantly, I caught up with my team and started to sweat about our deficit. But for those first few seconds I couldn't help thinking it was vindication, at last, for Kelly's lifetime of missed first pitches.

• • •

LAST LICKS.

Timmy Moriarty, of all people, hit a moonshot the likes of which I'd never seen come out of him before. Kelly's ninth-inning fatigue had a lot to do with it, but Timmy milked the moment. He cockily stretched a double into a triple, dusting himself off as he stood like he'd long been the MVP.

Back at the top of our lineup. Renewing her focus after an unlikely wake-up call, Kelly struck out Billy the Kid. "I shouldn't have swung at that high one," he screeched to himself, kicking up clods of dirt on his walk back to the dugout. He threw off his helmet and tugged on his hair. "What was I thinking? Idiot, idiot, idiot!" Ryan came over to soothe him, wary of more umpire interference, and we turned our attention back to the batter's box.

Kelly's pitching was all over the place. Next up was Pete, who smugly hung back, concave over the plate, bat resting on his shoulders. Errant balls—way too inside, way too high, one in the dirt—soared past him. He looked at Kelly, the gash of his mouth nearly tilted into a smile, but not quite. He sent her a silent message: *I'm just going to let you tire yourself out, honey.* Sooner than he could get into an actual stance, Kelly whipped two perfect strikes at him, forcing him to reposition. Her next pitch was so far outside, no one could aspire to hit it. But Pete had been sufficiently rattled and swung at it anyway. *Two out.*

Robbie followed Pete, observed four straight balls, and studiously jogged to take his base. With the tying run on third and the winning run on first, it came down to me. Batting against the girl of my youth in the World Series.

It had been years since we spent time with each other and longer still since we were friends, privy to the nuances of each other's gestures and tics. So much had changed that it should have been impossible for me to read her, but it wasn't. I could still follow her strategies like I was tracing a subway map.

First ball was high and tight, so I let it go by, even doing a dramatic little hop and smile, which I knew would bother her. Second one was low and away, which she knew I'd swing at and miss. I tipped the next pitch for a strike, followed by another high one I just looked at.

The crowd got to their feet, even Leo, clapping and whooping. Everyone sitting on the Moby Dicks' side partook in the traditional two-strike *get her outta there* clap while those on the Ringer's Bialys side cheered, knowing just a light tap could send Timmy home, close our one-run gap, and send us into extra innings.

Extra innings at the World Series, I thought to myself, savoring the sentiment. *God, you'd really do anything to prolong this game, wouldn't you? Anything so you don't have to think about what comes after this.* I couldn't picture it. Couldn't imagine getting in my car, doing the same drive I'd taken that morning in reverse, with or without the trophy. I couldn't imagine going back to New York; I couldn't imagine staying in Glen Brook at my father's house. I couldn't imagine getting into Crispin's car and driving to the beach. I still couldn't believe our last drive east was truly the last time.

Just as I became convinced I could be satisfied going on like this forever—stuck in a continuous loop of the ninth inning, always in a showdown with my rival—I found myself swinging. The ball popped against the end of my bat, and I could feel it reverberate in my wrists, down to my elbows, and into my chest. There was power behind it. *I could keep going on like this*. It soared to the right of Kelly, just far enough over and high enough above her head that her intercepting it appeared mathematically implausible. But Kelly loved to win as much as everyone else loved to tell the story of winning. She leapt to meet the ball and fell to the ground with it in her glove.

When she picked her head up, she realized what she had done. She quickly got on her feet to show the umpire, the squad, and the crowd: She had the ball in her hands. The final out of the World Series.

When the umpire called it, she tossed her head back to the sky, put her arms behind her, and screamed. It was a primal scream of victory. The rest of the Dicks ran toward her, dogpiling on top of her, spraying Gatorade indiscriminately. Tommy and the girls ran out, and he kissed her while they scaled her side. She couldn't stop smiling. They chanted for her like she was Reggie Jackson. I watched from home plate, bat in my hands propping me up like a tripod, unsure how to move from that spot or how to breathe. Or how to face my father.

If any onlookers caught me at that moment—planted at the plate, back to my teammates, tears leaking from my eyes—they'd assume I was being a bad sport. *A sore loser*, we'd say about the kids who cried when their Little League teams lost. I blinked back my tears and fought against the thought spiral that threatened to pull me under: *This was all for nothing.*

Then, my father appeared at my side.

My body tensed, bracing for whatever he was preparing to lay on me. I was at least in for a loud Tom Hanks *there's no crying in baseball* soliloquy. Probably something about my stance on that last swing, or how I set myself up for failure with that posture, missing the opportunity to let the ball hit the fat part of the bat. He was silent for a moment, just watching the Moby Dicks celebrate around the pitcher's mound. Then he pushed himself up by the handlebars of his scooter and turned to me.

"Look at me, Caro," he said, taking my tearstained cheeks into his rough, thick hands. He held me there for a few seconds, looking into my eyes, before planting a kiss on my forehead. "You made my most far-fetched dream come true, something I never thought possible these days. We made it to the show. *You* made it to the show. Thank you for getting me here. For bringing me with you."

We embraced—my force nearly knocking him down, my snot and tears soaking the shoulder of his yellow Bialys tee. "No Casey Stengel quote?" I muttered into his back. "No Yogi Berra wisdom for something like this?"

He pulled back from me and placed his hands on my shoulders. "How about this one instead: *Wait 'til next year.*"

He grinned. "No attribution, just an old Brooklyn proverb." I knew it well. The rally cry of the Brooklyn Dodgers each year after they lost three consecutive World Series to the Yankees. They flipped the script in 1955. My father's citation of the quote was an act of optimism. Faith in the existence of another year, of more baseball seasons to come.

It was time to line up and shake hands. I joined my men on the field in a neat, albeit dejected, single-file line.

Googamegoogamegoogamegoogame.

The Dicks, drenched in sweat and sports drinks and glory, shook our hands with grins and earnestness, using both hands to cup one of ours, some pulling in others for hugs and claps on the back. For all my *what's next* panic, it somehow didn't occur to me until then that no matter how the World Series ended, baseball was over for the season. It was like getting caught up in the whirlwind of Halloween and forgetting that it would be November the next day. The grief that tugged at my chest had an ancient quality to it, reminiscent of the way I felt as a child: I was bereft without baseball.

Googamegoogamegoogamegoogame.

Kelly and I were the last in each of our rows. When we met, she looked me straight in the eyes. Hands clasped, she held mine there for a beat before she smiled and said, "Good game, Caroline." My face mirrored hers.

23

ON TUESDAY NIGHT, I arrived early enough in Asbury Park to catch the sun still hanging low in the sky, relentless against the threat of autumn. I had a vision of myself showing up at Crispin's show in something as outrageous and flashy as a sequin in the night. But he didn't seem the type to appreciate a grand gesture—or drama at all, for that matter. We were opposites in that way. I opted for simplicity, realizing my presence might not be welcome or, at best, only merely tolerated: blue jeans and sandals and a white cutoff tee that read *GOOD OL' GRATEFUL DEAD* in a faded orb in the center of my chest.

With time on my hands, I walked the boardwalk through Ocean Grove. The tinny, haunted circus music of a chain-smoking, top-hatted busker on a keyboard tinkled through the air. The flat thump of children's feet gently rattled the boardwalk. I paused to read the inscriptions on the benches. Methodist well-wishes to those who were long departed, or simple markers of sustained existence: *The Calloway Family, Summer 2006.* "Where Paul + Soni fell and *stayed* in love!" Each bench was surrounded by beach-daisy carpets and bursts of scarlet Asiatic lilies.

When I passed through the casino and crossed over onto the Asbury side, I tried to remember how it all looked when Winnie and I were younger and wilder. The boardwalk hadn't been lit up; the street art wasn't commissioned. The casino stretched out farther down the beach, a whole other building housing the ghosts of amusements past. They'd torn it down since I'd been gone, but I wasn't quite sure when. What remained was a spooky monument to glory days gone by—beautiful but impotent. The hollow face of it still maintained its art deco green, the same muted mint shade of the carousel building that abutted it. If Asbury Park were a color, it would be that precise shade of green.

The sky on the ocean side of the boardwalk was still digesting its stripes, pinks and purples stacked on top of one another, while the sky on the street side had congealed into one big bruise. The marquee outside the Pony read: HOT ROLLERS ALL WEEK LONG. Unemotional and definitive. Serene Jackson was a true prodigal daughter among us, and hope for her mainstream adoption was renewed with the release of her new album. The mantle got taken up by the people of Asbury Park every time she put out something new. They were once again certain of imminent success.

Serene had been featured in *Bangs Ave*, the local zine that the music store and all the businesses on the block distributed, talking about getting sober and loving Nashville and making peace with her career trajectory. Southside Johnny interviewed her for the piece, and then they took Polaroids of each other and taped them down and hoped for the best where the copier was concerned. She also got a favorable write-up in *Rolling Stone* and a generous rating on *Pitchfork*, and the forthcoming Brooklyn Steel show even got a small shout-out in *The New Yorker*'s "Goings on About Town." Winnie had an in with one of the editors.

A small nimbus cloud of cigarette smoke hovered over the side of the Stone Pony. In the distance, I could start to trace the figures. Sarita O'Brien was there, laughing and waving her long tattooed arms in the air. She leaned against Hannah Murphy, who was a head taller than her and had her arms firmly wrapped around Sarita's waist. As I approached, I heard the depth of Serene's unmistakable voice: "That's why we're lowkey calling it the *I'm a Pepper* tour," she laughed, taking a sip from a highball of cola. "Everyone on the bus is sober! We've gone from trashing hotel rooms and getting arrested to making three cases of Dr Pepper the only item on our rider."

When I stepped into view, the girls all turned to face me. I braced myself for judgment but was met with warmth as smiles melted across their faces. Sarita gave me a little bark of excited approval in the moonlight—*ow owww*—and Hannah pulled her in tighter and gave me a little wink. "Why, welcome," Serene said witchily, like she'd been expecting me, like I was a recruit for a coven she'd been building.

A couple of men tumbled out of the side entrance then, for one last cigarette and glimpse of the lights against the night sky before the show was underway. The final breath before the tour began. They were all dressed up like Brooklyn cowboys in tight-fitting jeans and tucked threadbare shirts, punctuated by black-fringe suede details and embossed leather boots that'd been thrifted. When Crispin stepped out—palming his hair back, the shape of his curls retained by drying sweat— the girls looked at him expectantly, waiting for him to see me. They watched me watch him, waiting for him to react. They knew something I didn't, but I knew I was about to be in on it.

When he spotted me among them, the muscles shifted behind his face. A tension in his brow came unknit. "Look who showed up," Sarita cawed, smacking her chewing gum and laughing. He paused before moving toward me. He trained his eyes to be level with mine. He parted those lips that I'd meditated on, in this life and in the last: "Hey, you."

●　●　●

SERENE AND SARITA had the good sense to take their last drags and their Dr Peppers and herd the crew in through the stage door. *Show's starting soon*, they reasoned, but mostly they knew to give Crispin and me a few minutes alone. I took a tentative step toward him. He moved his eyes across the outfit, my hair. He opened his mouth to say something, but I started first.

"Don't be mad at Sarita for telling me," I told him, taking one hand in mine and clasping it. "But mazel tov on your one year. It's a huge accomplishment. How does it feel?"

He moved his free hand in his pocket, looking down with a clamped, grateful smile. "It feels like . . ." He laughed and thought about it for a moment. "It feels like I've spent a year building all this scaffolding around my life and now it's time to take it all down and see how I hold up. You know what I mean?"

"Yes," I said, looking up at him. His eyes were clear, his shoulders relaxed. "I think I know exactly what you mean."

"I feel like, alright, let's take this bird out and see if she can fly!" His smile shifted as his face rearranged his features into something more serious. "I owe you an apology," he said, sliding his hand out of mine and taking a step back. "I haven't been honest with you."

I braced for what might be on the other side of that tip toward confession: A plan to leave New Jersey and never come back. Some unknown siren he had been in love with this whole time. A sneaky hatred of me that bloomed within the bit of space I'd given him. My mother always called this species of thinking "catastrophizing," but I couldn't help myself. Everything I'd experienced in love and longing so far pointed to imminent catastrophe.

"I said I'd be here, and I didn't show," I said, trying one last time to make a case for myself. The volume of my voice climbed as the plea unfurled. "The rest—"

But he cut me off. My birdlike heart beat its wings against the cage of my chest. "I've just been afraid this is a one-sided thing," he said, and I swallowed hard, worried I might start crying. "I keep thinking, I just have to get it over with and tell you how I feel so we can both move on."

I felt acutely aware of how heavy each of my limbs were. A parched sensation prickled the back of my throat.

"I've been terrified for months now knowing that at some point, I'd need to come clean to you," he said, running a stressed-out palm through his hair. He paused as his grip lingered on the back of his neck. Then he released it. "But now I find myself wondering if maybe I'm not alone in how badly I want this."

I could feel the flash behind my eyes, the naked expression on my face. *I want this*. The words hung between us, clouding my field of vision as he took two steps toward me.

"You had no way of knowing how badly I wanted you here that night," he said. "How badly I want you here every night."

My face softened, yielding to the unbridled joy that accompanied the thought of him wanting me anywhere, in any capacity. He'd taken my hand back into his, close enough now to feel the heat transferring off his skin, radiating in little waves down onto me.

"Am I alone in this?" he whispered.

No, I mouthed back, looking up at him. He smiled, and my legs felt like a tuning fork.

"Caroline," he said, tentative and soft. "Is it okay if I kiss you?"

I nodded my head yes, tucked the loose hair around my face back behind my ears, and tried to remember to breathe as I angled my chin toward his.

But instead of leaning in, he pumped my hand in his twice like a beating heart then broke away to enter through the stage door.

• • •

SERENE JACKSON HAD a lot of nerve, crafting a set list that perfect on the first night of the tour. Someone should have warned her about front-loading all that energy, making the first night out the gate too good. I was thirsty and had to pee at the same time but didn't for a second think about leaving my post, pressed against the stage with Sarita and Hannah like exhausted swimmers. We were gripped as she tore through her discography, a homecoming and a kickoff all at once.

"Alright," Serene said, out of breath after ten or so songs, guzzling from a water bottle, "now, we've got something special for y'all here tonight." She shrugged off the blue crushed velvet tuxedo jacket she'd been wearing to reveal a ruffled white button-down shirt and black bell-bottom slacks held up by thick black suspenders. She plucked the pearl barrette pinned to her head and let down a cascade of her black velvet hair. Wisps of it stuck to her forehead in sweaty little ringlets.

She pulled Crispin over by his elbow, and they turned their heads to murmur to each other away from the microphones on their stands. They peeled away with a smile. She pulled a piece of crimson chiffon out of her back pocket, wrapped it around her hand, and leaned into the mic. "Hey, by the way, do you guys know Crispin Davis?"

The crowd, high off the set thus far, erupted as they would have for any stranger. No one screamed louder than I did, though, my otherworldly enthusiasm made socially acceptable by his stage presence and the sea of Hot Roller fanatics around me. "Good, good, good," she laughed. "Crispin is an old friend of mine, and he's new to the group, and we're, uh, taking him on the road with us for the Sober October tour." She paused and looked at him as he raised his gleaming bottle of Diet Dr Pepper to the crowd in a toast before swigging some. "Or whatever we're calling it now. Anyway, he's here, he's great, and right now we're going to do a song we've never done live before. And we're going to do something else we've never done before and dedicate it to someone special."

Serene looked down directly at me when she dropped an

octave and said *someone special*, and it made the embers of my cheeks burn. Hannah and Sarita looked at each other with wide wild eyes, then at me. Before she could clarify who the someone special was, Crispin pulled Serene back to murmur another secret in her ear.

"Sorry," she corrected herself, still giggling, then flashed a peace sign. "This song goes out to *two* special people. They go by the names of Todd Rundgren and Courteney Cox."

Just as the girls screeched "*What?!*" into each of my ears, the band launched into the cannon blast of Meat Loaf's twinkling epic, "You Took the Words Right Out of My Mouth." Produced, of course, by Crispin's hero, Todd Rundgren. A song like that could go one of two ways with the crowd: confusion or total embrace. But the Pony was packed with enough people who lived through the 1970s that it was a success. We were an audience of Asbury misfits, intermingled with blue-collar Shore folks and a few snappy suburbanites all dancing together as one undulating mass.

Crispin shared front and center with Serene as she belted the words with such depth and purpose, for a split second I forgot the song wasn't actually hers. With her ruffled shirt and sweaty bangs and wide-eyed animation, she looked like—I hated to admit it—a hot-girl version of Meat Loaf. I could see now, with her outfit and their dynamic, they were doing a send-up of the song's low-budget soundstage music video from the pre-MTV days. Crispin, I supposed, played the role of Karla DeVito. He kept the bass line going as Serene slinked up against him and they harmonized.

They parted as she launched into the bit about her lipstick shining and dying just to ask for a taste, and Crispin quickly removed the bass from around his torso. Without a hitch, Serene took it and picked up where he left off. He turned to face the crowd head on. More specifically, he turned to face me. I was standing in my small cluster of three when he looked down, smiled, and animatedly reached his hand out to me. I had no way of knowing what my face looked like at that moment. I seemed to have vacated my body as the girls pushed and he pulled and then I was onstage with the Hot Rollers at the Stone Pony—where Bruce and Patti and a hundred other idols of mine once stood.

Crispin smiled as sincerely as I'd ever seen him and eased me into a little Springsteen-esque dance, shuffling back and forth with elbows bent at ninety-degree angles. *He's trying to make my dreams of being Courteney Cox at the concert come true*, I thought. I couldn't believe my luck, or what was about to transpire in front of hundreds of people.

And then you took the words right out of my mouth, Serene sang, and it hit somewhere between a whisper and a moan. Crispin had his hands on my waist then, bringing me in closer.

Oh, it must've been while you were kissing me. His eyebrows flickered; the smile stayed. I took a deep breath to make sure I could and that made him laugh. Then he pulled me as

close as I could get. The damp air between us was all sandal-
wood and sweat and a whisper of Dr Pepper.

You took the words right out of my mouth, she repeated as
he brought his lips to mine.

Crispin was the low-key to my loud, the anti–drama queen
king. Private in a cool way, always courting an aura of mystery
without dickishness. I liked attention. I liked batting cleanup. I
liked dancing center stage. That night, he met me in the spotlight to let me know I wasn't alone there. He assuaged the fear
that had plagued me for half a year: the iceberg of my feelings
beneath the surface didn't make me dishonest if he had the
same thing going on.

Oh, and I swear it's true—I was just about to say I love you.

We kissed, and even though I'd never been there before, it
felt like coming home.

Serene came over to replace his bass and, in a magnanimous gesture, handed me a tambourine. She laughed and gave
my hand a little squeeze, then ran the scarlet chiffon over my
head like she was casting a spell before launching back into
her vamping. The song continued, Crispin and I dancing
close—laughing at each other's little shimmies and attempting to mitigate gigantic, goofy smiles. Grateful to be on the
inside of the same joke.

When the song ended, Crispin dropped his bass and kissed
me once more—this time quieter, more tucked away from the
spotlight. Just between us. Serene pulled Sarita and Hannah

and a few others out of the audience and onto the stage—
Courteney Coxes in their own right—as a couple of roadies
dragged an old king-size mattress onto the middle of the floor
and set up pillar candles and potted lilies around the perimeter.

"Thank you, my loves," Serene murmured into the microphone as she sipped cola on ice from the lip of her glass. "I'm
Serene Jackson, these are my Hot Rollers. If you haven't been
to a Hot Rollers show before: we don't do encores, we just do
sing-along finales. If you have been to a Hot Rollers show before: welcome back, you beautiful bastards. You know what
to do. I love ya."

The Hot Rollers replaced their instruments on racks and
in gig cases off to the side, finding spots on stools or on the
mattress or surrounding it in concentric circles on the floor.
Crispin took a seat on the edge of the mattress, pulled me into
him so that I sat between his legs, and wrapped his arms
firmly around my waist as he planted a kiss on the slope where
my shoulder met my neck. Serene was the only one with
an instrument—an acoustic guitar that once belonged to Roy
Orbison—and she led us in "You've Got a Friend," the James-
Taylor-by-way-of-Carole-King hit. We sang together, soft as
the candlelight that surrounded us, and the chorus sounded
like a prayer.

Epilogue

THE LAST THING Crispin said before falling asleep that night was said with a quiet laugh, bathed in moonlight while tracing shapes across the expanse of my bare back with his fingertips. I faced away from him, looking at the facade of the Steinbach Building, restored to glory and lit from beneath in such a way that it looked like we were beneath the Colosseum.

"What are you laughing at back there?" I asked, turning my head over my shoulder to catch a playful glance of him.

"I just have that song stuck in my head now, after that, after all this. You got it stuck in my head . . ." he said, trailing off.

I flipped over, propped up on my other elbow, breasts out and unselfconsciously sloping. "What song?" I asked. "'Fat Bottomed Girls'?"

He laughed, said no, then regained his composure. "It's that Faces song, maybe Ronnie Wood sings it? It played on rock radio a lot when we were kids. The one that's all about wishing I knew what I know now when I was younger."

"Mmm," I said, plucking a curl from in front of his eye and tucking it back into his thicket of hair. "I know the one."

"That's what you've got me wishing, Caroline Kline. Thinking I could've gotten through all the bullshit with a lot more grace if I knew it was leading me to you."

He fell asleep first, so I was left to consider in the dark how much more I knew in that moment than I had a year before, even a few months before. How much more I knew than even at the beginning of that evening. I knew in the twilight he felt the same way about me that I felt about him. I knew, at last, he didn't feel deceived or undermined that I'd been harboring this for so long, because he'd been holding on to a symmetrical affection the whole time.

I knew, after that night, a series of tiny intimacies I had craved. I knew what kind of toothpaste he kept next to his sink. The clean taste of him. The small animal noises that escaped him when his body was pressed into mine or when he slept. The trickling tone on his iPhone alarm that he preferred to wake up to.

What I didn't know yet was the full scope of what was to come. If, when Serene pulled me aside after the show that night, asking me to join them on the road and start training as their tour manager, I'd be any good at it. I didn't know what it would be like to travel with Crispin and be in such close quarters so soon after the beginning of our relationship. I only knew I'd regret it if I didn't say yes.

I didn't know the depth of what Kelly and I had incited. The screen-printed *WORLD SERIES: BATTLE OF THE BABES* T-shirts that were made and then sold out on the league's website. The interview on the front page of the local paper, where Kelly credited me with challenging her to step up her game from the time we were in Little League. I didn't know that Gary Feingold would work through the offseason to ensure the changing face of the league—setting term limits on the board, removing the word *Men* from the league name, and garnering 20 percent of spring season sign-ups from local women.

I didn't know that Rubin "Ruby" Winnick—a substitute player in one softball game only, setting the precedent for which injured players may nominate family members as temporary replacements—was a man. Nobody knew until Robbie Walker included his obituary at the end of a newsletter later that year and revealed the truth to everyone who followed. I didn't know that the precedent would then be renamed for me: the Caroline Kline amendment.

I didn't know about the experimental trial Claudia would

fight to get Leo into, attempting to slow down the degeneration. I didn't know that he would take up Transcendental Meditation to help him accept and navigate his condition— not because of the practice's long and storied reputation, but because he once heard Howard Stern talk about it and decided to give it a go. I didn't know if I would regret leaving home knowing he was sick, not knowing what condition he would be in when I returned.

I didn't know that I'd cease obsessing over what I didn't know. That my lifelong anxiety about *what comes next* could be assuaged by the company of someone who put a high premium on basking in the *now* of it all.

But that night at Crispin's apartment, I gave myself permission to wonder, even just for a moment. I spent the quiet hours wedged before dawn letting myself peek through the keyhole of what was next. The rush I could feel as the lights went down in the venue before the first show out on the road. What hearing my father's voice over the phone from thousands of miles away might feel like, no matter what kind of news he was calling to deliver. Seeing Winnie's face in the Santa Monica sun or Harper's kids running up and down the wharf.

I let myself imagine how it could feel to come home to this, to Asbury Park, and feel like I was at ease. Like I was at home. How I might walk up to the beach from beneath the hollowed-out casino late in the night, the frosty waves rolling slowly, a greeting from the shore. How the sunrise might look from the sliding glass doors in Crispin's bedroom, lighting up the gold bricks of the Steinbach Building at dawn: like promise, like victory.

Acknowledgments

At some point my childhood shower Oscar speeches evolved into a dream of one day writing acknowledgments for my debut novel, and I cannot believe the day has finally come. Writing is a solo act, but publishing is a team sport. None of this would be possible without the extraordinary people I'm surrounded by.

To my agent, Jade Wong-Baxter. The first yes of this process and the greatest, loudest yes of my life as a writer. Thank you for your singular brand of wisdom, guidance, and zeal. For fielding every "unhinged" idea I have with a prompt "send it over!" I'm so grateful to walk alongside you in this and all that is still to come. You've made my greatest dream come true.

To my editor, Gaby Mongelli. I cannot imagine what giant

mitzvah I did in my last life that I karmically ended up with you as my Jersey girl dream editor in this one. Thank you for so beautifully shaping this book into its final form, for your excitement and vision, and for loving the *Dolls and Guys* of it all. You had me at James Gandolfini Rest Stop.

To my literal dream team at Putnam: Kristen Bianco, Shina Patel, Jess Lopez Cuate, Ashley McClay, Alexis Welby, and the great Sally Kim. I cannot believe I get to know and work with you—how is this my life? To the latest and greatest additions to the roster, Tara Singh Carlson and Aranya Jain, with much gratitude for getting *Caroline* across the finish line and much excitement for all to come! Thank you to everyone who made this book into a stunning finished product: Vi-An Nguyen, Alison Cnockaert, Leah Marsh, Andrea Monagle, Chris LaForce, and Brianna Lopez.

The authors who so generously endorsed this book are my idols, and I'm so lucky for their precious time and praise. My undying gratitude and admiration to Katie Runde, Marcy Dermansky, Becky Chalsen, Annabel Monaghan, Amy Poeppel, Margarita Montimore, Laura Hankin, Beck Dorey-Stein, Bobby Finger, Kirthana Ramisetti, and Steven Rowley. To Mandy Berman, for your eyes, enthusiasm, edits, and endorsement—I'm so grateful to have you in my orbit!

To the team at Frances Goldin Literary Agency—it's the honor of my life to share a roster with the great talent at this agency and to share the values of its namesake. To Nicole

Weinroth and Hilary Zaitz Michael at WME, for the excitement and all the possibilities.

I'm endlessly grateful to the people who guided me when I wasn't sure this book would see the light of day. To Dan Conway, for your generosity and early encouragement. To Kerry Cullen, who is an amazing editor and writer and an even better friend, and to Lauren Adelman for connecting us. To Meta Wagner, for your support and everything you've taught me. To Sarita Gonzalez, my favorite Mets fan, and living proof that writing workshops produce essential friendships! To my writer friends who responded to every panicked email or DM with sage advice, especially Megan Barnard and Jana Casale.

To Courtney Maum, for helping me shape a great pitch and for writing *Before and After the Book Deal*, aka the Bible for writers. To Bianca Marais, who celebrated with me the day I signed with my agent and whose podcast *The Shit No One Tells You About Writing* was my companion throughout the query process. To Jami Attenberg, whose #1000WordsOfSummer writing challenge helped me finish the first draft of this novel in the weird and wild summer of 2020.

To my TE family past and present who watched this process unfold over a decade and cheered me on—especially Susan Morgan, Jarrett Cobbs, Kurtis Pemberton, Jane Kim, and Shawn Francis. To Kamaria Gboro, what are the odds the universe put two writers in each other's path like it has ours? You are next! To Coltrane Curtis, who never misses an opportunity to call me a novelist in front of our clients. To Lisa Chu and Valerie Chiam, for giving me the chance to build a career I love.

To Emily Smith and Jillian Eugenios, for every late-night chat, every moment of inspiration and commiseration, every workshop, every Saab story, and everything else. To Chloe Caldwell, who answered my truly unhinged fan letter and became my teacher and my friend. Core Four forever. To Heather Hasselle, for bettering and brightening my life since Tin House 2016—we are the lasses who cannot be tamed!

To all the friends who spent years cheering me on, especially my real-life Winnies: Melissa Middleberg, Heather Settles-Cultice, and Brittany Zaretsky. I owe my wild and idyllic girlhood to you, and knowing you is the greatest gift of my life. To Abby Rose and Will Rhinehart, for being excited with me. To Matt Vick, who makes my life a series of the funniest stories I'll ever get to tell. To Kathryn Milograno Vick, for the sanity checks and for making me write IT WILL SELL on a Post-it. To Twiggy Marie, my first reader always and half of the greatest book club on earth. To Mariel Sirota, my first friend on earth and the very first person to preorder this book! To Hannah Walker and Victoria Wong, who made Asbury Park home for me and reaffirmed that magic is possible when you loiter at a bookstore.

To Cassie Castellaw, for spending another perfect day on

the Asbury Park boardwalk with me. To the Peach Blossom girlies for making me author-photo-ready, especially Michelle Middleberg and Bri Vengersky. To Kerri Sullivan—I'm so grateful to build a Jersey literary community with you! To Kate Czyzewski: I could never thank you enough for your support and friendship. I'm so lucky to know you and to have Thunder Road Books as my home!

To Vincent Scarpa, whose friendship and generosity have shaped my life, and whose brilliance continues to shape my writing. For mailing me back that marked-up manuscript. To quote Lorrie: without you, my world would grow dull as Mars.

To Rachel Harrison, without whom this novel would simply not exist. Thank you for telling me this was the right idea. Thank you for every Friday phone call, brainstorm, and gut check. I can't believe we get to do this together. Let's keep making Carrie and Penny proud.

To my entire family for their love and support, especially Mark Dudley, Maria Thomas, and the entire Dudley/Brockelman/Schmelz contingent. To the extended Zedlovich universe—especially Pauline, for her early and constant encouragement. To the Galione/Barry/Davidson dynasty: there is no one I'd rather have in my corner and there is no family abubus.

To the second set of sisters I'm lucky to have: Aniya Atasunseva, Nicole Galano, and Juliana Galano. To my stepmother, Stephanie Galano-Preiss: I'm so grateful for your presence in my life, and I plan to spend the rest of it begging you not to sue me over Claudia's character. To Roseann Pirozzi-Preiss and in memory of Larry Preiss, who have always loved and embraced me since I was a tiny lunatic singing off-key Billy Joel songs in public.

To my siblings, Jordan, Alexa, and Lucas Preiss. Thank you for sitting on the floor of the Cookman Ave. apartment on Thanksgiving Eve and letting me transcribe the funniest things you'd ever seen on the ballfield. I'm so grateful we have each other to bear witness to everything we do in this life. I only aspire to tell great family stories because I come from a great family. "We're the home team!" (Helen Holm voice.)

To my mother, Lauren Galione, for always encouraging me to find myself and to be true to myself. Your guidance and love create the path I follow. This dream and this life are impossible without you. Ti amo sempre.

To my father, Scott Preiss, for telling me in every moment of doubt that I will not be okay, but great. For every baseball game, whether it's in the Bronx or in the backyard. I would not be a writer or anything at all without the life you've given me. I love you.

To Max Dudley, my greatest love and cosmic ally. For making the coffee. For teaching me about rigorous honesty. For being the architect of the shared life that made writing this book possible. I love you so fucking much. This, everything, is for you.

About the Author

Photograph of the author © Cassie Castellaw

COURTNEY PREISS was born in Brooklyn and raised in New Jersey off the same Highway 9 Bruce Springsteen sings about on "Born to Run." She graduated from Emerson College with a BFA in Writing, Literature, and Publishing. She lives in Asbury Park, NJ, with her husband and their rescue dog, Barry. *Welcome Home, Caroline Kline* is her first novel.

VISIT COURTNEY PREISS ONLINE

courtneypreiss.com

🐦 CocoGoLightly

📷 CocoGoLightly